DARK HORSE

ALSO BY RORY FLYNN

Third Rail

DARK HORSE

AN EDDY HARKNESS NOVEL

Rory Flynn

Houghton Mifflin Harcourt
BOSTON   NEW YORK
2016

For James Ryan

Copyright © 2016 by Rory Flynn

For information about permission to reproduce selections from
this book, write to trade.permissions@hmhco.com or to Permissions,
Houghton Mifflin Harcourt Publishing Company, 3 Park Avenue,
19th Floor, New York, New York 10016.

www.hmhco.com

Library of Congress Cataloging-in-Publication Data
Names: Flynn, Rory, (date) author.
Title: Dark horse : an Eddy Harkness novel / Rory Flynn.
Description: Boston : Houghton Mifflin Harcourt, 2016. | Series: Eddy Harkness ; 2
Identifiers: LCCN 2015037255| ISBN 9780544253247 (hardcover) |
ISBN 9780544253155 (ebook)
Subjects: LCSH: Police — Massachusetts — Boston — Fiction. |
Drug traffic — Massachusetts — Boston — Fiction. | BISAC: FICTION /
Mystery & Detective / General. | GSAFD: Mystery fiction.
Classification: LCC PS3556.L92 D37 2016 | DDC 813/.54 — dc23
LC record available at http://lccn.loc.gov/2015037255

Book design by Brian Moore

Printed in the United States of America
DOC 10 9 8 7 6 5 4 3 2 1

Everybody's got a little hole in the middle,
Everybody does a little dance with the Devil.

— EMILY JANE WHITE

1

DETECTIVE EDDY HARKNESS sweeps his hand along the inside of the windshield to clear the fog and searches for stragglers or thrill-seekers. He finds only dark windows, empty sidewalks, and street signs shaking in the wind. Albrecht Street is already a raging river and the emerald sky dumps more water by the minute. Cardboard boxes and suitcases, lost during the frantic evacuation, circle in the brown water, rising fast now that the sewers have given up.

Harkness slows the squad car to keep the engine from flooding.

"No one left, Harky," Patrick says. "Whole neighborhood's empty. Everybody's gone, like they're s'post to be."

A roiling clump of brown fur and glinting eyes swims past. "Except the rats."

"Bad sign when the rats start leaving, right?"

"Oh yeah." Harkness keeps the squad car moving so they can finish the last blocks of the neighborhood check and head back to Narco-Intel.

Just before dawn, a weakening tropical storm meandering off the coast of Rhode Island hit a wall of cold air and turned ambitious. The winds ramped up to hurricane force and the storm took an unexpected jag northwest. The National Weather Service didn't even have time to name it. Now Hurricane X churns over the North Atlantic, about to make landfall near Boston. Mayor O'Mara shut down the airport, trains, and trolleys. He ordered all citizens to *shelter in place,* evacuating only the Lower South End, protected from the storm surge by a rotting wood and earthen dam at the end of an abandoned industrial canal. If the Channel Dam gives way, the rising waters of Boston Harbor will sweep through Albrecht Square, empty now.

Almost empty.

A gunshot echoes over the frantic windshield wipers and the drumming rain. Harkness pulls the squad car to the curb.

"S'post to be a drive-by," Patrick says.

"Yeah?"

"So keep driving by, boss. Let's get the hell out of here."

"Can't pretend you didn't hear that."

"Hear *what?*"

Another gunshot cracks above them.

Harkness stares into the darting eyes of his partner, so much happier back in Dataland than out on the street. "So what was that?"

"Some yahoo exercising his Second Amendment rights?" Patrick holds up his hands. "Let it slide, Harky. For once."

Harkness shoulders open the door, and trash-laden brown water swirls into the patrol car. He picks up a crowbar from the floor and steps out into the knee-deep river raging down the street. "C'mon."

"*Gross.*" Patrick squeezes his eyes closed and opens his door. He trudges through the cold water to the sidewalk and climbs up on a lamppost base. The wind rips back their orange raincoats, and rain soaks their uniforms. "So we gonna go door to door," Patrick shouts, "all community-outreach-like?"

Harkness nods, eyes almost closed against the rain, dark hair whipping across his face.

"We don't even know where those shots are coming from, Harky."

Another shot sends glass raining down on the sidewalk from a hotel's top-floor window.

Patrick just shakes his head.

"Let's go." Harkness rushes to the front of the building — door locked, entryway clogged with bloated bundles of the *Globe*. Back when Harkness was a beat cop, a semi-recovered crackhead named Chai ran the Hotel Blackstone, more shabby than chic, where aspiring rockers, poets, and ill-informed European travelers rented rooms by the week. The coffee shop served piles of sweet potato fries that worked as reliable beer sponges. The maids and bellboys did a lucrative side business in short-term love. Now the Blackstone's a drug-infested SRO nightmare that the city's been trying to shut down for years.

They pop open the door with the crowbar and step inside. A light flickers in the gloom from the empty desk clerk's booth, where rows of plastic-tagged keys hang above an overturned red plastic chair. Harkness and Patrick follow a thin path where trudging footsteps have etched away a layer of grime across the lobby to reveal white tile.

Harkness clicks his radio to call in, his "Investigating shots fired" lost among dozens of urgent reports from across the rain-soaked city. Cars are abandoned on flooded Storrow Drive. A power station just exploded and shut down the Back Bay. Looters are smashing boutique windows on Newbury Street.

"Upstairs," he says. They cross the lobby and climb the steps, the still air thick with the sharp smell of aging piss. At the top floor, Harkness counts the doors until they come to the center.

Harkness nods Patrick toward the closer side of the door and he takes the other. They press their backs against the cracked yellow plaster.

"Sure this is the right one?" Patrick whispers, still huffing from the stairs.

A shot rips through the door between them and dim light filters through the splintered hole.

"Seems likely." On a normal patrol, they would have called for backup and waited. But this is no ordinary day. Harkness smacks the crowbar on the door. *"Police,"* he shouts. "Drop the gun and open the door, hands in the air. Now."

Another bullet cracks through the door.

Patrick gives Harkness a flat stare, clicks his radio to leave the channel open, not that anyone's paying attention. "Party time."

"Cover the door." Harkness cuts down the hallway to the other wing of the hotel. He pops a door and it flies open to reveal a dim living room, empty except for a jumbled pile of bicycle frames. He walks slowly to the far corner of the room, where a row of windows faces an air shaft. He grabs a tattered green T-shirt from the floor and wipes the window to clear away the grime.

Looking across the air shaft into the apartment, Harkness sees a young boy leaning against a radiator, tethered to it by a thick, shiny chain around his waist. He waves a gun with one hand and scratches his back with the other. Sensing someone watching, he turns. The boy can't be more than fourteen but looks exhausted as an old man, eyelids drifting down as he stares at Harkness and wonders why there's a cop in the empty room across the air shaft.

They look at each other for a moment. Then the boy holds up his hand and lets the gun drop.

Harkness nods, turns to retrace his steps.

Patrick's face glistens with sweat. "Harky, we got to get out of here, like now."

"Hang on." Harkness kicks open the bullet-pocked door and they take cautious steps into the apartment. Guns drawn, they walk past a sagging couch and a wooden table crowded with bottles and cans. A flat-screen flickers in the corner, the Weather Channel showing clouds swirling and wind-whipped weathermen in slickers shouting silently. Patrick cuts right to check out the kitchen, Harkness left to the bedroom. No one lurks in the trashed rooms, narrow hallways, or closets. They reconnect and inch toward the living room, where the skinny boy stands next to a white radiator, a body sprawled on the floor a few feet away.

"All clear. Just the kid." Patrick holsters his Glock.

"And a dead guy." Harkness leads the way across the living room, tinted green by the storm's aquatic light. The floor is thick with McDonald's boxes, scratch tickets, and wadded clothes.

The boy backs against the radiator.

Patrick walks up to the body. "*Shit,* man. This sad motherfucker's still warm."

"Check him out," Harkness says. "I'll talk to the kid."

Patrick nods, pulls on thin plastic gloves. "I get to have all the fun."

As Harkness walks toward the boy, he bends down to pocket a snub-nose, its grip wrapped with grimy medical tape. "It's okay, kid," he says softly.

The kid's face is light coffee brown with the scared blue-gray eyes of a German shepherd puppy. He's about ninety pounds of raw nerves, wearing a gray T-shirt and cheap jeans that hang limply from his narrow hips. All Harkness feels is shivering bones. The boy says nothing as Harkness pats him down.

"Got a name?"

The boy stares at him, pale eyes glowing in the gloom. He reaches around and scratches his back.

"Lord said to Noah, there's gonna be a floody, floody," Patrick sings to himself.

"Find anything?"

"No blood, wounds, whacks," Patrick says. "Just a wad of cash in his pocket and a big honking needle mark on his left arm. Don't take a genius to come up with the cause of death."

"ID?"

"Nothing yet." Patrick peels off his gloves and throws them on the floor. "Leave it for the techs."

"No one's coming back here for days." Harkness turns to the boy. "Who's that?" He points at the body.

The boy just keeps staring.

"Kid don't have much to say, does he?" Patrick tosses over the dead man's key ring and Harkness reaches up to catch it. He opens the cheap lock and unwraps the shiny chain from around the boy's waist.

The boy darts toward the door.

Harkness reaches out an arm to snag him. "Hold on a second."

The quiet boy's breathing like he just finished a marathon. His eyes ping back and forth and then linger on the couch.

Harkness is a legendary finder of drugs, money, guns, shell casings, cell phones, and the other well-hidden debris of the drug trade. But this hide is easy to spot. The kid might as well be pointing a finger. Harkness walks over to the couch and pushes his hand beneath the cushions. Nothing. Then he reaches back in the gritty space between the cushions and feels a slit in the lining. Reaching farther, he feels plastic. He pulls out a thick quart-size bag jammed with rubber-banded bundles of packets, each stamped with a blood-red horse.

Harkness holds out the bag to Patrick.

"Mother lode, Harky. That's more than a kilo."

Harkness stuffs the drugs in a yellow evidence bag and tosses it to Patrick.

He catches the bag, holds it up. "Know anything about this, skinny kid?"

The boy says nothing.

"Waiting for his lawyer, I guess."

"The kid's deaf," Harkness says.

"How the fuck do you know that?"

"Been watching my lips when I talk. Most kids would have just shouted instead of shooting out the window. And how many people around here keep the sound off on their TV?"

"Like none."

Harkness kneels down in front of the boy and his hands move in fluid motion, telling him that everything's going to be okay.

The kid signs back, hands a blur. He says the dead guy's his uncle, and that other people, bad ones, are on their way to the apartment.

Harkness tells him not to worry, they're leaving.

Patrick's eyes open wide. "When'd you learn that?"

"Taught myself a little American Sign Language one summer when I was a kid, back in Nagog."

"Must've been one boring motherfucker of a summer."

"You have no idea," Harkness says. "Give him your candy bar."

"How do you know I got one?"

"You're Patrick Fitzgerald, aren't you?"

Patrick reaches into the pocket of his jacket and holds out a Mars Bar like he's feeding a tiger. Deaf Kid takes off the wrapper gingerly, sniffs the candy bar, then devours it.

"We really gotta clear out of here, Harky."

"Okay, okay."

"Like now."

Their radios blare the department-wide emergency tone for the first time Harkness can remember and they stand still for a silent moment listening to the dead air before the dispatcher's terse voice echoes through the room. "All units. Channel Dam breached, major flooding expected. Leave evacuation zone immediately and await further . . ."

Harkness picks up Deaf Kid, throws him over his shoulder, and runs toward the door, Patrick following. Their footsteps echo down the dank green stairwell, walls darkened by hundreds of trailing hands.

Outside, the brown water's halfway up the squad-car door. Harkness wades in up to his waist, Deaf Kid slung over his shoulder, and looks into the flooded car, laptop and radio already underwater. Dunkin' Donuts cups swirl like cheerful boats in the back seat.

Patrick pauses in the hotel entryway. Cars are starting to break loose in the rising water and drift down the street. "Hey, Harky," he shouts over the howling storm.

"What?"

"Don't know how to swim."

"*Now* you tell me." Harkness nods toward the hotel. "Inside, quick. Get back upstairs."

The water running down Albrecht Street reverses, flowing away from the square — slowly at first, then faster. Harkness turns to see what's happening.

The seething wave blossoms, fat with trash. Plastic bottles fleck its crest. Foam blows like spit. Cars rise up its face and smash with the crunch of metal and glass. Harkness keeps Deaf Kid turned so he can't see the wave rushing at them — five blocks away, then three blocks, two . . .

Waist-high in whiskey-colored water, Harkness reaches for his belt and unclips his handcuffs. He wraps one cold steel cuff around his wrist then clicks the other closed around Deaf Kid's narrow ankle as the wave sweeps over them.

2

THEY THRASH THROUGH the tempest, swept underwater and dragged down with the cars, trashcans, and stinking debris, the dirty water pulling at them with greedy hands. Harkness struggles toward the dim light above them, swimming with one flailing arm and dragging Deaf Kid cuffed to the other.

Harkness grabs the door handle of a Town Taxi floating by and climbs aboard, pulling Deaf Kid up on the roof by his leg. Skinny chest heaving, the boy sprawls on the slippery surface and coughs up a spume of sepia water.

Harkness takes Deaf Kid by the shoulders and looks into his dimming eyes. The boy's stunned and about to go into shock. Harkness reaches in his pocket for the key, unlocks the handcuff around Deaf Kid's narrow ankle. He nods at the OFF DUTY light and the kid latches onto it.

They ride on the taxi's roof past warehouses and apartment buildings, the street a raging river, the cab a lurching, rudderless barge. They're half drowned and lashed by rain but grinning. For one stolen moment they revel in just being alive.

Then the street tilts down and the cab rushes past apartments, corner stores, and a payday-loan office. Ahead, Albrecht Square glows orange from a burning apartment building, black smoke billowing from every window. Darker shapes dot the water, some flailing and screaming, others floating face-down.

A man leans out of the second-floor window of an apartment building, long dark hair hanging in wet tendrils as he shakes his head at the chaos and destruction — a musician, waiter, night watchman. Doesn't matter. He looks alert and strong. They lock eyes as the cab floats closer. Harkness points down at Deaf Kid then toward the apartment. The man nods, ducks inside, and comes back with others, who lean out the row of windows.

Harkness stands on the roof, gets his footing, then waves at Deaf Kid to get up. Standing but shaky, he angles his dirty Keds like he's on a surfboard. Harkness grabs the kid by the waist.

Deaf Kid looks confused. Harkness smiles, then lifts him up in the air like a sack of leaves and gives him a precisely timed toss toward the waiting hands. Strangers reach out to pull him inside the apartment.

Harkness watches as Deaf Kid squirms in a window and disappears. Then the long-haired guy shakes his head and waves his hands in front of him as if trying to ward off a demon. As Harkness turns, a sizzling black cable coils around his neck and pulls him from the roof of the taxi.

Looking out into the dim, rain-slashed afternoon, Harkness sees a battered white trailer bob in a construction site like a child's toy. Water laps against the stained-glass windows of the red-brick chapel for merchant sailors. Wayward sailboats and floating cars cluster around the courthouse. Only the roof deck remains of the late-night whiskey bar, no loss there — the drunks kept May awake.

Next to the Northern Avenue Bridge, three Harbor Patrol boats, blue lights flashing, surround the harbormaster's shack. Harkness thinks it's strange — that building's been empty for decades — then his gaze wanders to an orange emergency raft gliding through the seaport's streets, now more like canals. Harkness focuses, remembers lying in the bottom of one of those rafts, a Harbor Patrol officer shouting down at him in the rain. But he doesn't know how he got home or how long he's been here in their apartment, staring down at his flooded neighborhood.

He's not even sure anything he sees is real. Is he back in their apartment or dreaming about it?

The parquet floor shifts and sways like the basket of a hot-air balloon. Harkness touches the wall to still it.

When he closes his eyes he sees Albrecht Square flooded and

9

burning and wonders if it was all just a nightmare. Then Harkness raises his hand to touch the bandage on his chest. He pulls away the white tape and lifts the bandage to reveal a silver-dollar-size circle of blackened, blistered skin just below his collarbone, the raw wound covered with clear ointment.

He winces and presses the bandage back in place.

Light footsteps slide across the floor, and the bedroom door inches open.

"Hey, you're supposed to be asleep." Candace's dark eyes look concerned, her face even more pale than usual. She's wearing her good-luck outfit — Celtics sweatpants and a time-thinned Misfits T-shirt — and she clutches a splayed copy of *All for One*, her comfort book.

"I'm awake, right?"

She puts her arms around Harkness and holds him close, tears trailing down her cheeks. "*Jesus*, Eddy. You stepped in it this time."

"I'm okay," he says, voice hoarse. He's swallowed seawater and gutter water, sewage and gasoline, who knows what else.

"Better be."

"How long have I been here?"

She squints. "You don't remember anything, do you?"

"Not really." Harkness shakes his head slowly.

"You got smacked in the head, zapped by a live wire, and half drowned," she says.

He nods, remembers fragments — the orange emergency raft, a doctor's neutral face hovering in a white room.

"You're lucky to be alive, Eddy."

Harkness says nothing.

"You were in the hospital for three nights," Candace says. "They were worried about brain swelling but it didn't happen. You've got a concussion but they said your head would start to clear in a week or so. You're just supposed to chill out and keep your head elevated. Plus you're on pain meds, antibiotics, and a bunch of other drugs."

"How'd I get here?"

"Ambulance from the hospital," she says. "Your friend Lattimore made it happen." Candace nods toward the window. "Neighborhood's all messed up. They're calling it the Inundation District now," she says. "Remember all that fancy Dutch flood stuff they told us about when we moved in here? The reservoir beneath the building, the electrical room on the upper floor?"

Harkness nods, has no idea what Candace is talking about.

"It worked. No water. No problems. Like the flood never happened."

But it did, Harkness thinks.

Candace puts her book on the bedside table and holds out an Elvis-worthy handful of pills in her working hand. When she was seventeen, Candace lost her left hand in a small-plane crash that killed her mother and sister. The accident seems prophetic to Harkness now though he can't say exactly why.

"Time for more drugs," she says.

Harkness stares at the bright capsules in her palm, and then Candace's hand is empty and the water glass on the nightstand is drained. He wonders if this is what Alzheimer's feels like.

The apartment seems too quiet. "Where's . . ." He searches his sputtering mind for Candace's daughter's name. "May?"

Candace tilts her head. "She's downstairs at Nate and Shawna's, playing with Jenna. Wanted to keep the noise down so you can rest."

"She okay?"

"May's fine," Candace says. "To a three-year-old, being trapped at home during a storm is an adventure."

"Oh."

"You know you asked me the same questions about May like an hour ago, right?"

"Don't remember that."

"Check this out." Candace holds up the front section of the *Globe* and waves it, trying to bring back fast-thinking, relentlessly focused Eddy. "Building manager dropped this by a couple of days ago. He thought you might want an old-style copy, for your scrapbook or something."

Harkness stares at the giant headline that screams FLOOD. In a black box at the top the mayor warns people to stay off the streets until further notice.

Candace opens the paper. "You're a bright spot in the storm." There are photos of the Charles River rushing across the Esplanade, rows of commuter trains underwater in the South Station rail yard, the UMass Boston campus cut off from the mainland by the storm surge. Then he sees a black-haired cop who looks like he just got sprayed with a fire hose standing on the hood of a floating cab, a scrawny kid hovering just above him in mid-toss while waiting arms reach down to grab him.

"I don't remember anyone taking pictures."

"Cell phones, Eddy. Someone's pretty much always taking pictures."

Harkness wonders where Deaf Kid is now, and Patrick. He turns to Candace. "Hey, help me find my uniform."

"Got to be kidding," she says. "They cut off what was left of it in the ER."

"There's another one somewhere." He tries to remember where.

"Eddy, you're supposed to take at least another week off to recover. You got whacked around. And you're not acting normal yet, just so you know. Even for you."

He closes his eyes, sees nothing but water and fire.

"Anyway, you can't go anywhere. No one can. The mayor says we all have to stay put until the electricity's back on and the flood starts to go down."

"When's that supposed to happen?"

"Pretty soon," she says. "Wasn't as bad as it could have been. Dodged a bullet, that's what they're saying."

"Who's saying that?"

The room shifts again and Harkness lurches toward the bed. He hears Candace talking in the distance. The room darkens as a cloud crosses the dim sun hovering over Chinatown.

A high oscillating note, warm as a Stratocaster playing through a vintage tube amp, rings in his right ear then moves to the left. George got a Strat for Christmas once, Olympic white with a tortoiseshell pick guard. Harkness wonders where his brother's guitar ended up, reminds himself to ask. It's probably worth a pile now and George always needs more money . . .

Harkness's knees give way and he sprawls on the bed. "Sorry, really tired." Candace lifts his head gently to put a pillow underneath it, then covers him with a blanket. *Like a body at a crime scene,* he thinks as he drops into deep, black sleep.

⋅ ⋅ ⋅

That night Harkness patrols the streets of the Lower South End before the flood, his drug-slowed dreams summoning up the neighborhood he knew when he was a rookie — restaurant-supply stores, a tearoom for readings, old-style Irish pubs, cheap hotels and apartments that rented by the month. Albrecht Square had the worn charm of Dirty Old Boston. It was the Scollay Square that the city fathers couldn't tear down.

Then the light over the neighborhood shifts to verdigris and the streets stream with stinking water, sweeping him away. Harkness's legs uncoil in his sleep as he sinks underwater and tries to swim.

Churning her narrow legs, Little Dorothy kicks closer, her pink dress billowing like the poisoned scrim of a jellyfish. She turns her head to reveal the vernixed oval of bone where her face once was before she became just another dead girl. Years ago, Harkness found Little Dorothy hidden behind the wall of a Fenway meth lab, her stiff, starved body stuffed head-down in a bucket of sodium hydroxide.

No matter how many years pass, no matter how many other bodies he sees, Little Dorothy still travels with him, a memory he can't drink away.

The underwater revenant points a pale finger at Harkness and opens her tattered mouth to give out a burbling laugh, a message to Harkness and all of the other survivors.

The storm may be over. But the damage is just beginning.

3

A DIVING MASK HANGS from the coat rack in the corner of Harkness's office and a striped beach towel waits in the center of his desk topped with a Post-it note that says *Gone Swimmin.'* Harkness smiles and shakes his head. He's back at work at Narco-Intel headquarters, four floors above Boylston Street. Patrick and the others have had a week to mess with his office.

"Thanks, people," Harkness says to the detectives hanging around his office door. "I'm amused and honored. Now get back to work."

They drift back to their cubes. Harkness looks out his window at cobblestoned Copley Square, ornate Trinity Church to the left, somber Boston Public Library to the right, the shimmering blue spear of the Hancock Building rising behind them both. Generators roar on Boylston Street, sunny and hot now that the last of the storm has spiraled out over the North Atlantic. Hoses spew murky water from basement bars. City workers in emergency vests shovel mud into green plastic barrels, feed downed branches into roaring chippers. Students, scholars, and bums step carefully along the crooked wooden walkways that cross the watery edges of the square.

Harkness turns to find Esther Vieramenos standing in his doorway. She's tall and birdlike, wearing a gray sweater on a hot day, dark bangs falling in front of darker eyes that lurk behind thick black-rimmed glasses. Her ID hangs from her narrow neck on a summer-camp rawhide lanyard. She looks like a detective someone bought on Etsy.

"I tried that shit, boss," she whispers.

"What shit?"

"Dark Horse."

"You mean you gave it a little taste, right?" Harkness busted her years ago when she was a coke-dealing Brandeis chemistry major. Now she's the Narco-Intel lab rat.

She shakes her head. "Nope. Swiped a gram from Evidence and snorted it low and slow all during the flood. Savored it like a wine taster."

Harkness looks up at the ceiling. "I'm going to have to unhear that."

Esther's their canary in the coal mine. She thinks like an addict because she used to be one.

Or maybe still is.

"I was stuck at home in Waltham, boss. Couldn't go anywhere. Sheltering in place was a big bore. Moody Street was flooded. Internet was out. Wanted to see what all the fuss was about."

Harkness holds his hand up. "Still unhearing." When Harkness drafted Esther for Narco-Intel she promised to stay on the straight edge. "Backsliding?"

"Nope," she says. "Just doing some not-so-scientific research."

"Sure."

"Dark Horse is messed up."

"You mean deadly," Harkness says.

"Way too strong for what it's going for on the street." Esther shrugs. "Maybe they're getting people hooked, then they'll jack up the price. I'll take a closer look at it in the lab."

"Do that. But just a look, okay?" Harkness steps toward Esther and stares into her dark brown eyes, checks that her pupils aren't constricted. At least she's not high on the job. He couldn't have let that slide. "Still getting tested?" Esther's contract includes random drug testing.

"Yeah?"

"If you ever test positive I'll have to fire you, you know that, right?"

Esther shrugs. "Don't worry about me, boss. I got buckets of normal pee. People're peeing for me all over the city."

"Thanks for that," Harkness says.

Now Patrick's hovering at his office door.

15

"I want full lab results next week, okay?"

Esther nods and turns. She runs her hand along Patrick's chest as they pass. "Hey, Patrick. I may be half Cuban but I'm all yours." She beams an unhinged smile at her office rival.

"I don't hang with freaky chicks who collect pee."

"Your loss." She clicks the door closed.

"Welcome back to the garden of misfit toys an' shit," Patrick says.

"Glad to be back."

"Feeling better?"

Harkness sits down at his desk. "Kind of. What'd I miss?"

"A week of flood duty with some clown lieutenant from A-One," Patrick says. He points down at the square. "We guarded a burnt-out power station. Cordoned off the flooded T station over in Maverick Square. Shoveled fish in the North End. That was a really fun day. The city's going to stink forever."

The roiling green clouds of the hurricane rained biblical hauls of fish down on the city — cod, stripers, small sharks, rays, and thick globs of jellyfish. Sucked up from the Grand Banks, now they clog alleys and dry on rooftops.

"It'll pass," Harkness says. "Everything goes away."

"Deep, boss. Think I'll write that down," Patrick says, but doesn't.

Harkness nods toward his dual computer screens, one playing the local news with the sound off, the other crowded with DEA trend data, the OD list from Boston City Hospital, and hundreds of unanswered e-mails. "Trending?"

"Just junk, junk, and more junk," he says. "Startin' to look like the Salvation Army around here. Every now and then I actually miss good ol' Oxy. At least people knew what they were getting with pills."

"We need to flag Dark Horse," Harkness says.

"Why? It's just old-style black tar. Crap heroin from California."

"Esther says it's weird."

"I say Esther's weird."

"Agreed, but we're getting more confirmed overdoses." Harkness points to the screen. "Send out an info request to the network. I don't want to keep finding Dark Horse bags next to dead people."

Patrick holds up his hands. "Done, boss. Department-wide?"

Harkness thinks. "Put it out to the whole network."

"Whatever you say, Harky. But this one's not worth the trouble. Black tar ain't nothing new."

"We'll see."

Narco-Intel's mission is "to take an unconventional, more effective approach to drug interdiction." Just how unconventional is an ongoing topic of discussion among Boston Police Department commanders, who regard the Bad Boys of the BPD with a mix of respect, eye-rolling, and worry that they'll go too far, again.

The Narcotics Information Network was one of Harkness's first innovations, a network of unlikely sources—bodega owners in Dudley Square, single mothers in Bromley-Heath, neighborhood dog walkers on Castle Island, art students in grimy Fenway basement apartments. Thousands of eyes on the street will turn up everything from empty heroin packets to cell-phone photos of users to addresses of potential dealers—all fed into a database that Patrick calls Big Data on Drugs.

Patrick reaches for the card taped to a bottle of Jameson on the briefing table. "Least you could do is open the note, Harky."

"Was just about to do that."

Patrick rips open the tiny envelope. "Card says 'Fantastic job, as usual. Get well soon. Apply this to affected areas.'" Patrick holds the card up to the light. "Bet one of his doofus helper dudes wrote it—the commissioner's just not that funny. Looks like he really signed it, though."

"Quit reading my mail," Harkness says, not looking away from his computer screen.

"All's I get is hardware catalogs and postcards from the gym."

"Maybe you ought to go sometime."

"To the hardware store?"

"To the gym. Or at least the swimming pool."

Patrick flails his hands in front of him. "Now that's just crazy talk, Harky. We ain't gonna see another hurricane like that for years, that's what they're saying on TV."

"Who, Fox?"

"No, real people."

Harkness stands and the room blurs and sparkles. He wavers, then sits back down, pressing his fingertips on his desk to keep from keeling over.

"You okay?"

Harkness gives a small nod, eyes closed. "From that concussion. Supposed to take it easy for another week or so." A question surfaces in Harkness's sputtering mind. He opens his eyes. "What about the kid?"

Patrick thrusts out his phone. "Seen this?"

Onscreen, Harkness throws Deaf Kid over and over from the top of a floating cab into the waiting arms of strangers who seem to be several floors above, thanks to editing that adds yards to the toss. The screen blazes with the words HE SHOOTS, HE SCORES!

"What the hell's that?"

"Animated GIF thingy," Patrick says. "You're a meme already. Gone viral."

"Can't antibiotics kill that off?"

"Most people would love that kind of attention."

"That's the problem."

Patrick watches Deaf Kid go airborne one last time then pockets his phone. "Deaf Kid checked out clean from the hospital, except he's underweight. And stone-deaf, course. You called that one. Kid doesn't even have a real name."

"What?"

"Birth certificate says Unnamed Boy. Mom never got around to fixing it."

"Relatives?"

"Dead junkie sprawled next to the radiator actually was his uncle. Went by the name Levon Ashmont."

"His uncle chained him to a radiator, really?"

Patrick shrugs. "Had like a dozen priors. Violent offender. Big-league dealer, which explains the value pack of junk stuck in the couch. Anyhow, you got to admit, the kid's kind of a wildcat."

"Weren't we all," Harkness says. "Any other family around?"

"Father got shot dead last year in Dudley. Mom's crazy, ended up in MCI. Got diabetes something awful. They ran out of things to amputate."

"Where's the kid now?"

"Department of Youth Offenders has him."

"DYO?" Harkness shakes his head. "He didn't do anything wrong. They won't know what to do with him." DYO is legendary for no-

18

show caseworkers who let kids fall through the cracks. He gets up from his desk and stalks toward the window to stare down at Copley Square. "Let's get him out of there."

"When did we get in the deaf-kid business?"

"Since we found one."

Patrick joins him at the window. "You and your strays, Harky. Got to say, I'm thankful, being one. On the other hand, I think you got enough already."

Harkness goes silent, narrows his gaze at the steps of the library.

"See something, say something." Patrick intones the Homeland Security creed without enthusiasm.

"That guy coming out of the library? Recognize him?" Harkness points to a short guy with a backpack, his smoke-bush hair swaying in the wind.

Patrick shakes his head. "Looks like any other dumb-ass student."

Harkness grabs his badge and throws on his gun belt and leather jacket. "Looks like Mouse. Dealer out in Nagog. Remember him?"

"Oh yeah, that guy. Major douche. Sold that nasty smart drug." Irresistible, expensive, and deadly, Third Rail is a Narco-Intel Hall of Famer.

"Mouse owes me."

"Owes you what?"

Harkness holds up his left hand, most of its index finger missing. "A finger."

4

HIS MISSING FINGER ACHES, Harkness could swear it does, as he runs across Copley Square toward the library entrance. That would be impossible—no finger can remember who did the severing.

But Harkness does.

He's coming up behind the hairy guy in a black denim vest. As he gets closer, Harkness reaches for his gun out of habit, then forces his hand away.

"Hey, Mouse."

Mouse turns, looks at him, then starts to run, the planks and his short legs slowing his progress. Harkness tackles Mouse, taking him down like he's a hipster piñata.

"You can't just, like, do that."

"I smell probable cause." Harkness rolls Mouse over and rummages through his muddy backpack, finding only a sticker-covered laptop and a stack of crumpled papers.

"Hey, man, that's not any of your —"

Harkness holds up his left hand, its index finger neatly severed at the first knuckle.

Mouse stops suddenly when he recognizes Harkness. "Oh, wow. Dude. It's *you*."

"You almost killed me." Harkness reaches down to pull Mouse off the ground and half drags, half walks him away from the crowd to a dark alcove next to the building's entrance. "Before I haul you in, I want to hear an apology, loud and clear."

In the shadow of one of the library's guardian statues, where scholars smoke, lovers kiss, bums piss, and book thieves compare tactics, Harkness shoves Mouse down, presses his boot crossways on Mouse's throat, and leans on it until the air starts to wheeze out of him like a pawnshop accordion.

Seeing Mouse rolling in the rot drags Harkness back to a Halloween party in a muddy field. A riot, screaming kids high on Third Rail, Candace searching for May—it isn't a time that Harkness wants to revisit.

Mouse waves his arms like he has something important to say. Everyone does when he has a boot on his throat.

Harkness lets up.

"Heard you were living with Candace now," Mouse croaks. "That's pretty weird."

"When I want your comments on my personal life," Harkness says, "a neon sign that says *Your Comments Here* will light up over my head, okay?"

"I mean, you *killed* Dex, dude." Mouse continues, ignoring the lack of neon. He fails to mention that Dex, Candace's ex-lover and May's father, was shooting at Harkness at the time. "That guy was a fucking genius." Mouse's hushed tone implies that Harkness, a mere cop, will never even come close to being that intelligent.

"Okay, heard enough out of you." Harkness puts his boot back in place.

"Stop. I'm sorry, I'm sorry. *I'm sorry!*"

Harkness nods, moves his boot away.

"It wasn't my fault, anyway." Mouse sits up, tries to brush the mud from his vest. "I have ESD."

Harkness just stares.

"Empathetic-sideman disorder," Mouse says, as if announcing that he has pancreatic cancer.

"That a real disease?"

"Should be."

"'Splain."

"It's when you're around someone who makes you do things you wouldn't ever do if they weren't around. Heard of Bill Evans?"

"Not much of a jazz guy." Harkness spent his youth in sweaty clubs listening to one-minute songs of the faster-louder variety.

"Bill Evans turned into a junkie for years," Mouse says. "Not because he *was* a junkie — 'cause, dude, he was like the straightest white guy in earth. But because of Miles Davis. Miles made all his sidemen get weird."

"So that's your excuse? Dex made you a freak?"

"Made me violent."

"The only thing I know about you is that there's still a warrant out for your arrest for assaulting a police officer." Harkness reaches back for his cuffs. "That would be me."

"Come on, man," Mouse says. "It's ancient history."

"Wasn't even a year ago."

"In Internet time, that's forever."

"Tell it to the DA." Harkness bends forward and grabs a hairy wrist. He's about to cuff and Miranda Mouse when the cobblestones shift beneath his feet and the cooling afternoon air sputters like water drops hitting a hot skillet.

"Harky? *Harky?*"

Harkness wakes lying on the dirty cobblestones, concerned faces clustered in a tight circle above him — Patrick, Esther, other Narco-Intel cops, a handful of office workers on their lunch hour, but not Mouse.

"Hey, get that guy," Harkness slurs. "Guy with a beard and a backpack." Harkness tries to stand but Patrick puts out a hand to stop him.

"That's like half the dudes in Boston, Harky."

"There's a warrant out on this one."

"Well, he's gone now." Patrick clicks his radio and puts the word out. "Now we're just going to get you back to the office so a doc can check you out."

Harkness tries to stand, his head heavy, legs wobbly.

"That cop's drunk," someone mutters.

"Figures," another says. "They're all drunk."

"Guy's a hero, smart-asses. Got a head injury in the line of duty," Patrick shouts. "Scatter. I mean it. Shoo!" He waves the people away like they're the swampy smell wafting over the square.

The crowd disappears and Harkness stands. Some papers from

Mouse's backpack are scattered on the cobblestones, and Harkness tries to pick them up.

"This is where you get in trouble, Harky," Patrick says. "Putting your head down low. Makin' all the blood rush." Patrick squats down and collects the papers. "You're going back to the office for some desk duty until the doc says you're back to normal. Or normal enough."

Harkness says nothing, just leans on Patrick as they stumble along the crooked planks that stretch across the square.

5

A WAITRESS COMPLAINS THAT her meds are in her apartment and the city won't let her back in her cordoned-off neighborhood. A crying young girl says her cat, Teddy, is still locked in her flooded apartment. A convenience store has been looted down to its bare shelves. "Whatever the water didn't ruin, they come and took," its owner says to the TV reporter in knee-high rubber boots. The camera shows empty Lower South End streets, still flooded weeks after the hurricane.

The story shifts to Brighton, where a storm-damaged biomedical lab is without power. A somber reporter delivers the update in front of the lab, thick with emergency crews in hazmat suits. "A frightened neighborhood still wonders, When will the frozen specimens in this lab start to thaw? Will the flood unleash smallpox, Ebola, or other deadly viruses?" Harkness clicks and the storm porn disappears.

His cell phone rings. It's his brother's number. Harkness considers not answering.

"George."

"Eddy. Get my message?"

"Been kinda under the weather. Literally."

"What happened?"

"Got head-butted by a car during the hurricane. And electrocuted, thanks for asking."

"Saw that thing on the Internet! Nice job, bro. *He shoots, he scores!* You're like a fucking hero again."

"Hardly."

His brother pauses and takes a slow inhale, gearing up. Every call from George comes with a demand. "You and Candace should come out and have dinner with Nora and me in Nagog. Got some family stuff to figure out."

This rare nonfinancial request takes Harkness by surprise, makes him wonder what George is up to. His brother decided to keep the family company afloat after the small-town Ponzi scheme of their late father, Edward "Red" Harkness, came unraveled. The survival of Harkness and Sons is all George thinks about. But maybe there's still a brother beneath the businessman.

"Sure," Harkness says.

"Good."

"Got to get back to work, George." Harkness's thumb is edging toward the End Call button.

"And I need your help with something," George blurts out.

Harkness clicks his phone off.

The stray papers from Mouse's backpack, stacked on the edge of his desk, catch his eye. He flips through printouts of books from the 1700s. Harkness stops when he comes across pages from *A Compleat Record of the Laws Pertaining to Nagog, Massachusetts*. Why would Mouse care about the ancient laws of a quiet colonial town? That Nagog is also his hometown makes Harkness even more curious. He puts the papers in his notebook and clips on his badge.

Patrick looks up from his computer screen when Harkness walks past his desk.

"Just going to the library," Harkness says.

"Don't get into trouble."

Harkness smiles. "How much trouble can you get into at the library, really?"

"You? Plenty."

Harkness walks quietly down the middle aisle of Bates Hall, the Boston Public Library's enormous reading room, its ceiling vaulted like a basilica of books, long wooden tables lit by green-glass lamps. Diligent high-school kids study, businessmen stare at laptop screens, and street people mutter in their sleep. Harkness opens the green door marked *Rare Books* and sidles past rows of barrels filled with flood-sodden books. He climbs a marble staircase, its narrow windows facing a dim air shaft, tan paint flaking off the walls like dried mud.

On the third floor, the maze of shelves ends at a large, windowless room, more laboratory than library — the Rare Books Department. Technicians in white coats huddle over a sophisticated scanner, the shelves behind them lined with leather-bound books locked behind glass.

A technician with close-cropped blond hair walks closer. "Can I help you, Officer?" The ID tag hanging around his neck says GLENN SIMON, SENIOR CURATOR.

"Sorry to bother you," Harkness says. "I just have a quick question."

Glenn squints. "Eddy? Eddy Harkness?"

"Right." Harkness tries to place the stranger, hopes he isn't someone he busted.

"Graduated a year after you."

A vague memory of a younger, scrawnier version of Glenn surfaces, an intense freshman striding across the elm-cosseted Harvard Yard.

Glenn can see that Harkness doesn't really remember him. "Not a problem, Eddy. I pretty much lived in Widener."

"Yeah." Harkness spent most of his time in basement clubs full of noise and skinheads. Widener Library was for naps in the reference room or sex in the stacks.

"Looks like we both went for the big money, doesn't it? A cop and a curator. Both working for the city. Not exactly Goldman Sachs."

"No, not at all." Almost a decade after graduation, even Harkness's coolest friends have ended up working at investment banks.

"But we managed to avoid the magnetic allure of lucre." Glenn smiles at his own cleverness. Harkness can envision him in his spotless Cambridge condo drinking single-malt late into the night as he sings along with Stephen Malkmus.

Harkness hands Glenn the stack of printouts from his pocket. "What can you tell me about these?"

"Where'd you get them?"

"From some guy who tried to kill me last year."

"Wow, what happened?"

26

"He didn't kill me."

Glenn flips through the papers. "Looks like part of *Revolutionary Records*. Finished the scanning right before the flood. About thirty handwritten legal record books from Lexington, Charlestown, Nagog — all the Revolutionary-era towns."

Harkness holds up a page from the *Compleat Record of the Laws Pertaining to Nagog*. "Grew up in Nagog."

"Lucky you. Nice little town."

"Debatable," Harkness says. "Look, why would anyone care about this stuff?"

Glenn tilts his head. "People like reading about obscure laws. They're like terms of service from the past. Like not letting sheep out on the town green after eight in the evening. You can't shout on the Sabbath. Kissing in public is punishable by an hour of whipping. Stuff like that. Every couple of years, the History Channel does a story about the laws that are still on the books around here. One of those 'quaint old New England' feature stories. Maybe your guy was doing some research?"

"Maybe." Mouse doesn't seem like a closet historian.

The scanner sends out an eye-searing blast of light and Harkness nods toward it. "What's that all about?"

Glenn rolls his eyes. "New initiative. O'Mara wants to digitize everything in the Special Collections. The hurricane got the mayor all worried about the city's priceless intellectual treasures." He puts air quotes around the last words.

"This place looks pretty safe." Harkness glances around the busy lab. "Anyway, you're up on the third floor."

Glenn shakes his head. "Protecting the books is only half of the story." He searches his worktable and then tosses Harkness a pair of white cotton gloves. "Put these on for a second."

Harkness pulls on the gloves and Glenn stacks books in his hands.

"Here's a *Nuremberg Chronicle*. Here's a book printed by William Blake." Glenn piles on more books, then unlocks a glass case and takes out a small volume. "And here's the *Bay Psalm Book*, the first book printed in America."

Harkness steadies the wavering stack.

"There," Glenn says. "You're holding about a hundred million dollars in rare books."

"Had no idea."

Glenn carefully removes each book. "Well, the mayor, our mutual employer, definitely does." The scanner sends out another blast like lightning striking the small room. "They're like money in the bank."

"Except they're not in a bank," Harkness says.

Glenn raises his eyebrows. "Exactly."

6

PATRICK BARGES INTO Harkness's office and stares out his window down at Boylston Street. "Commissioner! Commissioner!" Arms flailing, he rushes back to his cubicle to shovel all his desk debris into a trashcan. The other detectives pull off their headphones, sit up straight, and concentrate on their computers with new rigor. Commissioner Lattimore commands fear along with respect, thanks to his blistering tongue and on-the-spot demotions.

"People." Commissioner Lattimore strides through Narco-Intel's front office, a phalanx of aides in tow.

Everyone stands, salutes crisply.

Lattimore puts his hand on Harkness's shoulder. "Feeling better, aren't you?"

"Yes, sir." Harkness nods.

"Ready to get out of the office for an hour or so, aren't you? Get a little air?" Lattimore always encodes the answers into his questions, a habit from years of interrogations.

Harkness smiles, says what the commissioner wants to hear. "That would be great, sir."

"Excellent," he says. "Because I could use your help with a . . . situation. And there's someone downstairs who wants to see you."

Deaf Kid sits inside the commissioner's SUV like a tiny time traveler in a glossy black spaceship. Seeing Harkness, he starts smacking on the smoky glass with both fists. When the door opens, he flings himself forward and throws his skinny arms around Harkness's shoulders.

Harkness signs that it's great to see him, asks whether everything's okay. The boy just shakes his head no. He pinches his orange Department of Youth Offenders sweatshirt like it's toxic. Harkness climbs inside next to Deaf Kid. They're thrown back in their leather seats as the SUV hurtles down Boylston. The driver takes a hard right on Dartmouth and their caravan crosses into the expensive part of the South End, with its home-goods stores and farm-to-table bistros.

"A month later and it's like the flood never happened," Lattimore shouts from the passenger seat. "The city is in major denial. Everyone got all bent out of shape about the smallpox thing and you know what?" Lattimore doesn't wait for an answer. "Nothing happened. The emergency generators kicked in and the bio lab's fine. End of story."

Harkness nods. The things people worry about usually don't happen.

"But the Lower South End? We're getting pounded there, Harkness. Citizens throwing rocks at us because we won't let them back into their apartments."

"That's not our decision," Harkness says.

"Try telling that to a screaming mother with three kids," Lattimore says. "They're calling us storm troopers on Twitter. Ha-fucking-ha-ha."

Lattimore keeps going. "That guy's making all the wrong moves, if you ask me. No press conference. No reconstruction plan. He manages from the neck up. No heart. All dollar signs. Won't even return my calls."

Harkness nods. *That guy* is the new mayor, Michael O'Mara, who emerged as an unexpected winner in last fall's election after tacking together a pro-business coalition. Harkness doesn't mention that he voted for O'Mara, who seemed more competent than his opponent, Sam Reed—a perennial Mr. Nice Guy on the city council.

The commissioner turns around to shout directly at them. "We ought to be getting the city up and running again. Instead, this guy's got us standing around like the National Guard at Kent State."

Deaf Kid looks confused by the commissioner's anger. Harkness signs that he'll explain later. It'll be a crash course in Boston politics.

When Councilman John Fitzgerald had to drop out of the preliminary election thanks to worse-than-usual corruption charges, Michael O'Mara left the helm of his venture-capital firm and elbowed into the race. Parish-loads of church ladies all over the city voted for O'Mara because his name sounded Catholic. We Love MOM! — his campaign slogan, spread via every medium from bumper sticker to Twitter — made political analysts cringe. But it helped a dark-horse candidate eke out a razor-thin second-place win in the preliminary election and then a surprise upset against front-runner Reed in the general.

Lattimore supported Reed from the start, saying he was a friend of law enforcement. Now that O'Mara's mayor, the rumors around Narco-Intel say Lattimore's a short-timer.

Lattimore holds out a clipboard. "You used to be a beat cop around here, right, Harkness?"

"Yes, sir."

"Well, take a whack at my comments. They need to be more, you know, local and spontaneous. Add some real stuff." He points to his aides in the jump seat, Central Casting prepsters in blue blazers and white shirts, their striped ties varying slightly. "The Two Stooges spend most of their time playing squash at the Harvard Club."

The aides roll their eyes skyward. A file cabinet full of abuse comes with every BPD admin job.

As the SUV pulls over in a muddy street, protesters circle the car. They're carrying signs that read *We Are Boston* and *We Matter Too*. Harkness spots a short, bearded guy in round sunglasses standing in the background waving a sign. Mouse. Harkness takes a closer look but he's gone.

"The smarty-pants in Cambridgeport get a little water in their basements and the mayor's there. The Lower South End gets pounded, a dozen people die, and the mayor doesn't even show up, ever. Property over people. That's the line on O'Mara out on the street. Done with that speech?"

Harkness hands him the clipboard.

"Thanks." Lattimore reaches for his door handle. "Okay, people.

Showtime. Everyone dial it up to ten — eleven if you go that high. Stooges, try not to piss anyone off."

Lattimore takes a bullhorn from his driver and jumps on the hood of the SUV. The BPD regulars close in to protect him but he waves them away, takes a quick glance at his clipboard, and launches in:

"I'm Commissioner Lattimore of the Boston Police Department and I'm here to tell you that something's very wrong in the Lower South End."

Lattimore would reject the comparison, but Harkness senses a Kennedy vibe in the air, the good part of the legacy, the tough Irish honesty from before politics devolved into optics and messaging. The crowd falls silent.

"You're not being treated fairly and I'm sorry. Storms cause chaos. Be assured, our patrolmen aren't here to guard property. They're here to help people. They're here to help you."

Deafening silence from the dubious protesters.

"We're setting up a command post right over there in the lobby of the Hotel Blackstone. We'll escort residents back into their apartments as soon as the building inspector says they're safe. In the meantime, we'll be distributing all the aid that we can — water, food, and emergency funds. And we'll be working in close partnership with the mayor —"

Scattered boos here. The new mayor isn't earning any political capital in the Lower South End — but that's not his constituency.

"There's only one Boston, friends. Lots of neighborhoods. But only one city."

Lattimore gives Harkness a nod for this line, which gets scattered cheers.

"We have to stick together during tough times like this. Boston Strong, right? It may not seem fair to you — some parts of the city are fine, yours got hit hardest of all. That's the way storms work. They're not fair. No one predicted this hurricane would hit here at all, but we can all help fix its aftermath and rebuild. Fairly and impartially. And I guarantee you, some good will come from this terrible storm."

He nods toward Deaf Kid.

"As proof, take a look at a young man from your neighborhood, born into chaos and poverty. His mother never named him, but his friends call him Vince. Father was killed in a shooting in Dudley Square. His uncle was a dealer who overdosed on heroin. Vince barely escaped the flood."

A couple of guys shout, "He shoots, he scores!" Harkness gives a small wave to shut them up.

"And now the Boston Police Department is going to remove him from the custody of the Department of Youth Offenders — because, after all, what was his crime? He was just in the wrong place at the wrong time. We'll be paying for his care at the world-renowned Hamilton School for the Deaf in Waltham out of our educational fund."

Lattimore gives Harkness an astonished glance at this new paragraph. Harkness and the rest of the crowd applaud the commissioner's generosity.

"Because we believe that any neighborhood is only as thriving as its most vulnerable resident. And as this neighborhood recovers from a terrible storm, we'll be doing all that we can to help everyone in need. Thank you."

The crowd huddles around Harkness and Deaf Kid, who clings to him like a marsupial. Lattimore sidles up behind him and whispers, "So where's this so-called educational fund?"

"Thought you might know, sir," Harkness says.

"I ought to take it out of Narco-Intel's operating funds."

"Sure," Harkness says, "if you want to explain another spike in heroin overdoses."

"Okay, okay. We'll bury it in next year's budget."

"The Hamilton School's expecting him at three this afternoon," Harkness says.

"*What?*"

"The *Globe*'s meeting you there. Texted a guy I know. They're doing a feature. News channels too."

"Great publicity," the Stooges blurt in unison.

Harkness nods.

"Best of all," Lattimore says, warming to the idea, "O'Mara ends up looking like a heartless bastard."

7

THE BLOOD-RED HORSES spread through the city as Patrick presses a key on his laptop in the Narco-Intel conference room. It's almost midnight and everyone has gone home except Harkness, Patrick, and Esther — the ad hoc Dark Horse task force.

"What're we looking at?" Esther drinks black coffee from her chipped blue BPD mug.

"Known Dark Horse sightings that came in from the network. The darker the horses are, the more confident we are that the data's good. Darkest ones show confirmed overdoses." Patrick points to the first screen, where there's only a small cluster in the Lower South End. "See here? Starts showing up in June." He clicks and the numbers increase and darken, filling the neighborhood. "Really hits the streets in July and August. And then . . ." He clicks again and the scatter pattern of dark red horses dwindles with each click. "*Kaboom*. Pretty much disappears after the flood."

Esther shrugs. "What's so weird about that?"

"What's so weird about you?"

"You're up next, Esther," Harkness says. "Just let him finish." He's already regretting putting Patrick and Esther on special assignment together.

"Since when have you seen a drug that stays inside a neighborhood like that, girl?" Patrick says. "People may be all *buy local* and shit, but that's for microgreens and heirloom squash, not junk. This

Dark Horse stuff pounded the Lower South End. Then it's like game over when the flood hits."

"Flood must've washed out a big supplier," she says.

Patrick shakes his head. "The pros always bounce back."

"What does this all mean, people?" Harkness asks.

"Dark Horse is a neighborhood threat that's run its course," Patrick says. "It's old-style black tar someone dragged in from California, and it's over. The data don't lie, boss."

"Not so fast." Esther unplugs Patrick's laptop and plugs hers in. "Been taking a look at it in the lab."

"You mean snorting it up your pointy nose," Patrick says.

Harkness raises his hand. "Enough. You're on the same team. Got it?"

"Okay, okay." Patrick rolls his eyes.

Esther unleashes a virtuosic flurry of keystrokes and pulls up the lab results. "On the left, Dark Horse. On the right, weapons-grade heroin from Afghanistan via Baltimore. It's the purest known heroin found on the street in the last decade. The gold standard for junk." Esther looks at Harkness and Patrick. "The difference?"

"Dark Horse looks kinda brown to me," Patrick says. "On account of it being black tar."

Esther shakes her head. "Black tar would show a lot more acetylated morphine derivatives, mainly six-MAM and three-MAM, when we put it in Gwen."

Patrick looks up. "What's *ma'am*?"

"Monoacetylmorphine," Esther says. "Let me know if you want a fascinating explanation of the Wright-Beckett process and its shortcomings."

Patrick squints. "And who the hell's Gwen?"

"The centrifuge," she says. "I named it Gwen. The scanning electron microscope is Jerome. And the —"

It's Harkness's turn to roll his eyes. "Let's move on. So if it's not black tar, what is it?"

"It's incredibly powerful heroin, about ninety-nine percent pure, putting it up there with Afghan White," Esther says. "But it's cut with cheap brown lactose."

"What kind of dealer disguises high-grade junk so it looks like crappy junk?" Patrick says. "And sells it for about the same as a jumbo bag of Skittles?"

"Patrick's right. Doesn't make sense," Harkness says. Usually it's the other way around. Crystal meth bleached to look like cocaine. Mexican shitweed sprayed with angel dust for kick. Low-grade heroin boosted with fentanyl.

Esther shakes her head. "All I can tell you guys is what we found in the lab," she says. "Beyond that, I really don't know."

"Well, you better start finding out." Patrick says.

"Correction," Harkness says. "*We* better start finding out. All of us. I want both of you to dig into this one — more research, daily updates, collaboration with the DEA. Because if Dark Horse surfaces again, it's going to find a lot of new customers looking for a cheap thrill."

"You talking about students?" Patrick says. "But they're too young, cool, and smart to die. Just ask 'em."

Harkness nods. "Low tolerances, high potency. If Dark Horse hits the campuses this winter, we're going to end up carrying a lot of dead students out of their dorm rooms."

In the freighted silence, Harkness's cell phone rings. It's a familiar number. "Got to take this one. Task force meets again tomorrow night, same time."

Patrick and Esther drift away, pacing themselves so they don't reach the office door together.

"Harkness."

"Eddy, it's me." It's the voice of Captain Watt out at Nagog police headquarters. "Got a big problem out here."

"What's going on?"

"Got a pissed-off guy cuffed and screaming in the back of my squad car."

"What'd he do?"

"Attempted B and E."

"Sounds like you got your man. What's the problem?"

"It's your brother, Eddy. It's George."

36

8

HARKNESS DRIVES WEST from Boston at ninety miles an hour, lights flashing, early Swans blaring from the Chevy's blown-out speakers. He knows the twelve-mile trip all too well. He races through the Concord rotary, swerves onto the Nagog exit after a few minutes, then speeds through the outskirts of his inescapable hometown.

The windows of the Nagog Five and Ten are dark, the green clock above the Coffee Spot blinks on and off, and the banks at the center of town face each other in a silent stare-down. Except for SUVs instead of horses and paved roads replacing dirt streets, the town looks about the same as it in Colonial times. In 1775, town militiamen forced the British out several weeks *before* the Battles of Lexington and Concord — making Nagog popular with tourists and misery-inducing for teenagers growing up surrounded by too much history.

Harkness speeds by the Unitarian Church, its rainbow banner hanging over the peace labyrinth: ALL ARE WELCOME! BRING YOUR BELIEFS. His father used to tell a joke after a few gin and tonics: "How can you tell when Unitarians are mad at you? They burn a question mark on your front lawn."

This was before most of the town started demanding that Harkness's father be burned at the stake. Stealing Yankee money arouses a special kind of anger, since each penny is so carefully pinched.

It's after midnight and the stores and handful of restaurants have been closed for hours. No cars line up at the meters on Main Street.

There isn't any overnight parking after September 15. Harkness remembers this and many other details from a penitential year he'd spent with the Nagog Police emptying parking meters and fighting to get back to the BPD.

Harkness drives over the Nagog River Bridge and winds around Nagog Hill until he sees the familiar driveway. A software entrepreneur transformed the house, adding a stone turret at the end of each of two long wings befitting a prep school, gold-painted cement lions standing guard at the front door, and a Palladian central atrium with a mammoth chandelier in the entryway.

The enormous copper beech trees he once climbed with George and Nora have been cut, replaced by a line of young maples along an epic driveway. In-ground lighting adds a false importance to the trees, shivering in the cool night air and dropping their yellow leaves like cheap skirts on the grass.

The house looks like a retirement home for lesser reality-TV stars. Now it's flashing blue from the Nagog Police cruiser parked in the driveway.

Harkness slams the door, and Watt ambles down the driveway toward him, giving a small wave.

"Let me talk to him." Harkness tries to slip around Watt, who throws out a thick arm to stop him from yanking open the back door of the cruiser, where George is marinating in his misdeeds.

"Eddy, just hold on a second," Watt says.

"He's my brother." George slumps and turns away when he sees Harkness.

"And he's in a shitload of trouble."

"What'd he do?"

"Broke a back window and climbed in. Tripped the alarm system. Caught him prowling around inside, going through the home office." Watt leans closer. "I know George has been in a tight spot for a while. But robbing a house?"

"We used to live here," Harkness says. Somewhere inside all the gaudy renovations lies the Harkness family's simple white Colonial with its drafty windows, low ceilings, red-walled study, and an attic that rattled with squirrels at night.

Watt pages through his notebook. "Well, that might explain it, I guess."

"What?"

"Why George kept arguing that he wasn't doing anything wrong. That he was, quote, 'just looking for something that got left behind,' unquote."

Harkness says nothing.

"You're just going to talk to him, right?" Watt holds up his hand in the three-fingered Boy Scout salute. "Not kick his ass?"

Harkness nods.

"You got a couple of minutes, Eddy," Watt says. "The homeowner's on his way. And he's wicked pissed."

George wears black cargo pants, a puffy down vest, and a backward Sox cap that make him look like a Little League umpire. The charcoal he's rubbed on his tumid face is furrowed with sweat lines.

"Got to say, all black is working for you, George." Harkness slips into the back seat next to his brother. "Elegant and super-slimming."

George goes into a full-body spasm as he wrestles with his noxious accumulation of anger, frustration, and embarrassment.

Harkness just stares at his brother's latest meltdown.

Finally, George sputters out a comprehensible sentence. "This whole thing's your fault."

"*What?*"

"I needed your help." He points to the house. "I mean, this isn't my kind of work."

"And because I'm a cop, I'd be good at breaking into our old house?"

"Right." George nods. "You'd know how to shut off alarms and shit like that."

"Just so you understand, that's not what cops do," Harkness says. "In fact, it's pretty much the opposite of what cops do."

"All I'm saying is that Dad hid a couple of million dollars somewhere in our old house. You're supposed to be good at finding stuff. Why couldn't you just help me out for once instead of hanging up on me?"

Harkness presses his fingers against his temples. "George, we've been through this over and over. Dad *did not* hide any money anywhere. He fooled his investors and drained the company. Left everyone holding the bag. Including you. It's really not that complicated."

"What the fuck do you know? You don't spend all day dealing with the aggrieved parties." New sweat drips down George's sloppily charcoaled face, pale jowls peeking through. "Teachers' unions. Local businesses. They're all really angry."

"They should be," Harkness says. "Dad ripped them off."

"And I'm trying to pay them back!" George shouts. "But the deal we worked out with the regulators is fucking impossible."

"That's *your* problem, George," Harkness says. "You're the one who decided to try to keep the company from going under. And correct me if I'm wrong, but I think you kind of like playing golf with your banker buds and acting like a big shot."

Radio squawks from the front of the patrol car fill the silence. Up in the driver's seat, Watt pretends to be filling out paperwork while he listens in.

"What happened to brothers helping each other?"

"George, I've bailed you out so many times I can't even count them." Harkness stares out at the front lawn, perfect and flat as a putting green. "You can't tell me you're actually mad that I wouldn't break into our old house for you, can you?"

"When you put it that way . . ."

"There isn't another way to put it."

George leans closer, whispers, "Just get your pal Watt off my back."

"I'll try, George. But really. Cut it out. There's no money hidden in our house. Or anywhere."

George sits still, his mouth working like he's chewing gristle. Then he gives a slow nod.

Watt's radio starts up again on the other side of the Plexiglas divider. "Suspicious persons, forty-two Crescent Street."

Watt clicks his radio. "On it." Then he clicks it again. "Got Eddy here. Say hi." He holds the microphone toward the divider.

"Eddy!" The dispatcher shrieks so loudly that the speaker breaks up.

"Hi, Debbie. Great to hear your voice." Harkness used to hear it every day, calling in the litany of small-town problems — wandering dogs, shoplifting teenagers, befuddled elders, lost tourists.

"Stop by and see us," she shouts. "We miss you."

"Miss you too." Harkness actually does miss Nagog, where a couple of smashed mailboxes constitute a crime wave.

Watt hops out to open the back door. "Hit the road, pronto, George. Before the homeowner pulls in. Consider tonight a warning."

George's eyes open wide and he starts to climb out. "Really? Thanks."

"And George?" Watt focuses his blue eyes on George as he struggles out of the back seat. "If I ever catch you doing something this stupid ever again, I'll make sure you get charged."

George holds up both hands and gives them a half-assed shake.

Watt slides back behind the wheel of the green squad car and pats the passenger seat. "Up here, Eddy. Just like old times."

9

THROUGH THE SQUAD-CAR window, Harkness sees a parade of streets where he used to skateboard, houses of long-gone friends, and the walking trails where he and George raced their dirt bikes. History, American or personal, soaks every inch of Nagog's ten square miles.

"George was king of the high school," Watt says. "Class president, valedictorian. I always remember him driving your dad's cool old sports car, maybe it was an Alfa Romeo?"

"Vintage forest-green Karmann Ghia," Harkness says. "He wrecked it on the Cape after guzzling six Narragansett tall boys."

"I remember he used to have a sausage pizza delivered to the lunchroom every day because he didn't like the food." Watt shakes his head. "Who does that?"

"A guy who's going to be overweight."

"How the mighty have fallen."

"Always further to go," Harkness says.

"Thanks for that."

"Any time." Harkness points at the side street. "You can take a shortcut here."

Watt cuts through Crescent Street, which, true to its name, curves slightly. Nagog's street names have a Yankee directness or, as outsiders might say, a lack of imagination. Main Street is the main street. Central runs through the center of town. River Street runs next to the Nagog River.

Watt hits the spotlight and runs the beam along the edge of the road until they get to number 42.

The homeowner is already in the driveway when they pull up, waving them forward like an air traffic controller.

"Guy looks concerned," Harkness says.

Watt turns and gives Harkness a flat stare. "Everyone's concerned lately, Eddy—taxes, zoning, leash laws. So much to be worried ` about."

Before their boots hit the gravel, the homeowner's already talking at them. "Hey, guys. Tom Jacobson, Forty-two Crescent Street. Thanks for coming." Tom pumps their hands like they're here for a marketing-team meeting.

Harkness sizes Tom up. He's bald, in his late forties, with the steaky stalwartness of an aging suburban dad. Tom's wearing khakis, a white polo shirt, and a thin green jacket with a lightning-bolt logo over the pocket. Probably a tech guy, but not flashy new tech. More like a product manager at a hardware or software outfit somewhere on Route 128. The stickers plastered on the new silver Prius in the driveway tell their tales. Tom and his wife are hikers (Appalachian Mountain Club) and parents of an MIT student. They love their Tibetan terrier.

"I'm Captain Watt, Nagog PD. And this is Detective Harkness of the Boston Police Department. Why don't you just tell us what's going on."

Tom starts talking, the words splorting out in clumps. "They're in the garage and they won't leave, Officers. They have no right to just camp out like that. Without permission! And it's not even camping out when they're—"

Watt holds his hand up. "Please slow down, sir."

Tom Jacobson, owner of an upgraded Dutch Colonial with a towering sugar maple in the front yard and rows of leafy hostas lining the stone foundation, takes a couple of deep, cleansing breaths. "We came home from dinner in Boston about an hour ago and saw the lights on in the garage. It's not really a garage anymore. We remodeled it into . . . flex space, kind of. Our kids and their friends used to hang out there. We work out in it—there's an elliptical machine. And sometimes guests stay there, though we didn't tell the town that. Do you have to tell the town about that? It could raise our taxes."

"No, we don't have to tell the town about that," Watt says. "Did you go out to the garage and check it out?"

"No, that's why we called you."

"You sure it's not someone you know? Friends of your kids, maybe?" Out here, ten miles west of Boston, home intruders are usually UPS guys or neighbor kids smoking weed.

Tom shakes his head. "My wife's a birder."

They say nothing, wait for Tom to make sense.

"She has powerful binoculars," he says. "We've been watching from the back deck. There's two of them, I think. Maybe more. But no one we recognize."

They walk down the driveway to a squat building that still looks like a garage, except its large doors have been replaced with a normal door flanked by a bay window.

As they get closer, Tom's shoulders start to shake. "You've got to—"

"Just take a few steps back and give us a chance to talk to them, sir." Watt knocks loudly.

A tall, speckle-skinned young woman with long straw-colored hair answers the door. A male version of her stands a few yards back.

"Yes?" Graceful, easy smile, slow green eyes — the woman looks familiar to Harkness.

"Nagog Police, ma'am," Watt says. "Need to see your IDs, please."

The woman pulls a wallet out of her jeans and hands Watt a couple of licenses. "I'm Jennet Townsend. That's my brother, James."

James stands with his shaking hands hovering halfway between his belt and shoulders, as if the floor's shifting beneath his scuffed brown boots.

"We're not going to shoot you, James," Watt says. "We just want to know what you're doing out here. Because it looks like you live in the city." Watt holds the licenses out to Harkness.

Harkness reads the same address on each license, an apartment building on Burgess Street, just north of Albrecht Square. "Downtown," he says. "Lower South End."

Jennet steps forward. "We're allowed to stay here," she says, handing Harkness a wrinkled printout topped by a familiar title — *Compleat Record of the Laws Pertaining to Nagog.* "Nagog town bylaw forty-seven, known as the billeting bylaw, allows"— she points at a section and reads —"'citizens to seek shelter in Nagog outbuildings during times of emergency in the city of Boston.'"

No one says anything.

"We're taxpaying citizens of Boston," Jennet says. "The hurricane flooded our apartment building and the city's dragging its feet getting the neighborhood cleaned up. So that's a time of emergency." She turns to Tom, steaming in the background. "I know what you're feeling, Mr. Jacobson." She fixes her green eyes on him and gives a disarming, confident smile. "You're wondering, *Who are these people and what the hell are they doing here?* Just so you know, we both have jobs. My brother's a carpenter. I'm a dressmaker and seamstress. We don't do drugs or drink. We just don't have a place to stay. And it doesn't look like you're using this garage." Jennet waves toward the sheet-shrouded exercise equipment, the tumble of books along the wall, and the clothes piled next to a blue plastic sled. The Townsend siblings are probably the first people to set foot in the garage in months.

Tom walks over to Watt, trying to read the looping script of the billeting bylaw. "They can't really do this, can they?"

"I'll check with the town manager," Watt says. "But for now, I think you'll just have to figure out a way to make things work."

"What the hell do you mean, *make things work,* Officer!" Tom's heating up to a boil again. "This is our property. People can't just come along and stay here because they need a place to stay. For free!"

"No offense, sir," Harkness says. "But why not?"

Tom's eyes widen. "And you are who, again?"

"Detective Supervisor Harkness, Boston Police," he says. "I was in the Lower South End when the hurricane hit. It'll be a while before that neighborhood gets back to normal. Maybe letting these two stay here temporarily wouldn't be that bad." Harkness turns to Jennet and James. "You're going to take good care of this guy's garage, right?"

The Townsends nod. "We'd be glad to clean it up for you," James offers.

"And as soon as the city lets us back into our place, we'll leave," Jennet adds.

Tom seems almost satisfied by the plan. His furtive glances at Jennet tell Harkness that maybe he wouldn't mind an attractive young woman within binocular range.

"So why don't you just talk to your wife." Harkness reins in Tom's libido. "Work out an arrangement. At least until the town manager looks at the regulation and decides what to do."

"The regulation's still in effect," Jennet says, a little too quickly. "Law's been on the books since the late 1700s and no one took it off. Revoking it can only happen at town meeting." She's definitely done her research. Harkness stops himself from asking if she knows a drug dealer turned historian named Mouse.

"When's town meeting this year?" Tom reveals himself as a newish arrival. Anyone who grew up in Nagog knows the answer. It's a high spot on the town calendar, along with the Harvest Days, Headless Hallows Eve, the lighting of the Christmas tree on the town green, and the Ice Swap. And it's always on the same day.

"November first," Harkness says.

"Everything okay until then?" Watt asks Tom.

"I guess so."

The Townsend siblings look at each other, eyes connecting as if by Wi-Fi.

"So they'll be out of here in a couple of weeks, then?" Tom's acclimating to the town-sanctioned home invasion happening right here in his backyard. The Townsends aren't squatters or criminals. They're just clever city dwellers taking advantage of a friendly colonial town with archaic bylaws. Jennet's pretty and James looks harmless.

"Depends," Harkness says.

"On what?" Tom squints.

"On how the people of Nagog vote," Jennet says.

Harkness nods. "That's right." Jennet has all her facts straight. She and her nervous brother have figured out a legal way to claim an outbuilding as their own.

But clever only takes you so far in Nagog.

· · ·

"I know Jennet Townsend from somewhere," Harkness says as Watt drives him back to the Nagog police station.

"Well, she definitely wants to get to know you, like, biblically." Watt drives with his knee, raises both hands, and holds the tips of his index fingers close. He makes the sputtering sound of electricity.

"Cut it out."

"I saw the sparks fly."

"Not from me."

"Whatever you say. So, where do you know her from?" Watt puts his hands back on the wheel. "Did you bust her?"

"No, I'd remember that."

"Did you fuck her? I think you'd definitely remember that." Watt bends forward, so amused with himself he can hardly stand it.

"*Jesus*, Watt." Harkness reaches down to the floor and throws Watt's lunch bag at him.

Watt dodges. "Well, you better watch out. *Lovely green eyes tell beautiful lies.* My grandmother used to say that. Maybe Jennet's working an angle."

"We'll run her address and license number at Narco-Intel and see what she's up to."

"You memorized her license number?"

Harkness nods.

"I can't even remember my wedding anniversary," Watt says. "Must be nice to have such a great memory."

Images flash through Harkness's mind like shuffled cards — his father face-down in a pool of his own cooling blood, Little Dorothy dissolving in a bucket of acid, dozens of dead dealers and users sprawled in apartments and alleys.

"Not really."

Long past midnight, Harkness wakes to Candace's hand running down his chest. In the dim light, he can see that she's already arranged the pillows and sheets between their bed and the open doorway that leads to May's room. The sex wall, she calls it.

Having sex while May's sleeping fitfully down the hall requires a Special Ops level of stealth. The moment any activity resembling sex begins, adult brains send out a tone that only toddlers can hear, one that signals the possible creation of a rival sibling. At least that's how Candace explains the phenomenon.

Whatever the reason, May often broadcasts abattoir screams from the baby monitor after one furtive kiss or stumbles into their bedroom when they're in mid-act with the bad timing of a community-theater trouper. A crib or a closed door is no match for May, a toddler Houdini committed to a campaign of parental abstinence.

The first rule is to move slowly, easy since Harkness is only recently healed, at least enough for somnambulant late-night sex. He holds himself back, careful to inch inside Candace, so that they seem to be holding still, just spooned together in chaste half-sleep.

The second rule is harder to follow. No appreciative sighs. No fast breathing. Nothing. Candace bites her lower lip. Harkness imagines that he's on a surveillance gig and can't make a sound. He kisses the back of Candace's neck, remembers sitting in the Nagog High library watching a younger, paler Candace clomp past him in battered Doc Martens, silver headphones clamped over her dyed black hair.

The first few minutes pass without May waking.

Then there's rustling from down the hall.

May's first, quiet "Mama?" goes unanswered. Harkness and Candace stay joined but holding still, hoping she'll fall back asleep. But it's followed by cries of escalating urgency, the kind that could wake the neighbors. Or the entire city.

Candace shakes her head slowly, admitting defeat.

Behind the wall of pillows, they uncouple, pull on underwear and T-shirts, and rise to walk through the apartment — lit by the gleaming lights of the city — to check on May.

10

L ONG LINES SNAKE through the greenway — business-people, hipsters, and students waiting to buy pulled-pork sandwiches with fried pickles, bowls of pho with fresh basil, and locally harvested oyster poboys. Each bag of food delivered to a smiling customer means just one thing to Harkness: his city is changing. The cheap and sometimes toxic food of Buzzy's Roast Beef, Durgin-Park, and the Hoodoo Barbeque has given way to pricey, artisanal fare.

Sitting on a bench next to the food trucks, Harkness worries about the rarefied, eclectic tastes of Bostonians. It used to be that the city's unpalatable food, like its bad weather and worse driving, was considered character-building. His city is turning soft and ripe for a gutting. Jacked in and smug, sitting in front of their laptops in coffee places, organic salad bars, and herbal-cocktail emporiums, what did these clever young citizens have to complain about any-more? What would make them actually stand up for their beliefs instead of just getting another tattoo or piercing?

At thirty, Harkness is almost a decade older than most of the others clustered around the food trucks. He already senses the void opening up between *still young* and *not that young anymore.* They work for companies he's never heard of, use new apps, listen to bands he probably wouldn't like, and hang out in clubs and bars he's never set foot in. On bad days, Harkness thinks of the city as a brutal machine, hungry for hot new blood to grease its mercantile gears.

Deaf Kid tugs on his jacket, pulling Harkness back. His colleague on this breezy morning has already eaten a bowl of pork belly on sticky rice from De Pho, the Vietnamese truck, and an order of poutine from O Canada! Harkness signs, asking how much food he can put away.

The boy shrugs, takes one last pull from his elderflower lemonade, and tosses the plastic cup in the trash.

They stand. Time to get to work. The deal with the Hamilton School lets Vince miss only half a day. Harkness told the headmaster he was taking him on a field trip. And Vince made it clear that he hated being called Vince, leaving him nameless for now.

They walk down the greenway to where Harkness has ditched the shit-brown Narco-Intel Chevrolet surveillance car. Inside, Deaf Kid stares at the newspapers and McDonald's wrappers on the floor with barely disguised disgust. Then Harkness presses a button and a laptop screen rises out of the plastic divider between them. Deaf Kid smiles. A couple of clicks later and he's watching Comedy Central with the closed-captioning on as Harkness drives down the expressway.

It's always good to keep an informant as comfortable as possible.

Harkness parks the beat-up Chevy on Southampton Street and shows his badge to the cops on duty keeping out looters and disaster tourists. They wave them into the Lower South End. Here, the crisp fall day gives way to a hellscape of stinking debris and abandoned buildings. They're wearing knee-high rubber boots, and Harkness carries a .22-caliber pistol, suitable for shooting rats, in the back pocket of his jeans.

Deaf Kid glances from one end of Albrecht Street to the other. Like Harkness, he's trying to reconcile what he's seeing with what he remembers. Every flood washes away the *before* and leaves a destroyed *after.* Most of the streets are drained now, deep water replaced by shallow, fishy muck. Tattered plastic grocery bags flutter from sagging telephone wires. Cars are piled in low corners like so many smashed toys.

The deserted neighborhood looks like a ruined stage set. They pass a couple of men in overalls hauling wet furniture out of an apartment building. A woman sits on the curb, shouting into her cell phone. Furtive men in hoodies skulk into alleys. Harkness's right hand awakens slightly, ready to reach back for the reassuring power of his gun. The Lower South End feels like it's given in to disorder, and every cop knows where that leads.

The concerted recovery effort that the commissioner promised has been stuck in bureaucratic netherworld, triggering new protests on the Common, angry speeches by city councilmen, and an exodus of all but the most tenacious residents.

Harkness asks Deaf Kid to show him where he used to pick up the money. The boy pauses and his eyes lower. He'd told Harkness that he'd been a go-between for his now-dead uncle and the neighborhood dealers, that he'd spent his days making drops and picking up cash, his nights tethered to the radiator. Using an underage nephew as a street dog was smart business, but dangerous and cruel. His uncle's big plans and threats died with him.

Deaf Kid tugs on his arm and they cut down an alley clogged with waterlogged trash that gives out a sour, thick rot. Flies swarm on the matted fur of a dead dog. Deaf Kid reaches up to open the metal door of an electrical box bolted to the back of an apartment building. He points inside. Harkness puts on a glove and pulls out a bulging baggie of sodden packets with their familiar logo — a ruined, puffed-up brick of Dark Horse. He drops the drugs in a yellow evidence bag, writes the location and time on it, and slips it in his backpack. He pulls out a laminated poster showing a row of coroner's photos of overdoses, their eyes black-barred for anonymity. First-timers to career junkies, black and white, young and old — Dark Horse killed them all. Beneath the dead, the poster's message is printed in large red letters above the Narco-Intel tip-line and text-message numbers:

DARK HORSE — CHEAP, COOL, DEADLY
$10,000 REWARD FOR INFO ABOUT DEALERS

Harkness staple-guns the poster to the electrical pole and they move on down the alley, continuing their old-style neighborhood sweep.

Deaf Kid's uncle used him on the street because he thought no one would ever suspect that a scabby-looking kid in clothes pulled from the Salvation Army donation bin could be carrying thousands of dollars in cash and drugs. Deaf Kid claims he doesn't know the real names of any of the dealers, though he's pretty sure he'd recognize them.

They walk the alley, pausing when Deaf Kid feels along the wall for a loose brick or digs in the debris for a metal lock box. As they move farther down, Harkness can spot the hiding place even before Deaf Kid reaches his hand toward it. Nothing hidden wants to stay that way.

Sometimes the hiding place is empty. Other times it yields a thick wad of cash or rain-soaked bundles of Dark Horse. Harkness staple-guns the posters on every corner. It's a long shot, but the simplest tactics can work better than all the data-scouring back at Narco-Intel. Patrick may be convinced that Dark Horse has run its course, but Harkness knows that when the Lower South End fills back up, it will take hold again — here and across the city.

"What?"

Deaf Kid is yanking on his sleeve like an insistent trout on the end of a fly line. He points to the corner, where three guys are pulling equipment out of a storefront. The sign above it says RAW POWER RECORDING STUDIOS AND PRACTICE SPACES. Deaf Kid tells Harkness that the guy with the long gray hair once handed him a wad of cash to pay for a half-brick of Dark Horse.

As they walk closer, Harkness signs for Deaf Kid to stay where he is, but he just shakes his head. Normal protocol would require calling in backup and waiting, but only Patrick and Esther know where he is today and Harkness wants to keep it that way. Besides, he recognizes the gray-haired guy.

Harkness crosses the sidewalk to the studio. "How's it going, Jack."

The musicians stop to stare at the unlikely duo.

Jack squints. "Eddy?" His long hair is clotted in sloppy pewter-colored dreadlocks, more like dirtlocks. His fingers end in burnished crescents of grease.

"That's right."

"Thought you were a cop now."

"I am."

"How come they gave you a partner straight outta middle school?" The two other guys laugh and then go back to sorting through a heap of trashed equipment.

Deaf Kid stares at his middle finger as it unfurls slowly.

Jack gives him a disapproving glance. "Shorty's got attitude," he mutters, then launches into a tirade about what social media's doing to kids. Jack's shrill voice triggers memories of self-righteous diatribes onstage back when he was the rail-thin, fierce lead singer of the Jackals, a hardcore band that never quite made it out of Boston.

"What the fuck're you doing down here, Eddy?"

"Working."

"Wish the cops'd been working here a couple of weeks ago when a bunch of assholes busted into the studio and took everything that the flood didn't ruin already." Jack gives Harkness a hard stare as if he alone is responsible.

Harkness says nothing. No excuses. No apologies. Jack isn't a friend, just someone he knows from years in bars and clubs. The past has a way of showing up without warning in Boston — college friends, seething ex-girlfriends, martinet bosses, guys from bands. They're relentlessly *around*, intercepting you long after you've graduated, grown up, and moved on.

They stare at the gear sprawled out on the sidewalk. The open-jawed cases reveal vintage guitars with peeling paint and warped necks. The amplifiers are trash-encrusted, like coastal rocks at low tide.

"Looks bad," Harkness says, finally.

"Dude. That's a '62 Strat. Or, correction, was one." Jack points, suddenly focused. "Over there, that's a '64 Gretsch two-tone Anniversary with a Bigsby. And a Rickenbacker twelve-string in custom flame orange, made everything sound like the Byrds." He gestures to the amps and other gear. "Bought this batch of Marshalls from Aerosmith after their first world tour. Recorded the Real Kids' comeback album with that sixteen-track board. Used to be vintage. Now it's just trash."

"Insurance?"

"Noooooo." Jack closes his eyes. "You know, after Katrina, musicians down in New Orleans sold their busted-up guitars to Planet Hollywood and the Rock 'n' Roll Hall of Fame. But I don't think anyone gives a shit about a bunch of ruint guitars from Boston."

Harkness asks Deaf Kid if he's sure Jack was the dealer. The boy nods up and down like a bobble-head on Adderall. Harkness holds a Dark Horse poster out to Jack. "Mind if I put one of these up on the wall here?"

Jack squints as he reads the poster. "Ten thousand bucks, really?"

"Yeah."

"Uh, what if the person who turns in the dealer, like, *knows* the actual guy?"

Harkness gives Jack a truth-inducing stare.

"Like, would that person still get the ten grand?"

"No, but his friend would probably get five to twenty years for dealing heroin, Jack, depending on the amount."

"Amount of what?"

Harkness wonders if Jack hit his head in the flood too. But harder. "Of drugs, Jack. It depends on how much heroin that person sold."

"Well, I mean, a bag's a bag, Eddy. Not like you can buy supersize bags of heroin like at Sam's Club or something." Jack gives a snorty laugh.

"But if you add up all those little bags, and it comes in at more than thirty-six grams, then the penalty's a minimum five years in Walpole. A cranky judge might give you twenty."

"Penalty for what?"

"Uh . . . for dealing heroin."

The other guys disappear into the dank storefront when Jack's ramblings start skittering into felonious territory.

"Well, let me ask you this, Eddy. Is it dealing if you buy something and just have it around, like, when people are doing something, like recording or practicing or just chilling? I mean, it's not like money's actually changing hands. Hypothetically, of course."

Deaf Kid asks Harkness whether all his friends are this stupid. Harkness points down the alley. Deaf Kid wanders slowly away, shoulders shaking as he struggles to contain his laughter.

"Look, it's still dealing, Jack. If someone buys a big batch of drugs, that person would be a drug dealer, and ultimately, the other people who use those smaller amounts? Those would be drug users."

Even this basic description of the drug economy seems to confuse Jack. "But . . . but okay. So, like, if someone just took the drugs that someone else left lying around, like, that's not really drug dealing, right?"

"Depends," Harkness says.

"So if someone told you about a situation like that, maybe they would still get the ten grand?"

Harkness just stares at Jack, relentless as a June bug bashing into a screen door over and over at night.

"Is that ten grand like a check or cash?"

"Look, Jack. Sounds like you, or someone you know, bought some Dark Horse and had it around the studio for people who wanted some, right?"

"What? Didn't say that." Jack holds up his hands. He's starting to understand that every word that passes through his crooked teeth might be taking him that much closer to jail.

"If it's enough to share with a band, it's probably over the felony limit. And if I remember correctly, you're only a couple of blocks from an elementary school. So that makes it worse."

"Why?"

Harkness skips the details, reaches into his jacket pocket, and holds up his shiny steel handcuffs. "What you've said so far is enough for me to take you into Narco-Intel for questioning."

Technically, not true. But the threat of being dragged into a police station gets Jack's attention. His eyes narrow and he backs away slightly. "Why the fuck would you do that, Eddy? Thought we were friends, dude."

"We just live in the same city," Harkness says. "One that isn't that big."

"All I can say is that you've gone to the dark side, man. The fucking dark side."

"Really?" Harkness says.

"Yeah, really."

Harkness gives him a moment to stew. "Here's the deal, Jack. I'm a narcotics detective now. That means I'm a guy who stops people from killing themselves — or other people — with drugs. Is that the dark side? I don't think so. No, I'm not a guy who goes to gigs anymore. Or who wants to hear about your latest band."

Jack looks shocked. "We're really good, Eddy. Called Jack's Joke Shop. Like the Upper Crust without the costumes and wigs. But way better."

"Jack, I don't care. A couple dozen people have overdosed on Dark Horse, a drug you seem to know something about. If you can name a dealer, I won't haul you in today."

The offer hovers in the air. But not for long.

"Tall, skinny black dealer guy named Levon." Jack looks around to make sure Deaf Kid's gone. "Worked out of the Hotel Blackstone down near the square."

"Excellent," Harkness says. "But that guy's dead."

"*Shit*, I knew him pretty well. I think he played bass in a cover band. Another musician goes down hard." Jack steeples his fingers in front of his heart and sends out a perfunctory prayer.

"Give me something else, Jack."

"Okay, okay." Jack works his mouth and scrunches his eyes in a credible imitation of someone thinking hard.

Harkness jingles the handcuffs for inspiration.

"There's another guy at McCloskey's, you know, that dive bar in Albrecht Square?"

"Oh yeah." Harkness remembers long bleary nights at McCloskey's with his previous girlfriend, the notorious Thalia Havoc, the crowded bar awash in cheap whiskey specials and imploding relationships.

"Flashy guy, always wears a nice suit," Jack says. "Used to be just another fake playa hanging on the corner. Now he's gone big league, looks like. If he's not dealing himself, he knows who is. He's the neighborhood know-it-all."

"This guy got a name?"

"Calls himself JJ — short for Jimmy Jazz."

"Like the Clash song?" Harkness says.

"Yeah, like that," Jack says. "And Eddy?"

Harkness shoves the handcuffs back in his pocket. "What?"

"Don't tell JJ that I ratted him out, okay?"

"Course not," Harkness says. "What're friends for?"

11

FIELD TRIP OVER, Harkness and Deaf Kid walk past soggy couches and stuffed black garbage bags piled on every corner, waiting for a trash pickup that doesn't seem to be coming soon. Harkness sees a couple of orange-vested workers tumbling out of a row-house entryway, tangled up like fighting cats. They hit the sidewalk and one man dusts himself off, then kicks his coworker in the knee, knocking him to the ground with a groan. Then he pulls a pipe wrench from a leather tool belt and moves forward, sending the downed man scuttling.

"Hey." Harkness runs toward them, signaling Deaf Kid to stay where he is. When he gets between the two men, the man on the ground stands and runs away.

"Get over here, lazy bastard," the guy with the wrench shouts at his coworker's sweat-stained green T-shirt, growing smaller. Then he returns his wrench to his tool belt. He shakes a Marlboro deftly from its box and lights it, smokes like he's starving.

He turns toward Harkness then takes a quick step back. "Shit, Eddy. What the fuck're you doing down here?" His voice sounds all buzzy and mashed, like he's humming through a mouthful of soft serve.

The close-cropped black hair and freeform teeth, the one gleaming obsidian eye and the other opalescent — it's Frankie Getler. "Looking around, Frankie."

Boston has moved on from being a city full of angry chowderheads. But not Frankie Getler.

Harkness hands the car keys to Deaf Kid and points him toward the Chevy, signs for him to wait in the car for a minute. Deaf Kid nods and wanders off, taking his time. He's in no hurry to get back to school.

Getler bends toward Harkness to put his good eye closer. "Is that kid deaf?"

"Yeah." Harkness gets a whiff of Getler's signature scent — cigarettes, stale towels, and a winy outgassing of last night's drinking.

"Shame. I'm one eye away from blind myself. Was working for Boston Electric stringing trunk lines along Columbus Avenue back in '85, I think it was, when all of a sudden —"

"I remember."

"Told you that one already, did I?"

"Yeah. Couple of times." Getler's opaque eye was blasted by an arcing transformer in an epic struggle at the top of an electric pole during Hurricane Gloria. He likes to recast the tale as an Ahab-like battle against electricity.

Getler shakes his head. "You let my apprentice get away, Eddy. Only lasted a couple of days. Can't find anyone who wants to do real work anymore, you know, with the big wires. Everyone just wants to peck away on their fucking phones all day like a bunch of chickens."

Harkness looks at Getler's truck, the ghost lettering from a Chinatown bakery barely visible under a sloppy coat of white paint. "Not working for Boston Electric anymore?"

"They fired my ass," Getler says, his buzzing voice like the sound of a pissed-off, alcoholic bee. "Said I was too dangerous. Couldn't afford the insurance on me." He gives a crooked grin. "Wonder why not?"

Harkness wonders whether Frankie Getler is shooting for the Shane MacGowan look or if whiskey, bad dentistry, and not giving a fuck are doing it for him. Despite Frankie's weird hum and lack of a moral compass, Harkness always liked him. Back when he ran the go-to crew for gray-area surveillance, Getler was always more than glad to shut off electricity to a suspected meth lab or do other jobs where cash worked just as well as a court order.

On the street, almost every man can be bought. With Frankie Getler, you knew exactly how much it cost.

"Working a sweet private-sector gig now," he says. "Manchester Group. Heard of 'em?"

"No."

"Big real estate guys outta New York. Tons of money." He raises his chin at Albrecht Street. "They own pretty much the whole neighborhood. Been buying buildings right and left."

Harkness points to the row house. "You fixing this place up?"

"Hell no." Getler shakes his head, opens the back of his truck, and reveals a jumble of rusted fuse boxes and ripped-out breaker switches. "We been tearing out the old shit," Getler says. "Easiest gig in the world, but can I get a fucking crew that sticks around?" He doesn't wait for an answer. "No, I can't. Maybe I should go on Craigslist or Amber's List or whatever."

Harkness writes the listing in his head. *Scary-as-fuck electrician seeks crew to work to the bone and beat when necessary. No minorities or union members need apply. Must enjoy epic tales of electricity gone wrong, cigarettes and coffee by day, whiskey and beer all night.*

"Started out with a dozen crews in May," Getler says. "After the hurricane, I got more to do than ever and I'm down to five trucks and maybe ten guys. You hear of anyone who wants to work like a dog and get paid like a king, send 'em my way, okay, Eddy?"

"I'll do that."

"Because this whole neighborhood is about to go sky-high," he says. "Mark my words."

"What do you mean?"

Getler gives a sly smile. "You'll see, Eddy. Can't keep primo real estate like this down for long. The market speaks."

"And as I remember, so do you." Harkness reaches into his jeans pocket and takes out his badge, then pulls out the crisply folded hundred-dollar bill he keeps behind it, just in case. He hands it to Getler, who beams out a broad smile.

"Yes, I do," Getler says. "I like to talk. Just give me a topic and I'm off and running."

"Dark Horse," Harkness says.

Getler's smile drops and he hands back the money.

Harkness stares at Getler's good eye and tries to will away whatever has him in its grip. It's not conscience. It's fear. "Look, I need your help," Harkness says. "I wouldn't be asking you if I didn't. A lot of people are dead already."

"No shit, Sherlock."

Harkness shuts up, lets Getler's febrile mind do the rest. One of Getler's thrice-told tales was about a favorite nephew who worked on a fishing boat out of Gloucester and overdosed in a shabby beach hotel during the off-season. Getler might be a corrupt, violent maniac, but he hates drugs.

While Getler's still thinking, Harkness unbuttons his shirt and pulls off the white bandage covering the burn wound on his chest, healing but still raw.

"*Shit*, Eddy." Getler shakes his head. "Nasty jolt. You'll be carrying around that scar for life, you know."

"Yeah, I know." Harkness also knows that common ground opens up a source like the flick of an oyster knife. He and Getler are scar-carrying members of the Almost Electrocuted Club.

Getler reaches out to snatch the cash from Harkness's hand. "Step into my office, Eddy." He points to the shitty white truck. "You just bought yourself ten minutes of talk."

12

HARKNESS AND PATRICK meet in the dead zone, the corner of the Narco-Intel offices unseen by the BPD's ubiquitous departmental surveillance cameras.

Harkness hands Patrick a piece of paper and he stares at it, bleary from camping out in the office all night again. Fall is a busy season for drugs. The shorter, darker days make people start to crave a little oblivion to get them through. Above them hangs the inescapable number, the one that Harkness tapes to the wall every morning — heroin overdoses this year in Massachusetts. Today's number is 956.

Patrick holds up the paper. "What's this?"

"Request for a detailed information search."

"How come you didn't just put it in the system?"

Harkness shoots him a look. "I don't want this one on the department's servers."

Patrick sighs, folds the paper, and slips it in his jacket pocket. "Looks like we're heading for another little skunk works. This one going to get us in big trouble?"

Harkness leans closer. "Maybe."

"Don't get me fired, Harky. Can't get a job anywhere else. I got preexisting conditions on top of preexisting conditions."

"It'll be fine," he says. "We're just doing our job. Plus some extra."

"Like what?"

"I need some info about something called the Manchester Group — executives, advisory board, investors." Lattimore's mantra for Narco-Intel is "All drugs, all the time." He wouldn't tolerate an investigation into why a real estate developer was already gutting the Lower South End months before the flood. But one dirty path tends to lead to another.

"Will do."

"And while you're at it, give their firewall a kick."

"Do I look North Korean?"

Harkness wonders if he's pushing Patrick too far. Then a heavy hand squeezes his shoulder. "Kidding, boss. I'll huff and puff and see what kinda security they got going. No problemo."

"Thanks." Harkness looks at the clock, then out the window at Copley Square. "Showtime."

Patrick walks over to strap on his gun belt and throw on his jacket and hat. "Cop up, people," he shouts across the office. "Time to show the mayor some love!"

Handsome, gym-thin Mayor Michael O'Mara strides onstage to applause and shouts of "We Love MOM!" He looks at ease on the low wooden platform. Copley Square is packed with news trucks, office workers on their lunch hour, curious tourists, a handful of protesters waving signs (*Boston Wrong!*), and plenty of city employees, the Narco-Intel detectives among them.

"Why are we here again?" Patrick asks.

"Because we got an e-mail from the mayor's office that told us we had to be here to show our support," Esther says.

"The dude's looking pro," Patrick says. "I'll give that to him."

They study the stage like they're watching a perp walk as O'Mara makes some opening remarks. He's wearing a dark blue, meticulously tailored three-button suit, a crisp white shirt, and a season-appropriate tie, red as a falling maple leaf.

Patrick points to the cops guarding the stage. "Yo, it's that guy, Lieutenant Landers from A-One."

"Lieutenant Landline." Esther shudders. "Douchey McDouche Douche."

"Last to know, last to go," Patrick says. "How come he's got a dumb-ass like that in charge of his security?"

Harkness shrugs. "Heard they knew each other back at Boston Latin."

"Takes his cronying seriously, does he?"

"Who doesn't?" Harkness studies the people around O'Mara. There's his press secretary, Jill Seybold, with her blond hair cut in a brutal bob, wearing a gold-buttoned Chanel suit more appropriate for a charity auction than a political announcement. On the other side, there's his chief technology officer, Neil Burch, his shaved head polished to a Carville-esque sheen. Thick black-rimmed glasses give Burch an MIT Media Lab vibe, though from having a couple of drinks with him at the mayor's inaugural party, Harkness knows Burch is more old-school, with a degree in mechanical engineering from Pawtucket Polytech.

As Harkness watches O'Mara onstage, he's glad that he voted for the guy. After almost a year in office, O'Mara's shaken off the taint of his venture-capital roots, which made him act like he was always standing in front of a PowerPoint presentation. He's more relaxed now, his dark hair tinged by a trustworthy frost of gray. His smile looks natural, with none of the tightness that used to make him open for online ridicule as a sepulchral grinner. His lips are thin and bloodless, but so it goes. Boston isn't the land of voluptuous lips.

O'Mara seems to be getting to the core of whatever he's here to say. Harkness waves at Esther and Patrick to get them to keep it down.

"People of Boston, we dodged a bullet when Hurricane X hit," O'Mara says. "If the storm had come at high tide, much of the city would have been flooded. And we'd be facing much more daunting problems. The Back Bay, where we're standing today, would have been inundated and badly damaged. I want to say one thing very clearly today — *no more dodging bullets.*"

Huge applause at that line.

"I'm here to announce two key appointments and one major initiative for our city," he says. "First, I've created a new position of storm czar. The individual who has that job will coordinate all of the flood-preparedness work that we need to do as a low-lying coastal city largely built on landfill." O'Mara points to a serious-looking guy in a blue suit, white shirt, black tie, and fancy eyewear. "I've asked John van de Velde, currently the city's chief of environment and energy, to take on this important role so that we'll be ready for whatever nature throws at us."

More applause. The czar takes a bow. He looks like a Dutch scientist or one of the German guys in the Notwist.

"So far, everything he's saying makes sense to me," Harkness says to Patrick.

"How come Lattimore hates him?"

"Has his reasons."

The crowd goes silent and the blogger microphones stretch closer to the podium to catch the next tweet-worthy quote.

"Mr. van de Velde will be looking to the future, of course," O'Mara says. "But what about now? What about repairing the considerable damage in the Lower South End?"

Shouts of "We matter too" come from the back of the crowd.

"I hear you," O'Mara says. "Your neighborhood is caught in an unfortunate battle with the federal government, which officially controls the Channel Dam area, a U.S. Superfund site. When the dam gave way during the storm, it did more than flood the Lower South End. It spread benzene, mercury, and other toxins throughout the whole neighborhood. Getting someone to take responsibility and begin the cleanup has been a major challenge. Given the inefficiency and gridlock in Washington, I'm not willing to wait. And families that are being kept out of their homes shouldn't have to wait either."

Massive applause at this line. Everyone is ready for the Lower South End to rebound.

"The guy's killing it," Patrick says. O'Mara's firing on all cylinders, like he's giving a TED talk instead of a mayoral speech.

"I'm appointing Robert Fayerwether, head of the Urban Reconstruction Council, to oversee the reconstruction and resurrection of the Lower South End."

The crowd applauds and a tall gray-haired man who could have been jet-packed to Copley Square from 1964 steps forward and waves. A public figure in the tradition of Frost, Lowell, and Moses, Fayerwether looks serious and smart — the kind of sage who could re-architect the Lower South End into the twenty-first century over lunch.

"So how are we going to pay for all the urgent work that we need to accomplish?" O'Mara holds his outstretched hands up to the sky as if addressing the universe. But in politics, there are no rhetorical questions. "The answer isn't in a bank," he says. He points at the library. "The answer can be found inside our much-beloved Boston Public Library."

The crowd's puzzled — bums and high-schoolers are found inside the library.

"Let me explain." The mayor points to the elegant doors of the Boston Public Library. "Our library, the people's library, has hundreds of thousands of items in its Special Collections," he says. "Cultural relics that never see the light of day. Fascinating books, artifacts, and paintings — but of real interest only to scholars."

Some boos from the audience here. Not a good idea to disrespect scholars in Boston.

"We've made a major investment in digitizing the high-value materials available in the Special Collections," the mayor says. Harkness remembers the stack of one-of-a-kind books waiting their turn in the maw of the relentless scanner. "These works are available now to the people of Boston and scholars throughout the world via the Internet. Digitization means democratization."

Hearty applause from the digerati, silence from the dozens of listeners wearing Boston Public Library employee badges.

"But what about the originals?" Again, O'Mara knows the answer to his own question. "I'm asking the library's board of directors to vote to deaccession selected items and auction them to museums, educational institutions, and private collectors. We anticipate that the sale of these books and artworks will raise an anticipated *four billion dollars* in unexpected revenues for the City of Boston — a windfall that will let us start rebuilding the Lower South End without waiting for state or federal funds."

The communal gasp that comes from the crowd indicates some are amazed that a stack of tattered books could generate that kind of money while others can't believe the mayor's selling the city's intellectual crown jewels. Harkness shakes his head at O'Mara's audacity.

He isn't the only one who's giving the mayor a skeptical eye. The crowd's murmuring and milling around. There's a lot of fumbling in backpacks and purses.

"*Now!*"

A furious rain of books flies at the stage and showers the mayor.

Reporters duck and cover. Banners fall. Microphones hit the ground and screech. The cops around the mayor jump off the stage and zero in on the book throwers like bouncers.

Patrick looks confused. "Harky, how come they're throwing *books?*"

Harkness sees Glenn Simon, the Special Collections curator, hauling back a hardcover like a Major League pitcher. He fires it off with an impressive overhand. The book's pages must be glued closed, because it spins straight toward the stage, taking a last-minute swerve and smacking O'Mara's forehead.

The mayor drops to the floor. Screams echo from onstage as handlers rush to his aid.

Harkness pushes through the crowd to tackle Glenn, and shoves him face-down on the cobblestones before he can throw another book. He's cuffed before he even recognizes Harkness.

"*Shit*, Eddy," he says. "That hurts."

"You're lucky it's me and not a normal cop," Harkness says.

As if on cue, a phalanx of BPD beat cops barge through the crowd, hunching down, guns drawn. They point their guns at Glenn until Harkness waves them off. "Cuffed him," he says.

"Good work, Detective." It's Lieutenant Landline, face blotchy, eyes wild with anger. No one wants the mayor getting knocked out on his watch, even by a book. "We'll take this asshole from here."

They lift Glenn and shove him through the crowd to a BPD van.

Onstage, O'Mara rises, holding a bloodied handkerchief to his forehead. Aides and cops lead him to a waiting ambulance, red lights flashing. The stunned crowd watches the ambulance glide away, then breaks into applause for the fallen mayor.

13

GLENN'S FREE AFTER a few days in jail and an early-morning arraignment along with the city's latest sports-bar fighters, storefront-window smash-and-grabbers, clueless-tourist scammers, and turnstile leapers. It's late afternoon before his bail bond comes through and the curator turned activist is released to blink in the sunlight like a vole spaded from a garden.

A reporter with a camera snaps a couple of quick photos as Harkness walks Glenn to the squad car. Harkness can already see the *Herald* headline: BOOK HIM!

"That's it?" Glenn leans back heavily in the passenger seat, his left eye swollen from his getting smacked around during processing. "One lousy photographer?"

"What'd you expect, Glenn — a press frenzy? You started the book riot. Not the money riot. Or the shoe riot. Or some other riot for something people care about."

"Fuck you, Eddy."

"How about 'Thanks, Eddy.'"

"Thanks, Eddy. Thanks for tackling me and almost breaking my arm."

"You'd still be in jail if I hadn't called down and moved the paperwork along," Harkness says. "Lieutenant Landline wanted you to do a couple weeks of chill time just for making him look bad." Harkness dodges the fast walkers crossing Cambridge Street — nurses on their way to hospital jobs, lawyers in tan raincoats. Just briefly, Harkness craves a normal job.

"What about the media, you know, CNN, *HuffPo*?"

"Online chatter is mostly snarky," Harkness says. "There's video showing the mayor getting conked on the head by the book you tossed. Most people don't seem to care about the whole rare-book thing as much as you do."

"So they don't care that the mayor just stole a couple billion dollars in priceless books from the people of Boston?" Glenn's voice frosts up. "They care more about tangible property than intellectual property?"

Harkness nods. "Pretty much. The usual academics and book people are outraged. Nicholson Baker. A guy from the Smithsonian. But regular folks? No big deal. I mean, you made high-res digital copies, right? Maybe it's enough."

"That's the problem. Today's digital files may be tomorrow's cassette tapes. No one knows how digitization is going to go. That's why you always keep the original. Like the Constitution. Or the Bill of Rights. Those aren't copies!"

Glenn's on tilt. He probably didn't sleep much in lockup and his white shirt is wrinkled and smeared with blood from getting knocked around. Harkness knows the radicalizing power of a good ass-kicking. Beat up a street dealer and you can almost guarantee that he's going to stay in the drug business forever. One thing's clear on this crisp fall morning — Glenn's not done.

"Where to?"

"The library, I guess." Glenn quiets. "While I still have a job."

Harkness cuts onto Tremont Street, where steam wafts from a tourist icon, the giant kettle that once graced the Oriental Tea Company, now hanging over the front door of a busy Starbucks. "Starting to think that throwing books at your boss wasn't a very smart career move?"

Glenn shakes his head. "I do *not* work for that guy." Glenn looks down at the rubber floor mat under his feet and drops into a solipsistic silence.

Harkness watches the fake steam rising from the teapot's spout, imagines it coming from Glenn's ears.

"I wasn't even aiming at O'Mara, you know," Glenn says a few minutes later as the Granary Burying Ground and Park Street Station drift by. "Throwing a book isn't exactly like pitching a baseball, Eddy."

68

Harkness turns to stare at Glenn. "Didn't say it was."

"I was aiming at Fayerwether."

Harkness nods. "Well, that explains a lot."

"What do you mean?"

Harkness cuts left down narrow Avery Street. He skids the squad car onto the sidewalk on Washington near the neon sign of the Paramount Theater. "You were one of those Hasty Pudding guys back at Harvard, right?"

"Yeah. So what?"

"Seems like a good time to do a little dramatic reading. I mean, we're in the theater district." Harkness shoves a couple of stapled pages across the seat at Glenn. "Here — your lines are highlighted in yellow."

Glenn picks up the pages and stares at them like they're a warrant. "What the fuck is this?"

"I'll be the voice of Robert Fayerwether IV, you know, when the phone rings at the Urban Reconstruction Council offices." Harkness closes his eyes to get in character, then opens them. "'You shouldn't call me here, Glenn.'"

Glenn says nothing, just shakes his head to clear it. "You recorded my phone call from jail? Really? What the fuck?"

Harkness shrugs. "Maybe you ought to get out of the library a little more, Glenn. Nothing's sacred these days. Privacy. Intellectual property. You name it. It's open season on everything."

Glenn's face tightens. He looks down at the script and focuses, then starts to read in a stumbling voice. "'You need to call someone and . . . uh . . . get me out of jail.'"

Harkness reads: "'Because?'"

Glenn squints at the page. "'I wouldn't be here in jail if it weren't for you. I helped you clear out Albrecht Square. Now you and the mayor are selling everything I ever worked to save. Fuck you, Fayerwether. Really, fuck you.'"

"Nice, potty-mouth," Harkness says. "Almost as convincing as the actual call — the one that got Fayerwether to front your bail bond. Discreetly, of course. Through a third-party signatory who happens to be his brother-in-law."

Glenn tosses his script on the floor. "Okay, Eddy, enough. What do you want?"

"It's easy, Glenn," Harkness says. "Some research."

"On what?"

"Let's just say *selected topics.*"

"Why should I help you?"

"Because you're about to get fired, and you're mad that all your pet books are heading to Sotheby's."

Glenn's head drifts slowly down until his forehead rests on the dashboard.

Harkness pulls a small black notebook from his jacket pocket. "First of all, how do you know Fayerwether?"

"Met with him in the old Trustees Room every month for seven years," Glenn says. "He's on the library's board of directors."

"The same people who get to decide whether to sell your books or not?"

Glenn nods. "Yeah. It's a rubber-stamp board. The mayor. Fayerwether. Some other business guys. Couple of writers, for show."

"What's he like?"

"Not exactly the nicest guy around," Glenn says. "Connected. Old money. Powerful. Been running the Urban Redevelopment Council for decades. Iron-hand kind of guy."

"What'd he want from you?"

"Right after the hurricane, Fayerwether cornered me at the end of an emergency staff meeting and asked if I could dig up a historical loophole that might help clear people out of the flooded parts of the city. Made it sound like it was really important. So I did a little research and gave him the goods on a bunch of colonial towns."

Harkness looks up from his notebook. "Lots of towns still have a billeting law on their books?"

"Sure," Glenn says. "Lexington, Concord, Andover, Nagog, couple of others."

Harkness wonders why the squatters chose Nagog, suspects it wasn't an accident, because nothing is.

"So Fayerwether wanted to clear out the Lower South End *before* the mayor appointed him?"

"Don't be stupid, Eddy." Glenn leans forward, getting worked up again, vibrating in his seat. "Don't you get it? These guys all went to the same colleges . . ."

"So what? We both went to Harvard, Glenn."

"But we're not up to anything."

"Really, book chucker?"

"They're all on the same boards and belong to the same clubs and live in the same neighborhoods. The mayor. Fayerwether. All of them." Exhausted, Glenn slumps back against the squad car's perp-pummeled leatherette. "That's just the beginning. I could tell you some stories."

"Next time we get together, I might just take you up on that." Harkness closes his notebook and slips it in his pocket.

They drive in silence down Boylston Street. Harkness circles the Public Garden then cuts down Commonwealth Avenue, trees already glowing with tasteful holiday lights. Glenn stares out the window as they pass the elegant, exclusive clubs that he was just ranting about — Bay State, Massasoit, St. Botolph, and St. Pancras.

Glenn exhales on the window and draws a smiling face in the fog. "What's the point, Eddy?" he says. "It's like fighting gravity."

Harkness pulls in front of the library, double-parking behind a food truck. "Look, you're tired and pissed off, Glenn," he says. "But what you're doing — the book riot, calling Fayerwether and yelling at him — isn't going to stop anything."

"Had to do something, Eddy."

"I get it. But if you keep bothering Fayerwether or the mayor, or go on an online rant, or mouth off at your hearing, you could get a couple of years in Walpole. Judges don't take kindly to citizens attacking the mayor. Even if the weapon was a book."

"I think it was *Two Years Before the Mast*. Solid binding, but a commonplace copy." Glenn's starting to cross the line between smart and smart-ass.

"Got a wife and kids, Glenn?"

"No," Glenn says.

"Anyone special in your life?"

"Not really."

"Okay, then. If you end up going to jail, that doesn't do anyone any good. You. Me. Your coworkers at the library. It just means the people you're mad at will win, again. Do you want that?"

Glenn says nothing.

"Just promise me you'll stay invisible for a while."

Glenn tries to open the door but it doesn't work.

Harkness reaches for the lock release. "We're not done, Glenn. You're a smart guy. I'm going to have some questions, the kind you might be able to answer. Can I count on you?"

Glenn turns and stares at Harness with bloodshot eyes. "No way, Eddy. No fucking way."

Harkness releases the lock. Glenn opens the squad-car door, slams it behind him, and stalks toward the Boston Public Library, a free man.

14

HARKNESS SLIDES OPEN his top desk drawer, reaches in the back for the black-velvet ring box, and opens it to reveal the engagement ring. Reflections from the small radiant-cut diamond glimmer on his office wall. It was his grandmother's ring, found when he, Nora, and George emptied out the house after their father's suicide. Their father never gave their mother the ring. He had larger-carat tastes. But it seems right for Candace — direct, unpretentious, beautiful.

If he were a more conventional man, Harkness might have written a list of the pros and cons of marrying Candace. He would simply review the list and make a decision. But the ring has spent the past couple of months in his desk drawer — not because he's afraid of commitment, dedicated to being single, or not sure he's in love with Candace. Like a crossword puzzle, these typical complications have answers. The reasons for his delay are harder to put into words.

As Harkness puts the ring back in the drawer and locks it, Patrick barges in carrying his open laptop.

"Harky, you gonna ask Candace the big question or just let that ring sit in there until it turns back into carbon?"

Harkness says nothing, just stares at Patrick so long that he starts talking again.

"I mean, you ain't gonna find anyone better than Candace," he says. "Someone willing to put up with all your Harky-ness-ness."

Harkness holds up his hand, palm forward. "You broke into my desk?"

"Needed keys to the storage rooms when you were out on sick leave."

"There's a lock on my desk for a reason."

"I take all forms of security as a personal affront and challenge," Patrick says.

"Don't do it again, okay?"

"Why would I?" Patrick shrugs. "Already took a good look around. Anyway, isn't it kind of a cliché to hide an engagement ring in the back of your desk drawer?"

"I'll hide the ring somewhere else. But I don't want to hear another word about it."

"Already let you know where I stand on the matter."

"I didn't ask you, just to be clear."

"Fair enough," Patrick says. "But if you want to talk it over anytime, let me know."

"I'll do that," Harkness says, knowing he won't.

Patrick points to his laptop. "For now, let's take a walk over to the dead zone for a few minutes. Got something for you."

The ever-escalating number of fatal overdoses, 980 today, hangs over their heads — a reminder that *opioid nightmare* is more than just media shorthand. As he talks with Patrick, Harkness can't help but wonder whether he's wasting departmental resources on a side project that won't keep the number from rising.

"So who are all these people?" Harkness points at the long list of hundreds of names on Patrick's laptop screen.

"They're the Manchester Group, categorized by employees, execs, and directors."

"Looks like a normal company," Harkness says. "Anything weird?"
Patrick tilts his head. "Not really."

"So they're just another straight-ahead business success story? Lots of employees, smart decisions, growth, profits, all that stuff the analysts like?"

"Pretty much." Patrick smiles. "Unless you take a closer look."

"I'm assuming you did that."

"Oh yeah." Patrick taps on the keyboard with one hand. "Cross-referenced all of 'em with prior offenders, outstanding warrants, and all the usual lists."

"And that uncovered?"

"Nothing," he says. "Barely a parking ticket in the bunch."

"So they're clean?"

"Not so fast, Harky." Patrick holds up a thick finger. "I set the database on auto-reference and went to sleep. While I was dreaming about taking a day off, hitting a million-dollar scratch ticket, and fitting into a size forty-four R again, this little honey scanned all publicly available records. And hit pay dirt." He rubs his laptop like it's a genie's lamp. "People are right. Sometimes you do some of your best thinking while you're sleeping." He spins the laptop toward Harkness, revealing a long list of names.

"What's this?"

"Cross-referenced the Manchester Group folks, past and present, with the City of Boston employee database," Patrick says. "They got to make that list public. Sunshine Law stuff. O'Mara's in there — on the board a few years ago. Fayerwether was on the board in the nineties. And that guy Neil Burch was head of security at Manchester for about a decade. The Manchester Group is like the farm team for the mayor's office."

Esther drifts into the dead zone. "How come Patrick gets to have all the fun?"

Harkness looks at Patrick. "Are you having fun?"

"Not really, unless you think data-mining is fun."

"You two have been meeting here for weeks," she says. "Let me help out."

"No way," Patrick says. "I'd rather eat kale."

Harkness shoots Patrick a look that reminds him to be nice. "There isn't a lab angle here," he tells Esther.

She shakes her head. "Doesn't matter. I'm a detective first, lab rat second. Just tell me what you need me to do."

"I may have something for you," Harkness says. "Side project, but part of the Dark Horse investigation."

Patrick slams his laptop closed and stalks back to his desk.

Esther steps closer. "So what's the assignment, boss?"

"Need information on Boston resident Jennet Townsend," he says. "Did an initial check on her." Harkness hands Esther a sheet of paper with Jennet's information on it. "She's an activist from way back. Lived in the Lower South End until she moved to Nagog with some of her friends."

"Heard about that," Esther says. "That wanderer thing."

"Yeah, *that wanderer thing* is starting to drive my hometown completely nuts. But that's not what I want you to look into. Jennet Townsend used to run something called the Community Store in the Lower South End back when I was a beat cop. There was some kind of minor scandal—I can't remember what it was about. Can't find anything on it online."

"Really, nothing?"

"Wasn't a big deal at the time. I just want you to check it out. See if it had anything to do with drugs."

"Hate to say this, boss, but Patrick's better at this kind of thing."

"Can you dig deep for a crumb of evidence? Can you read fast? Can you be charming?"

Esther thinks. "Yes. Yes. Maybe?"

Harkness writes Glenn's contact information on a piece of paper. "This guy works across the street at the library. He's about to get fired for starting the book riot."

"Didn't turn into a movement, did it?"

"Glenn's not exactly a charismatic leader," Harkness says. "But he's really good at finding obscure facts. Kind of an info-savant, from what I hear."

"So?"

"Back when I was a beat cop, there was a paper called the *Lower South Ender*. Local news. Opinion pieces about how bad everyone in city government was. Lots of whining and insider gossip—you know the type. All focused on the Lower South End."

"Micro-news before there was micro-news."

"Exactly. Came out every week until the editor gave up or ran out of money. If anyone knew anything about Jennet Townsend, it would turn up there. It was like the neighborhood sink trap."

"What do you want me to do?"

"Talk to Glenn, see if the library has copies. If they do, search them for anything about Jennet Townsend and the Community Store."

"You mean like doing a keyword search?"

"No, I mean like going through a foot-high stack of dusty local newspapers and reading every word, carefully. Taking notes. And drinking coffee to stay awake."

Esther deflates slightly, looks like she's already losing interest. "Can I write about it in my blog?"

"No. And I'm not going to explain why that's a bad idea." Last time Harkness checked, more than fifty thousand people were reading *Blab from the Lab,* Esther's blog about crime scene investigations, her Tonkinese cat, and the occasional recipe.

"Please."

"No means no, Officer Vieramenos." Harkness hands her the piece of paper. "Go. Let me know what you find. And do not, repeat, do not, share anything about this assignment."

Esther pantomimes zipping her mouth closed and tossing the invisible key across the office.

Harkness stands in the alley behind Boylston Street, drinking an afternoon coffee (splash of milk, no sugar) from a paper cup and staring at the reinforced back door of Narco-Intel, tagged with incomprehensible scrawls and drawings of unnatural acts. It's slathered with stickers from bands he's never heard of — winky-jokey retro-band names that make him wonder what's happened to the underground music scene. Would college students really line up outside a club to see a band called Mission of Irma?

He's rushed out this door hundreds of times on his way to find hidden evidence, interrogate a dealer about some nasty new entrée on the drug menu, or piece together the narrative of another drug-related death. Upstairs, today's incoming tide of memos awaits his attention. But before he walks back up the narrow steps to Narco-Intel headquarters, he dials the familiar office number of Harkness and Sons.

"Any of your golf chums in real estate?" Harkness asks George when he picks up.

"I'm at work, Eddy."

"So am I."

"I mean like work that pays money."

"I get paid to be a detective, George."

"But not much, right?"

"Okay, let me try again. I need your help, George."

"Don't lead with the need, Eddy." Their father used to mutter this phrase whenever George asked for something — more allowance, a ride to school — without offering anything in return. Red Harkness couldn't turn an honest profit. But he could definitely turn a phrase. "Tell it to Anne Frank," another maxim from his stainless-steel soul, stopped whiners cold.

"Cut it out, George," Harkness says. "This is serious."

No response.

Harkness takes a new tack. "You probably don't have any powerful real estate pals, do you? I mean the real players, not minor-leaguers with a couple of buildings?"

"Sure I do," George says. "I know Brian Donoghue, the asshole who's putting up Batterymarch Tower. You know, that new high-rise downtown? The one that overpaid tech guys are dropping like a million bucks to get an apartment the size of a closet? And I know a bunch of others, all major dickweeds. And they're taking it home in bags. The market's white-hot. Can't make shiny buildings fast enough."

"I'll text you some questions."

"About how to get rich like they are?"

"No, for an investigation I'm working on."

"Ooohhhh." George makes his tremulous snarky sound, the one that dismisses his brother to an outer corner of his limited consciousness.

"You owe me, George."

"Oh yeah?"

"Last time I saw you, you were freaking out in the back of a squad car like a big baby who got caught breaking and entering his old playpen."

"Oh, that," George says. "Those piker cops in Nagog would never get a B and E to stick. My lawyer would fillet them like a wild salmon from Whole Foods."

"Buying organic, are we?"

"I'm all about health. Health is wealth. You heard it here first, bro."

Harkness sees that a call is coming in from the Nagog Police. "Gotta go, George. One of those piker cops is calling."

After he clicks his brother away, all Harkness hears is frantic shouting. "Hold on. Can't understand what you're saying."

"Eddy? Eddy? Something really strange is going on out here." Usually slowcore, Watt's gone speed metal.

"What?"

"Like an invasion or something!" he shouts. "Need your help. Really."

Harkness presses his eyes closed. He knows where requests like this lead. But he can't desert Watt, who's as much of a brother to him as George, maybe more.

"On my way."

15

THEY RACE PAST the marble obelisk jutting from the center of the town green. It's late afternoon and Watt hits the siren and lights to clear what passes for rush hour in Nagog. Harkness stares out the squad-car window looking for any hint that the Civil War monument lay in pieces just a year ago, but sees none. Time erases the evidence, at crime scenes and in small towns.

"Okay, it started slow, but now there are three people living in the Gilmores' carriage house on Main, six in an empty rental house on Central, and dozens of others all over town," Watt says.

The radio crackles with other reports — a break-in on the Post Road, strangers spotted inside an artist's studio on French Street.

"They're calling themselves the *wanderers*," Watt says.

"That's what I hear."

"What're we supposed to do, Eddy? There's no protocol for this."

"Don't give in to small-town hysteria."

"What?"

"Maybe these wanderers are good for this town, Watt. Ever think of that?"

"No. Why?"

"All those extra spaces — the basements and garages — that's where the kids take drugs and get pregnant. The in-law apartments are where the husbands end up living after the wives kick them out."

"Whoa, hadn't thought of that."

"Nothing good ever happens in a remodeled garage, trust me."

"So you think we should just let all these strangers, these so-called wanderers, just move in?"

Harkness shrugs. "This town needs a little new blood."

"If you were still here you wouldn't be saying that, Eddy. You'd be trying to get rid of all these people. And trying to figure out where they're coming from."

"Did that already," Harkness says.

"Mind sharing?"

"Sure. Remember that place we went to on Crescent Street last week?"

"Guy's name was Jacobs or something? Looked like he still collects statehood quarters? Smells like Snuggle?"

"That's our guy," Harkness says. "Let's go talk to the brother and sister camping out in his garage."

"Why?"

"You'll see."

Watt and Harkness walk down the dark driveway to what Tom Jacobson called flex space—now home to Jennet and James Townsend. Peering through the window, they can see the transformation. There are a couple of Ikea beds, floor lamps, a reasonable-size flatscreen TV, and a retro teal couch. Watt raps on the door and Jennet comes to open it, followed by her brother. In the background, Tom Jacobson sits on the couch, watching the Sox.

"Evening," Harkness says.

"Officers," Jennet says. "Can we help you?"

"Just doing a quick well-being check," Watt says. "Wanted to make sure everything is okay here in, you know, the space you commandeered."

"That's not what we'd call it," Jennet says. "But we're definitely okay."

"Mr. Jacobson, you good with the whole thing?" Harkness asks the homeowner, his eyes glued on the playoff game. Late-season play hasn't been kind to the Sox and the fans are hoping for a miracle, again.

Tom Jacobson nods. "Sure, not a problem."

"That guy really likes baseball," James says.

"He really likes your sister," Harkness says.

"That's not true!" Tom Jacobson shouts.

Jennet smiles. "Is that why you're back here, Officer?" she says, turning coy. "To protect me from a middle-aged Sox fan?"

"They're known to be dangerous," Harkness says.

"That's funny," Jennet says, not laughing.

"I'm here to ask a simple question, Jennet. How many more people will be coming out to Nagog?"

She shrugs. "How would I know?"

"Because you organized the wanderer movement," Harkness says. "And you're leading more wanderers to Nagog."

"That true?" Watt asks.

After a long pause, Jennet answers. "Yeah, it is. So what are you going to do? Kick us all out onto the streets?"

"No," Harkness says. "You've got until town meeting, when the citizens of Nagog will probably do that for you. Until then, we just want to make sure that no one gets hurt. That holds true for the people who live here and the people who're moving here."

"Understood."

"So where's this all going, Jennet?" Even from preliminary research, Harkness knows that her long résumé is full of direct action and minor skirmishes — at anti-nuclear rallies in high school, Occupy Wall Street in college, the Ferguson protests after.

Jennet pauses, then relents. "There'll be a couple of hundred more wanderers coming to town," she says finally. "Maybe more."

"That's really what you're calling them, wanderers?" Watt says.

She nods.

"Sounds German or something," Watt says.

Harkness steps forward. "You'll tell them all to be respectful, right?"

"Absolutely. We had a training weekend in New York. And there's an online course."

"A course in wandering?" Watt says.

Jennet nods.

"If there's trouble, we'll come back here and find something to bring you in for," Harkness says.

She bristles. "Oh really?"

"Look, I grew up here, Jennet," Harkness says. "Nagog's got its problems. Like any other town. But people are generous. Don't take advantage of them."

Her green eyes stare, unblinking. "I won't."

"Stay in touch with Captain Watt," Harkness says. "He's a good man but he doesn't like surprises, do you, Watt?"

"No, I really don't." Watt hands her his card.

"And if it's about something in Boston, give me a call." Harkness hands her his card and Watt shoots him a look.

They turn to leave.

"See you guys!" Tom calls out from the couch, James perched awkwardly next to him.

Jennet walks them down the driveway under the sharp gaze of Mrs. Jacobson, who's sweeping leaves from the back deck in furious swipes. She doesn't need binoculars to see what's going on in her garage.

"Officer Harkness?" Jennet says.

Harkness turns and Watt keeps walking toward the patrol car.

"I just wanted to say thanks," Jennet says. "A lot of cops wouldn't have let us stay."

"Don't thank me. You're not breaking any laws, yet," Harkness says.

"You were a cop in the Lower South End, weren't you?" she says.

"Yeah. How'd you know?"

"I remember seeing you on the street," she says. "I used to run the Community Store, the food pantry on Stanton Avenue."

Harkness smiles, acts like this is news. "Oh really?" Harkness summons up an image of the store, the line in front. "Busy place."

"Been back to the neighborhood lately?"

"Couple of weeks ago," Harkness says.

"Terrible, isn't it?"

"Still a big mess."

"Someone's got it in for the Lower South End," Jennet says.

"Got slammed by the hurricane," Harkness says. "Takes a long time to fix a neighborhood."

"You can't tell me you believe that." Jennet tilts her head. "You know how it works. The city takes care of the rich and makes everyone else walk through the poor door."

"I'd like to think it's gotten better than that."

"Well, it hasn't. And if you think it has, then you're just another stupid cop." Jennet turns abruptly and stalks back to the garage.

Harkness stands in the driveway, stunned, then pulls open the squad-car door and gets in.

"What do you think, Eddy?" Watt says.

"I think you're in for a lot of trouble."

"Right back at you," Watt says.

The E-Z Mart line is long but Harkness is thirsty and there's no other place to buy beer in Nagog after nine. It's Friday and there's the usual assortment of old Nagogians standing in line to buy cheap plastic liters of vodka to get them through the weekend. Skateboard kids buy energy drinks. Burly guards getting off the midnight shift at the Concord prison order slices of grease-glazed microwave pizza.

A young bearded guy in a multicolored woven poncho stands at the front of the line. "So, yeah, five of the Easy Money tickets," he says, leaning on the counter. "Ten of the ones with General Grant on 'em. And American Spirits. The yellow pack." He takes out a roll of cash and pushes a stack of bills at the clerk.

A sharp, clear voice blares from the back of the line. "With that kind of money, maybe you should consider paying rent," the man says. "Instead of throwing it away on scratch tickets and smokes."

Harkness turns. It's Wade "WB" Buckholtz. He's one of the civic leaders who always shows up in the *Nagog Journal* doing something helpful — cleaning up a park with the Rotary Club or leading the All Hallows Eve parade. Tonight he's wearing faded Nantucket pants, a white T-shirt, a rumpled blue windbreaker, and a floppy white bucket hat — universal outfit of the Greatest Generation, New England division. At least the ones still kicking. WB's flashing gray eyes stare at Poncho Guy as if trying to reduce him to ash, starting with his bobbing man-bun.

Poncho Guy says nothing, just waits patiently for his change.

"You know what they call scratch tickets, don't you?" WB doesn't wait for an answer. "A tax on people who don't know how to do math."

He gets small, forced laughs from some of the people standing in line.

"But you're not stupid, are you, friend?" WB says. "You're working the angles. That's what it's all about these days, right? Crowd-sourcing, kickstarting, freeganing, bitcoining, and all that?"

People waiting in line go into subway mode, pretending like their ears don't work. Harkness wonders what happened to WB to make him so twisted and bitter.

Poncho Guy also seems afflicted by sudden deafness. He rakes his change toward him, stuffs it in his pocket, and heads through the E-Z Mart door. Just under six feet tall, Harkness notes, according to the perp yardstick on the door frame.

Harkness pays for a *Nagog Journal* and a quart bottle of Jack D'Or saison beer — the last remnant of his once-ambitious drinking. His father showed him where the road of excess might take a man and it definitely wasn't the palace of wisdom. Now Harkness and Candace like to split a quart of good beer on Friday night and watch the light fade over the harbor. It's enough.

Outside, the night smells cool and crisp, and vivid stars wheel in the cobalt sky as Poncho Guy tries to unlock his bike, a girl's model with a snap-on wicker basket.

"So you have enough money for gambling and cigarettes but not to pay your rent — is that it?" WB hovers over him like a relentless heckler at a comedy club.

Poncho Guy shakes his head. "Man, you have no idea what's going on."

"Not true, friend. Led the innovation group at DefensaTronics for more than thirty years. Put satellites in deep space. Drones in Syria. Just try me. I've got plenty of ideas about what's going on."

Silence from Poncho Guy, struggling with his expensive lock, the kind no blowtorch can saw through — and no bike owner can remove, apparently. Harkness wanders a few yards away from the store and pretends to check his phone.

"Say, here's an idea," WB says. "Why don't you turn that key clockwise and give the U-shaped piece a tug."

Poncho Guy pauses, then does as he's told. The lock opens. He puts it in the basket with his E-Z Mart bag.

"One last question for you, little wanderer," WB says, his voice imbued with equal measures of Vermont marble and Massachusetts coastal salt. "When did young men like you become such weak, ignorant bastards?"

As Poncho Guy stands and gets ready to straddle his girly bike, he gives WB a playground shove that sends the old man reeling backward into a parking meter, number 356 — prone to getting quarters stuck in its craw, Harkness remembers from meter duty. WB slides down its metal post until the baggy ass of his faded red pants smacks the sidewalk.

Harkness steps forward to grab Poncho Guy by the front of his wovenware. One lift and he's up in the air, then down on the sidewalk, face-up, Harkness's hands gripping his shoulders.

"You *do not* do that," Harkness says. "Not to an old man. Not to anyone in Nagog. You're a guest here, understand?"

Poncho Guy shakes his head quickly. But not quite fast enough. Plus, there's a dismissive eye-roll that rubs Harkness the wrong way.

Harkness moves one thumb to press the hollow above Poncho Guy's sternum, the secret enclave where all the nerves gather. Poncho Guy starts to whip back and forth on the sidewalk like a crazed inflatable cell phone in front of a wireless store on opening day.

Harkness lets him flail for a few seconds, releases him.

Poncho Guy makes a noise that Joan, one of the Harkness family cats, used to make when an impressive fur ball was en route.

"Who the fuck're you?" he says finally.

Harkness flashes his badge.

"Cops don't do shit like that."

"Well, I do," Harkness says.

"Edward?" WB rises from the sidewalk but he's tottering a little. "Edward Harkness?"

"Yes, sir," Harkness says.

Poncho Guy takes advantage of the distraction to jump on his bike and flee. His rainbow-colored drug rug flaps as he pedals furiously toward Main Street.

"Your father would be proud of you," WB says.

"Doubtful," Harkness says. "But thanks."

WB reaches down to grab his white hat from the sidewalk and beat it against his thigh. "These people coming to our town and taking advantage of our hospitality. It's like the Mexican border around here lately."

Harkness doesn't take the time to point out the dozens of differences. From what he saw, WB was the instigator, pushing a clueless wanderer a little too far. Besides, Candace just texted, wondering where Harkness is.

He's in his inescapable, irascible hometown. Again.

WB smiles and gives Harkness a cautious pat on the upper arm, which passes for unfettered emotion in Nagog.

"Glad you're back, Eddy," he says. "We need honest, brave young men like you to protect the peace." He leans closer. "When town meeting comes, we'll throw the bastards out, won't we?"

16

THEY PERCH ON plastic wicker furniture bought on sale at Pier One. May's asleep, so Harkness and Candace can give their limited sins free rein without fear. Out on their narrow cement balcony, they drink the quart of Jack D'Or and share a Marlboro Light. Little vices keep the big ones at bay, they tell themselves.

Seen from nineteen floors above the seaport, the city stretches out in a glimmering grid lit by constellations of streetlights, except one patch of darkness — the Lower South End. "You'll like this," Harkness says. "A bunch of people are leaving the Lower South End and invading Nagog."

"Why?"

"There's an old law still on the books that lets them move in." Harkness sums up the ancient billeting regulation, triggering laughter from Candace.

"The people are calling themselves wanderers. Or the wanderer movement. They're taking over all the remodeled garages and studios in town."

"Sounds like Airbnb, but without asking or paying," Candace says. "All those pissed-off, not-in-my-backyard people must be freaking big-time."

"Oh yeah."

"Maybe they need a little excitement." As a lifelong member of Nagog's nonconformist minority, Candace takes a certain satisfaction in watching her hometown tweek.

"We should check on your dad's house." Candace's father died last year after a drug-fueled car wreck, leaving her a drafty McMansion and an underwater mortgage.

Candace shrugs. "They can have that place. No one's looked at it in months. I should just put a *Welcome, Wanderers!* sign out front."

"Don't bother. They seem pretty good at finding places to stay."

"Well, this one comes with a ghost or two." Candace stares out at the harbor.

"What doesn't?" Harkness reaches over to pull her toward him. They kiss long and slow.

"It's so weird, Eddy," she says. "How we ended up here, and together. How anyone ends up together."

Harkness nods. It's definitely weird.

"I remember seeing your dad working in his office when I came over to your place in high school to . . . listen to music."

"That's what I told you we were going to do, was it?"

Candace smiles. "You had this headphone splitter thing so we could hang around your room listening to the same old Gun Club song and nodding at each other."

"I don't remember much else happening."

"That's because nothing did," she says. "You were a senior and I was a freshman. Wouldn't have been appropriate. Plus, you were shy."

"Hardly," he says. "Just in awe of your beauty."

"And . . ."

"Still am," Harkness says.

"So let's do something about that." Candace stands and pulls off her gray hoodie and drawstring pants. She steps out of her black thong, kicks it toward Harkness, and jumps up to sit on the cement balcony wall facing him.

"Isn't that cold? And dangerous?"

"It'll warm up." Candace balances herself with her good hand. "And you'll catch me."

Harkness stands and unbuckles his belt, dropping his clothes on the cement floor of the darkened balcony. He reaches out to cup Candace's pale breasts, to trace her inverted nipples gently with his fingertips until they emerge into the night air. Wrapping his arms around Candace, he's inside her in seconds.

"Beautiful night." She breathes faster.

"Getting even better."

They move together, Candace rocking on the edge of the balcony, nineteen floors above the street. Even during this delicate act of stealth sex, they're both listening for sounds of May waking up, rolling out of bed, and wandering through the living room.

But they're alone on the balcony, far from the crowds returning to the reopened whiskey bar, farther from the gleaming towers of the financial district.

Facing the city, Harkness can't take his eyes off the dark building perched on pilings in the harbor, even as Candace picks up the rhythm and presses herself urgently against him. Why are a dozen black limos waiting on the Northern Avenue Bridge next to the old harbormaster's shack? The inexplicable building beams out a silent semaphore, joined by Candace's amatory cry, echoing into the night.

Harkness is almost out of the bedroom when Candace stirs. "Eddy? What're you doing?"

"Checking something out." He's putting on a pair of rumpled cargo pants, a faded black T-shirt, and a creased leather jacket.

"What?"

"Traffic problem."

"Really."

"Building that looks weird."

"How the hell do you know?"

"Because that's the kind of thing I know."

Candace turns quiet. "Just don't be out long," she says. "And don't take your gun."

He nods. "Just surveillance," he says. "Fact-finding mission."

"Not a trouble-finding mission?" Candace lies sprawled on the bed, eyes half open.

"I've got more than enough trouble already."

"If you're talking about me, thanks."

Harkness heads out into the city, still wide awake late on a crisp fall night.

· · ·

Harkness stands on the retaining wall next to the harbor, just out of view of the last diners finishing dessert at the Daily Catch. He takes out the digital bee, the little drone that Patrick loves like a new puppy. Controller in one hand, bee in the other, he presses the tiny button and the bee springs to life, rising out of his hand and moving across the water.

The bee lets Narco-Intel go inside meth labs in Springfield, pill mills in Cambridge, and weed warehouses from Chelsea to Quincy. But tonight its rotors seize up and it drops like a rock down into the black water, its long career ending with an audible and expensive *plop.*

Harkness wonders how he's going to break the news to Patrick. Somewhere deep in the centuries of harbor murk waits a five-thousand-dollar bee-size drone created by humorless Swiss engineers. Harkness sticks the controller in the lower pocket of his black cargo pants.

He could walk back home where Candace sleeps, warm in their bed. Or he can walk over and take a closer look at the suspicious building that he watched from their apartment all summer, wondering what was going on inside. Dozens of workmen descended on the weathered building, turning it sleek — a new slate roof and bay windows, a dock stretching into the harbor. Now the place is empty during the day but packed at night, though there's not a word about it, online or anywhere.

From more than enough time spent in Chinatown dives, Kenmore Square clubs, and Southie taverns, Harkness knows that no good ever comes from an after-hours haunt in Boston. Resisting the lure of nestling in for the night, Harkness walks downtown, heading toward the sickly yellow lights of the Clam Digger, the worst seafood restaurant in Boston.

Customers who stumble into the Clam Digger looking for anything other than a beer sponge, more beer, or both, face several difficult decisions. Fried clams with bellies (for the adventurer) or just strips (for the squeamish)? Lobster roll with real lobster or the fake fish sticks dyed to look like lobster? The frost-burned stuffed quahogs or the potentially deadly steamers?

Harkness's father loved the Digger, with its porthole-shaped windows and nets on the walls dotted with an incoherent assortment of region-inappropriate aquatic life — varnished pufferfish, king crabs, conch shells — and enough tangled sets of car keys to fuel a neighborhood swinger night. Red liked to stop here on the way to the airport, mostly as an excuse to tank up on cheap preflight vodka tonics but also to etch away Nagog's high-toned veneer from his sons' worldviews. Hanging out in a dim bar with polyurethane-slathered tables embedded with coins was his version of *keeping it real.*

Tonight the Digger is packed with college students, the tables crowded beerscapes of Sam Adams longnecks. They're smart enough to know to skip the food. Harkness pays for a beer and a shot of whiskey, walks into the bathroom, and waits for it to clear out. He drinks a little beer then dumps some of the whiskey over his head and rubs it in like Vitalis, Clubman, or another old-style hair tonic.

Outside, he staggers onto the Northern Avenue Bridge, whiskey dribbling down his chin and onto his T-shirt. When he was a teenager, Harkness used to cross this bridge to get to the Waterfront, a cavernous club with great bands and lax doormen. Some nights when he walked past, Harkness would see old men playing cards in the harbormaster's shack, a dilapidated building perched on half-rotten pilings a hundred yards out in the water, connected only by a metal ladder and a walkway corroded with brown-red rust.

Now the place looks like a members-only nightclub, its lights steaming in the cooling air. Harkness wonders who's coming here night after night and what they're doing. The digital bee failed to find an answer. But Harkness is ready to try, even if it means stinking like cheap whiskey, again.

Harkness sways toward the security guards, weaving across the Northern Avenue Bridge, crowded with Mercedes, BMWs, and a black SUV that Harkness recognizes as the mayor's.

"Got some party goin' on, yeah!" he shouts, getting close enough to let his whiskey wind waft over the pair of guards.

"Private event," one of them says.

"Get the fuck out of here now," the other adds.

"What's going on, dudes, bros, dude-bros?" Harkness slurs. How people treat drunks says a lot about them.

"None of your business."

Harkness sways closer to try to get a glimpse inside the windows but the two guards move together like meaty doors. He notices a silver skyline on their black SWAT team vests, some kind of logo.

"Tha's cool," Harkness says. "Privacy, I'm down with that." He glances at the gleaming cars. "Mayor's here, huh? Voted for the guy."

"We don't care." The guard steps forward to shove Harkness against a steel bridge support still spray-painted with the names of long-gone bands. He takes out a metal nightstick with a pivot handle — illegal, Harkness thinks, as the guard takes a swing at his head. Harkness ducks. He wishes he hadn't listened to Candace about leaving his gun at home.

The guard jabs with the nightstick, hitting Harkness on the lower back and dropping him to the gritty road with a kidney shot, cheap but effective. Harkness pushes on his palms and rises slowly, the pain blossoming. "Not a very nice thing to do, hitting a guy who ain't causing any trouble."

"Get the fuck out of here or we'll arrest you. We're cops."

"You? You're not cops," Harkness says. "And you can't arrest anyone."

"Try us, asshole."

Harkness reaches into his pocket to take out his badge, then rises to his feet. Dropping the whiskey stagger, he walks straight ahead, holding his badge in front of him like a talisman. "Detective Edward Harkness, BPD," he says, slur suddenly cured. "Hands where I can see them, both of you."

They look at each other, deciding whether to believe Harkness or beat him some more.

"Don't believe me? Go ask Lieutenant Landers. He's here with the mayor, right?"

They're stunned. Private security guards don't get a lot of training. They just have to be linebacker-size and mean. They raise their arms as high as their musclebound bodies let them. "What do you want, man?"

"Answers."

"And then?"

"Then I won't charge you with assault, impersonating a police officer, or carrying an illegal weapon," Harkness says. "How's that sound?"

They nod in unison. It sounds good.

Harkness takes out his notebook. "First question — who's in there?" Harkness lifts his chin toward the old harbormaster's shack, now retrofitted into something more. "And I mean everyone."

17

THE INSISTENT BUZZ running through the Nagog High auditorium grows louder and the crowd stirs and focuses as the vote approaches. Dozing elders jostle awake as Wade Buckholtz creeps slowly to center stage, leaning on an aluminum walker. Harkness nudges Candace and she takes out her earbuds.

"I can't believe WB's still the town moderator," Candace says.

"Me neither." Harkness pictures him sprawled on the sidewalk in front of the E-Z Mart.

"WB's wife died of pancreatic cancer last year," Nora whispers. "She was in my unit. It was terrible." She shivers. "He was totally devastated."

WB takes the microphone from its stand and whips the cord around like a televangelist. "Now we come to the last vote of the evening," he says with reverence. "'Article 167: A Ruling to Uphold the 1798 Billeting Rule in the Town Bylaws.'"

WB totters forward, leaning on his walker, followed by two Scouts (one Boy, one Girl) carrying the American flag and the Nagog flag, which bears the date of Nagog's founding, 1635, and images of the somber-faced heads of nine redcoats arrayed in rows above the town motto: Nine Men's Misery for Thee!

"I'd like for everyone to stand," WB says quietly. "Those of you who can."

The crowd rises, papers rustling, bad hips creaking.

Nora watches the stage intently. "I don't think WB needs that walker."

"How can you tell?"

"No tennis balls on the bottom of the front legs," she says. "They make it slide. Otherwise it doesn't really work." A nurse at Nagog Regional, Nora knows plenty about old people.

Harkness stares at his little sister, impressed.

"You're not the only one who notices things, Eddy," she says.

"As we deliberate and vote on this final article," WB says, "we must remember that the passions of the moment are not always the best guide for our conduct in the future." For a frail man, his voice is reassuringly loud and calm. "And if a town-meeting action requires sacrifice by some, may it be only where the common goal is worthy of the sacrifice." He pauses. "Let us each approach this critical issue, difficult and divisive, with open hearts and minds. Like the tolerant community that the town of Nagog has always been."

Mild applause from the crowd at this noble but unrealistic assessment. As everyone sits back down, sharp glances ping through the room. The crowd includes closet drunks who career their whiskey-dinged Escalades through town, clipping every car parked along Main Street. There are real estate developers who built egregious apartment complexes on top of vernal ponds and burial grounds. There are investment bankers who divorced their bitter wives to remarry secretaries younger than their daughters. There are bored moms who had sweaty affairs with their Ukrainian fitness trainer, Demitri, the lanky lothario of the Nagog Gym.

There are neighbors who are just plain assholes and everyone knows it.

WB recognizes the first speaker, and a fleshy, bald man mounts the stage. It's Jim McGinnis, a former town selectman and owner of the Powderhorn Café, where the Rotary meets every Friday morning, because coffee refills are free there.

"*These people.*" He shouts into the microphone as if trying to communicate with someone trapped at the bottom of a well. "These people have invaded our town, seized our buildings, and cloaked their true mission. They're freeloaders intent on subverting our rights as landowners. I insist that my fellow townspeople vote no to abolish this archaic provision and send *the wanderers*"— he pauses to add air quotes —"back to Boston where they belong." He returns the microphone to WB, who relays it to the second speaker.

It's Miriam Ling — forty-something, diminutive, and wearing the distinctive red blazer of the Nagog Home Team.

"Why's she dressed like it's Christmas already?" Candace whispers.

"She's a Realtor," Harkness says.

Candace looks confused. "So?"

"They wear blazers," Nora says.

"Why're they red?"

"Because people like Christmas," Harkness says.

"The Nagog Home Team bakes an apple pie at every open house so it smells *homey*," Nora adds. "Did you know that?"

The couple sitting in front of them makes a sound like air escaping from an inner tube.

Miriam begins. "As many of you know, I'm in the home business." She gives a bleachy smile. "I think nothing's more important than loving your neighbor. No matter who that neighbor might be."

Eyes roll at this blatant biblical ploy, a Baptist move here in the land of Episcopalians, or God's Frozen People, as Harkness's father called them. Many in the crowd dismiss the idea of loving all of one's neighbors as an impractical myth, like the unconditional love that parents are supposed to provide but probably don't.

In flinty Nagog, no one loves the unlovable — at least not for long.

Miriam barges ahead as if she's breezing through a crappy sunken '70s den lined with knotty-pine paneling on the way to the five-star living room with an awesome home theater. "We are very blessed here in Nagog. Blessed with a beautiful town, hundreds of acres of conservation land, a rich history that dates to colonial times —"

"There was history here before the white people came," blurts out Larry Three Drinking Gourds, the town's sole supposedly Native American citizen, who claims he's part Wampanoag.

General eye-rolling of the here-we-go-again variety greets the latest outburst from Larry, a cheerless, morbidly obese man who glides in his flag-bedecked mobility scooter to an endless array of civic meetings, from the monthly free-for-alls at the zoning board of appeals to the committee meetings for the annual Ice Swap.

Miriam recovers. "Of course, Larry. And there'll be history here long after we're gone. And I'd like for us to be remembered as the

Nagogians who welcomed people in need into our community and into our hearts. Or at least into our converted garages, pool houses, and underused art studios. For this reason and many more I encourage you to vote yes on Article 167, preserving the hospitality for which the great town of Nagog is known for now and will remain known for long into the future."

The allotted thirty minutes of debate crawls on like a visit to the Registry of Motor Vehicles. The no-people are pissed off, as if the wanderers have barged into a sacred cave where their ancestors' bones are stored instead of just moving into their outbuildings for a few weeks. The yes-people are weepy do-gooders who see this vote as a referendum on the mutable soul of the community. Someone calls them climate refugees, a genius phrase that pushes the green thinkers in the crowd over to the yes side.

To Harkness, the general drift of the diatribes boils down to this: A yes vote preserves the benevolent and welcoming nature of small-town Nagog. A no vote protects the rights of landowners to do whatever the hell they want. It's the age-old fight between individual freedom and the collective good played out in a town just like any other — kind at its core, but wary of strangers.

At almost two A.M., the debate ends and the assembled citizens raise their clunky beige keypads to vote. Nora and Candace find theirs. But since Harkness no longer owns a house in Nagog, he's voteless.

"Listen to me, citizens of Nagog," Wade Buckholtz says. "All in favor of upholding the 1798 billeting rule from the town bylaws and allowing the wanders to stay should vote yes." He pauses. "All in favor of striking this regulation and banishing the wanderers should vote no. You may vote . . ."

He looks at his watch. "Now."

The keyboards clack and the total of yes and no votes tallies on the enormous screen behind him.

The numbers increase jerkily as people fish their reading glasses from their NPR tote bags and spotted fingers struggle to press the right key.

Candace waits for the total to materialize, then holds her beige keypad up. The vote stands at 259 yes, 259 no.

"Candace." Harkness reaches for her arm. "I think you need to . . ."

She's focusing on her keypad. "Right, I need to vote now," she says.

"Maybe you should leave it tied."

"No way," she says a little too loudly, then presses a key.

"All votes in?" Moderator Buckholtz asks, then waits a couple of beats. "Voting is complete."

The crowd swivels toward the screen. The number of yes votes turns slowly to 260.

"The article passes by one vote," he says. "The regulation stands. The wanderers can stay."

Half the crowd groans, the other applauds.

"Candace, you just passed the article," Harkness says.

"I did not," she says. "I just ended up casting the last vote."

"Okay, but we're not going to tell them that." Harkness points at the seething crowd. Half the audience might as well be waving burning torches.

"No one cares, Eddy."

"Oh yeah? Everyone cares."

Candace looks down at the front of the auditorium. "Hey, is that the wanderer you told me about?" She points to flaxen-haired Jennet, hugging her smiling supporters.

"Yeah." Harkness sees a bearded young man next to her and the annealed end of his missing finger starts to ache. *Mouse.*

"I want to talk to her," Candace says.

"Right behind you."

As they barge through the crowd, a couple of sharp elbows poke them.

"Cut it out." Harkness moves closer to Candace like a bodyguard.

By the time they get near Jennet, she's surrounded by her posse of earnest, bearded young men, though Mouse isn't among them. Candace walks up to her. "I want you to have these." She fishes in her jacket pocket and finds a set of keys. "My father died last year and we haven't got around to selling his house. It's a big one — you can probably put like a dozen people in it. It's two seventy-five Oak-tree Court."

"Thanks so much." While the two are entwined in a sisterly hug, Jennet stares over Candace's shoulder at Harkness for a long moment, her gaze laden with an indecipherable emotion, until Candace breaks free to talk to a high-school classmate.

Jennet walks slowly toward Harkness, green eyes fixed.

"You must be surprised about the vote," he says.

Jennet shrugs. "People doing the right thing shouldn't ever be a surprise." She reaches out to lay her hand on Harkness's shoulder, then lets it slide away. She leans closer. "I have to talk to you," she says.

"You have my card," Harkness says.

"It's private," she says.

"Shouldn't be."

A baby-faced reporter from *Nagog Journal* sidles up and starts interviewing Jennet. "How do you feel about the vote? Does this mean more wanderers?" Jennet gives Harkness an exasperated look and starts cobbling together quotable answers.

Harkness finds Candace and Nora. Together they drift to the emergency exit at the side of the auditorium and walk into the crisp air of the parking lot.

"Somebody likes you," Candace says with a musical lilt in her voice.

"What?"

"I think that wanderer woman has a hankering for Harkness."

"No way."

"Kinda cute in a speckly way. Julianne Moore can play her when they make *The Wanderer Story*." Candace switches to a deeper voice. "Critics give two thumbs-up to this heartbreaking story of a little town with a big heart."

"I'm sure Jennet would like that."

"Just don't go wandering with her," Candace says. "Or I'll have to strangle her with her nice hair." Her smile brightens at the thought.

Beneath the yellow lights of the parking lot, the crowd trudges between cars, headlights flash on, and a long line of Outbacks inches toward the exit. Everyone's glad to be escaping the meeting, though the occasional angry shout reminds Harkness that not everyone's happy about the final vote. Far from it. He stays in front as they walk to Candace's red Toyota, eyes darting left and right.

"Oh no!" Nora runs her finger down the deep scratches that stretch from headlight to taillight on the side of the Corolla.

"What the fuck!" Candace says. "How'd they know we voted for the wanderers?"

Harkness points to the bumper. "I think the Sam Reed for Mayor sticker probably tipped them off."

"That what?" Candace asks.

"That we're wanderer-hugging liberals." Nora shivers. "Wonder what they'd do if we were voting on something really important?"

"Lynch everyone who didn't vote the way they wanted?" Candace climbs in the car, shaking her head.

"There's still time," Harkness says.

18

K NOW ANYTHING ABOUT the Harbormasters?" Harkness waits. Glenn stops in midstride in the elegant inner courtyard of the Boston Public Library, stares up at the red-tiled roof as if it holds the answer.

"You mean historical or modern?"

"Both," Harkness says.

"I was afraid of that."

"Why?"

"You'll see." Glenn starts walking slowly through the inner courtyard, its low trees wrapped in burlap, fountain turned off for the winter. Under the marble-arched colonnade, students tap away on laptops, eat sandwiches, smoke. Harkness smells weed, considers finding the source, but why bother? No one cares about weed anymore.

"Let's start with some history," Glenn says. "Back in the early 1700s, before all the landfills made the city bigger, there used to be just one narrow path leading to Boston. A couple of guards stood on Boston Neck all day and night. If someone's boat just came in or people wandered into the city through the forest from the west, they had to face the Masters of the Harbor."

"And?"

"If they didn't like what they saw or heard — maybe the stranger was a Quaker or a woman who looked wanton — they had a big cedar stake buried in the ground next to them, sharp side up, and they would just lift 'em up and drop 'em on the spike, then listen to 'em scream as they bled out, just for a chuckle. They left the rotting corpses on the stake for years as a warning."

"Beantown is a mean town," Harkness says softly.

"Definitely. Paul Revere rode past a pole skewered with stinking corpses on his way to Lexington and Concord. That's the way Boston got started—the Masters of the Harbor picked who got to settle in the city and who got the spike. If they weren't sure, they made the new arrival wear a noose around his neck for a year. If any little problem came up, they just used the convenient pre-tied noose."

"Vigilante justice."

"Except the Masters of the Harbor weren't vigilantes," Glenn says. "They were in charge. And here's what you need to know, Eddy. They still are. They called themselves the Vault for a while—met in the vault of the Boston Safe Deposit Company once a month to plot the future of the city. Now they're back to being the Harbormasters."

"Recognize any of these people?" Harkness hands Glenn a piece of paper with a couple dozen names on it, all of the names that the security guards out on the Northern Avenue Bridge gave him.

"Well, there's the mayor, of course," Glenn says. "And Fayerwether." He points. "Katherine Aiello used to be on the library board, way before I got here. I think she made all her money as an exec with Digital or Lotus. Something old." He scans the rest of the list. "I kind of recognize some of the names. But I don't know any of them. Who are they?"

"The Harbormasters, circa now."

Glenn stops. "Whoa, you got a list of the Harbormasters? They're supposed to be super-secretive. How'd you do that?"

"Let a couple of security guards beat me up."

Glenn nods. "Probably worth it."

"So what do they do?"

"I have no idea," Glenn says.

"We can assume they don't toss people on spikes anymore."

"Don't assume anything." Glenn checks his watch. "I really have to get back to work, Eddy."

"How much longer are you going to be around?"

"Three weeks," Glenn says. "Maybe a little more. I appealed through the union. Getting rid of a city worker takes a while."

Harkness tries to imagine Glenn doing something else besides working in a library but can't.

"Talked to your girl Esther the other day," Glenn says.

"And?"

"She's almost weird and nerdy enough to work at the library."

"No argument here."

"Let her know that I think I tracked down a box of copies of the *Lower South Ender* in our Dedham archive. They'll be here in a couple of days — I'll text her when they come in. Mind telling me why a narcotics detective is taking such an interest in arcane chapters of Boston history?"

"It all comes back to this." Harkness takes out a folded Dark Horse packet from his wallet and hands it to Glenn.

Glenn studies the blood-red horse with an intense gaze, then rubs the package between his fingers. "There's something wrong with this," he says. "Here, I'll show you."

Back at Narco-Intel, Harkness hangs up his jacket and walks past Patrick's cluttered cubicle.

Patrick points to his office. "Warning. You got yourself a visitor."

Harkness looks across the room and sees the Two Stooges sitting in metal chairs on both sides of his office door. They raise their hands and wave in unison.

"What does he want?" he says quietly.

"No idea," Patrick says. "Not a happy camper. Want me to break out that Scotch?"

"I'll let you know."

Commissioner Lattimore stands at Harkness's office window, staring down at Copley Square. "Checking out crime novels on departmental time, Harkness?"

"No, sir, doing some research."

"That's what I hear." Lattimore turns and gives Harkness a disappointed stare. "I've told you over and over, Harkness. It's simple — Narco-Intel is about drugs. Finding drugs. Tracking down dealers. Stopping new drugs from hitting the market. Keeping users from dying. That's what you and your team are getting paid to do. Not to go wandering off-mission. Not to go to the library. Or the jail. Or even to the Lower South End."

"Yes, sir." Harkness wonders why Lattimore is taking such an interest in how he spends his time.

"I looked at the data on Dark Horse over the weekend," Lattimore says. "It's dead in the water. No confirmed buys. No overdoses in weeks. Nothing. Time to let that one go. It was a sideshow. And now it's over."

Harkness says nothing.

"From your silence, I'm assuming you disagree."

"Remember *Fire*?" Harkness says.

Lattimore shakes his head. "No."

"Club drug," Harkness says. "Showed up right after ketamine but before that turbocharged version of MDMA."

"Why do we care about Fire?"

"We thought no one would every buy Fire again after it killed off five people in a weekend. But it came back. With a vengeance. Knocked off a dozen students at an MIT frat. You know what I learned from Fire?"

"What?"

"You can't keep a good drug down."

"Well, something's keeping Dark Horse down," Lattimore says. "And it looks like it's going to stay down."

Harkness shakes his head. "Dark Horse is a category-killer. If it comes back, it's going to wipe out all of the mom-and-pop brands of junk and take over the East Coast."

Lattimore says nothing.

Harkness tries another angle. "Look, if Amazon sold heroin, it would be Dark Horse. Cheap. Powerful. Free two-day delivery to the morgue."

"I get it. I get it." Lattimore holds up his hands. "If it were up to me, I'd just let you keep running with it. But the mayor's team insists that we come up with some good news. Telling them that there's super-heroin on the street isn't exactly what they had in mind. They went through the Lower South End and took down all your posters. Said they made the city look bad."

"Look bad? We're about to hit a thousand overdoses this year. That looks bad to me."

"Exactly," Lattimore says. "The mayor doesn't want to have a full-blown drug crisis during his first year in office."

Harkness has to laugh at this.

"I know, I know," Lattimore says. "It's stupid posturing. Spinning a message. We ought to be admitting there's a problem and running an awareness campaign to stop it. That's the way I'd do it. But I'm not mayor. And I'm not exactly in the mayor's good graces. I bet on the wrong guy. Did fundraisers for Sam Reed, for Chrissake."

"Campaign's over," Harkness says. "Time to move on. Just like you said."

"Oh yeah? Well, that's not the way it works around here." Lattimore stares at the floor. "Sometimes I wish I was young like you again, Harkness. At least you can pretend that the world is fair."

Harkness catches Lattimore and his entourage as they're walking out of Narco-Intel. "One last question, sir."

Lattimore waves the Stooges on down the stairs, then turns to Harkness. "Yeah?"

"Heard of the Harbormasters?"

Lattimore's face shifts from surprise to anger to exasperation. "I assume you're not talking about the Boston Police Harbor Unit that patrols the harbor?"

"No, I'm not talking about cops in boats."

"Do *not* tell me you're fucking around with the Harbormasters."

"I don't even know who they are, sir," Harkness says. It's almost true.

"All I can say is they're way above your pay grade, Harkness — and mine." Lattimore looks up at the ceiling and takes a sudden interest in the water stains marking the tiles. "That's all I got."

"Really?" Harkness is amazed to find that Lattimore isn't a better liar after so many years in the public eye.

"You won't find out much about the Harbormasters, no matter where you look," Lattimore says. "They're not public. Kind of a private civic think tank, from what I know. Bunch of business leaders."

"So you do know something about them." Nothing is unknowable in a post-secret world.

"Look, they seem like a bunch of hail-fellows-well-met, as my father used say."

"I have no idea what that means," Harkness says.

"They're just a bunch of high-powered businessmen who get together to drink and pretend like they control the city. Maybe more of the former than the latter." The elevator door opens and Lattimore steps inside. "And Harkness?"

"Sir?"

"If you fuck with the Harbormasters in any way, I'll fire you personally. On the spot. Despite my complete respect for you. Got that?"

"Loud and clear, sir."

Harkness watches Lattimore and his crew marching down the stairs, then moves to a window to watch them walk down Boylston Street and climb in the black SUV.

He turns and walks across the office, stands in the dead zone until Patrick notices and joins him. Harkness hands Patrick the list of Harbormasters. "Check these out."

"Who are they?"

"Not sure," Harkness says. "More important people we're not supposed to bother."

"So what are we gonna do when we figure out who they are?"

"Bother them."

19

ARKNESS AND CANDACE stop at the pumpkin-carving tent, where adorable children and their less lovable parents shout instructions at high-school volunteers in orange sweatshirts, standing ankle-deep in pumpkin guts.

"The eye! Make it more slinty."

"More teeth!"

"Don't forget the ears!"

Candace lifts up May to look. "Since when do we outsource making jack-o'-lanterns?"

"Can't let kids use knives anymore," Harkness says. "Legal thing. So they have volunteers do it for them. With guidance from the parents, of course."

"Wow. Such fun."

As they keep walking across the leaf-strewn Nagog Park, Harkness senses the layers of history becoming delaminated. When he was a kid, Harkness used to swim with George in the park's outdoor pool, rigging up their towels as hammocks on the fence. He played baseball here back in high school. Now he's walking with his girlfriend and her daughter, dressed in a puffy lime-green parka. Before nostalgia can take hold, he remembers why history is a continuum — it continues ahead. He takes May's hand in his, then he and Candace lift May and swing her back and forth, triggering a burble of uncontrollable laughter.

Ahead hovers an enormous red hot-air balloon shaped like an apple, the Nagog Home Team's contribution to Harvest Days. Every few minutes, a fiery burner sends hot air roaring into the balloon, inspiring the apple to rise slowly.

A line of townspeople snake up to the basket, which carries passengers about twenty yards above the field on long tethers. After letting the riders hover for a few minutes above the park, the Home Team minders haul in the rope and the next group rises slowly.

"Ever wonder why some things get co-opted by other things?" Candace asks.

"Like hot-air balloons and Realtors?"

Candace thinks for a minute. "Green and decaf."

"Sunday and jazz."

"Bunnies and organic food."

"Maybe some things are just supposed to be together."

"Like me and you," Candace says.

"Yeah."

"Wasn't a question," she says.

As they walk through the fair, people in the crowd acknowledge their passing with lingering stares.

Candace leans close to Harkness. "What're they looking at?"

"We look like the kind of people who voted pro-wanderer. Some of them are probably still holding a grudge."

"Town meeting was last month."

"People around here have long memories," Harkness says.

"People around here don't have enough to do."

The vote did nothing to resolve the wanderer issue. It just split the town and brought media attention to Nagog, now a test case for community tolerance versus individual rights.

They walk past a crowded booth flying a red flag that shows a red house and two crossed rifles. The hard-eyed men and women gathered around the American Landowners Alliance booth are chanting "Sign our petition, send the wanderers to perdition."

"That slogan doesn't really work," Candace says, but she gives a queasy shiver and lifts May to her shoulder. "Shit, Eddy. Those people look really pissed off."

"Dada, dada." May reaches for Harkness and he takes her, holding her until they're clear of the booth.

"Here's the friendly opposition." Harkness points at a crowded booth with a hand-painted sign: HOST THANKSGIVING WITH A WANDERER! Earnest women, their gray hair bound in cruel braids, chat with a cluster of crusty wanderers.

They keep walking through the fair until they hear shouting behind them. Harkness turns to see a skinny guy in an AC/DC shirt and thin leather jacket yelling at the people gathered around the American Landowners Alliance booth.

Harkness's internal alarm is blaring. "You two go on ahead for a minute."

"Eddy, you're off duty." Candace's voice turns tight and small.

"I think it's Lee."

"The guy from the Nagog Five and Ten?"

"Yeah."

Candace points at a petting zoo set up on the edge of the field. "We'll be over there."

Lee jams his bony finger at the ALA booth. "Harvest Days is a Nagog tradition," he shouts. "It's for the people of this town. We don't need you yahoos coming here and turning it all political."

A small crowd's stalking around behind Lee, guys Harkness went to high school with, the kind who never left Nagog. There's Steve Dawkins, who runs the town snowplow; Randy Dupraz, who helps out around the firehouse; and Royal Hilliard, whose family has an expensive neighborhood named after it. He works at the water-treatment plant. Behind them, a little older but just as lost, stands Hank Steadman, the town animal control officer.

"Name's Calvin Addison." The guy standing in front of the booth has short hair and dark eyes and a face so flushed he looks like he might explode. "We're allowed to be here." Calvin's wearing jeans, cowboy boots, an ALA T-shirt, and a way-too-small-to-zip red fleece vest. "We came all the way from Texas to tell folks that no one should oughta take your home away." Even in the fall chill, sweat's running down Calvin's face.

Lee and his band of friends stare at Calvin like he came all the way from another planet. Some iteration of this gang — swamp Yankees with thin skins and an overdeveloped sense of outrage — has roamed Nagog for centuries.

Part fuck-up townie, part stalwart Nagog defender, Lee's not giving up. "Butt out, sweaty dude," he says. "Just leave. We don't need you trying to get people more riled up than they already are." Lee leans down and pretends to snatch one leg of the ALA table. He pauses, as if to say *I'd never do that*. Then his smile fades as he overturns the table, scattering their brochures, petitions, and T-shirts on the ground. Lee's friends lunge forward to trash the booth.

Harkness shakes his head. *Here goes.*

Calvin grabs the ALA flagpole and pokes at Lee. Lee grabs at the red flag and rips it from the pole then tosses it back to his friends, who throw it on the ground and stomp on it.

Seeing the ALA flag abused sends Calvin into a frenzy. He charges with the bare flagpole, tipped with a shining gold eagle with two outstretched wings that catch Lee in the shoulder. He gives out a garbled scream.

"Fuck you, man." Lee wanders out of the fray to peel off his leather jacket and sees his T-shirt, darkened with blood. Like a barfight veteran, Lee pulls off his T-shirt and presses it against his pale shoulder.

The sight of blood makes Calvin pause, then he sees Lee's friends regrouping and runs at them with his flagpole.

Harkness sidles up to Calvin, reaches down to grab one of his thick ankles with both hands, and yanks it, sending the Texan toppling face-first into the dust. A second later Harkness is on Calvin's back, one knee in his kidneys, bending his right arm behind him.

Calvin's a big guy so once he's down, gravity works in Harkness's favor. But he continues to struggle. His free arm keeps reaching back.

"I'm a cop," Harkness says. "Stay down and quit moving, and we won't have any trouble."

He doesn't. He's trying to get something out of his fleece vest's pocket.

"Sorry, Tex." Harkness yanks back harder on Calvin's arm and he starts screaming like an emasculated calf.

"Freeze!"

Harkness looks up to see a skinny kid wearing mirror shades and a Nagog Police uniform holding his service pistol at arm's length, advancing toward him.

Harkness reaches into his pocket for his badge.

"Hands where I can see them!" The kid's glasses and milky skin make him look like a larva with a gun.

"I'm a cop," Harkness shouts.

"Sure you are."

"No, I am," Harkness says. "Ask Watt." Watt told Harkness that finding good recruits was getting harder and harder. But really.

There's a pause as the Nagog Police Department rookie struggles to figure out what to do, Calvin screams, and Harkness freezes like a deer in the headlights.

There's nothing more frightening than a rookie cop with his gun out. This weary insight came from Sergeant Gene Baylor, Harkness's first supervisor back in the Lower South End. Baylor was a dead-end sergeant with a tractor ass, a drinking problem, and plenty of opinions, most of them wrong. But squatting on top of a whimpering keg-shaped Texan, staring down the shaking barrel of a Glock 17 in the hands of someone who's contemplating using deadly force for the first time — Harkness has to admit, that asshole Baylor was right.

Watt strides between them and takes charge. "Officer Troutman, put that gun away pronto. This man is a cop. Eddy — don't hurt that guy."

The fleshy-faced rookie can't seem to lower his gun. He might twitch off a shot or two by accident.

"*Jesus*, Troutman," Watt says. "Put that fucking gun down before you hurt yourself. This is Eddy Harkness. He's a cop. Legend around here."

The rookie blinks, then stuffs his gun back in its holster.

Harkness unfreezes when Watt walks over. "What's up, Eddy?"

"Need to cuff this guy." Harkness points down at Calvin.

"What'd he do?"

"Assault. I popped his shoulder a little but he should be fine. And frisk him carefully, he's got something in his pocket."

Calvin makes a low growling noise as Watt handcuffs him and calls for backup and an ambulance for Lee.

"What happened?"

"Lee and his buds started it all by heckling the ALA people. Then this guy decides to go gladiator and poke Lee with a flagpole. That's about all."

"I'm on it." Watt takes over.

Harkness stands and dusts himself off. "Gotta go. I'll come into the station and file a statement tonight."

Watt reaches into Calvin's pocket, pulls out a folding knife in a leather sheath. "Thanks, Calvin. Now we can haul you in on assault *and* carrying a concealed weapon."

More growling from Calvin.

A few yards away Lee's kneeling down, pressing his blood-soaked T-shirt to his shoulder while his friends comfort him with a tall can of Narragansett. As he walks by, Harkness gives Lee's unstabbed shoulder a gentle squeeze. "Ambulance is on the way. Get that stitched up and you'll be fine."

"Thanks, Eddy," Lee says. "See you 'round the store."

20

HARKNESS CATCHES UP with Candace and May at the petting zoo set up by a local farm. The black-faced lambs, breath steaming in the cold air, seem to transfix May.

"Where've you been?" Candace shivers. The crisp afternoon light is already fading.

"Just talking to Lee," he says. "How's she doing?"

"May?" Candace leans down to take the caramel apple and wipe her daughter's hand, triggering a squall of screams. "I think she likes caramel apples, lambs, and getting her way. Not necessarily in that order."

Harkness nods toward Nora and George, walking with their mother between them. "Look out, here comes the family. What's left of it."

"At least your mom's alive, Eddy. I got no one left."

Harkness raises his eyebrows.

"Except you, except you!" She kicks at him with her burgundy Doc Martens.

"Careful, don't get Eddy angry," George says as they walk closer. "Gets violent sometimes. Didn't anyone tell you?"

"Everyone keeps warning me," Candace says.

"And?"

"It just makes me love him even more," Candace says, pale face locked in a mall-photo smile.

"Hey, listen, Candy," George says.

"It's Candace."

"Sure," he says. "Can you keep an eye on Mom for a couple of minutes? We need to have a quick Harkness-sibling powwow."

"George, she's already watching May," Nora says.

"Just, uh, check out the apple-balloon thing for a minute," George says. "Mom likes it."

The hypnotizing rise and fall of the apple-shaped balloon brings order to their mother's cross-wired mind. Maybe it's the loud roar that the burner makes when it gusts hot air into the balloon. Or maybe it's because the balloon looks like a big absurd apple. Harkness wonders if she remembers the Indian summer afternoons when she used to pull her children out of school and take them apple picking out in Bolton. Then he pushes the past away, stops himself from falling into a nostalgia wormhole.

"Not a problem," Candace says. "May likes the balloon too." She takes their mother's hand and the three walk off together.

"You picked a good one, Eddy," George says. "Just look at that. She's got the ass of a fourteen-year-old boy."

"Shut *up*, George," Nora says. "She's great, Eddy. Maybe you two should get married."

Harkness pauses. "I'm thinking about it."

"In addition to the previously noted astounding ass," George says, "she's not crazy, unlike all your other girlfriends."

"Thanks for that, George."

"She's a really good mother," Nora says. "And you're both so comfortable together. I mean, not that I know much about compatibility." Nora dates doctors, her relationships rarely progressing beyond dinner in the hospital cafeteria. "But you seem to get along great."

"It would be a marriage of similars." George counts on his short fingers. "You both like terrible music. You both have fathers who killed themselves," he says. "You're missing a finger. She's missing a hand."

"Thanks for your astute observations."

"So she's okay with the fact that you killed that Dex guy?" George says. "Father of her daughter?"

"We don't really talk about it much," Harkness says. "As far as May knows, I'm her father."

"Maybe Candace is turned on by it, Eddy," George says, revving with perverse enthusiasm.

"By what?"

"That you killed her last boyfriend. Ever thought of that?"

Harkness gives George a soul-searing stare. He'd slap him around, except Nora's here.

"So do you have a plan?" Nora says, ignoring George.

"For what?"

"For when you're going to ask her."

"Sometime after the holidays," Harkness says, wondering if it's true.

"Good decision," George says. "Getting engaged at Christmas is tacky."

They reach the outer fringe of the fair — the overflowing trash-cans, boxes of apples buzzing with yellow jackets, the empty CPR-demonstration station — and turn around.

"You know, Suzanne and I are thinking of getting married some-time," George adds.

Nora rolls her eyes. "Well, when you buy her a ring, we'll believe it."

Harkness smiles, reaches out to squeeze the hand of his reasonable sister.

"No need to get pissy," George says. "Actually, I'm too busy for a serious relationship. I'm working sixty-hour weeks trying to save the family name."

"Tell it to Anne Frank," Nora says.

George sidles up next to Harkness as they walk toward the big red apple balloon of the Nagog Home Team. "Hey, those questions you sent me? Got some answers from my real estate friends, just like you asked me to."

Harkness stops on the path. Ahead, they can see Candace, May, and their mother watching the balloon as the heater roars and the apple rises.

"You go on ahead, Nora," George says. "Eddy and I need a min-ute." She nods and walks toward the balloon.

"What'd they tell you, George?"

"That shit in the Lower South End? Classic pay-or-plague move," George says.

Harkness resists the temptation to roll his eyes at his brother's repeating some phrase he's just learned as if it's common knowledge. "Mansplain that for me, okay?"

"My real estate developer friends told me that when you want to clear out a building or a neighborhood, the first thing you do is pay off the tenants. If they're renting, you get them another apartment somewhere else in the city and pay for their first three months' rent. If they own the place, you pay 'em way above the assessed value. If you need to, you just hand 'em some jaw-dropping money so they forget how much they like where they live. That's the pay part. Pretty obvious."

"And then?"

"Then things get ugly," George says. "You let the trash pile up. Cut the heat way back. Arrange a lot of annoying construction projects involving jackhammers at six in the morning. Shut off the elevators. Anything that makes daily life suck. That's the plague part. They call it that because it's like—"

"Visiting plagues upon them," Harkness says.

"Good, Eddy," George says. "Not bad for a cop."

Candace leads their mother over to Nora, triggering a confused look in the older woman. "Who are you?"

Nora looks her in the eyes. "I'm your daughter, Nora."

Their mother laughs. "There's no Nora at the school."

The three siblings exchange glances. Their mother's fast slide from tack-sharp school principal to confused walker still surprises them.

"Mom," George shouts. "Eddy's thinking about—"

Harkness grabs his arm and squeezes. Nora just shakes her head at George's almost pathological inability to keep a secret—so different from his father.

"Hey! Yeah, Eddy's thinking about taking this little critter up in that apple-balloon thing," George says, his smile inane. He reaches down and picks up May, holds her out like a squirming offering.

May squeals. Kids always like George. With his flubby body and gibbous face, he looks like a cartoon man.

"That's nice," their mother says. "That's nice."

Harkness reaches over and takes Candace's hand as they walk together, three generations without a lot to say, silenced by the dampening weight of loss. Their parents' marriage—once a mysterious

117

tangled ball of plans, dinner-table arguments, affairs, trips to Europe, dinners with dozens of friends, cases of Bordeaux, photos in the *Globe* during gala season — has unspooled into a cautionary tale of dementia for their mother, disgrace and death for their father. Mourning that loss is pointless, Harkness knows. His family's small tragedy pales by comparison with more vicious losses the world doles out.

They pass by the empty, ticket-strewn table at the entrance to Harvest Days, now ending as the weak afternoon light fades, the air cools, the booths shut down, and the crowd heads home — young and old, citizens and wanderers.

21

McCLOSKEY'S IS STILL a dump but on the day before it shuts down forever, the packed bar's thrumming like a Lansdowne Street club on opening night. Harkness slips in and hovers in the crowd for a moment, then takes a seat at the end of the bar, next to Jimmy, a young man in a yellow suit and snap-brim gray hat. Harkness makes it look natural, not like he's been hanging around outside the bar for hours, waiting for him to show up for last call.

Harkness orders a Harp and a shot of Jameson.

Jimmy looks over, squints at Harkness, doesn't say anything.

The bartender spins his beer toward him, clicks a shot glass on the scarred wooden bar, and pours a lengthening golden strand in it. Harkness nods in thanks, takes a sip of the whiskey, then the beer.

"Cop, right?"

Harkness shrugs. "Yeah. But I'm off duty."

"Sure, man."

Harkness watches Jimmy in the bar mirror, sees him struggling to figure out what to say, or if he should say anything even.

"Tried to find your gun, man," Jimmy whispers. "Remember? The one you lost. Looked everywhere."

Harkness acts surprised. *"Fubu?"*

"Ain't called that no more. Changed my look and my outlook. Re-fucking-branded myself. Now I'm Jimmy Jazz. I also go by JJ and J-Jaz. Always evolving. Like the Internet."

Harkness smiles. "You look like you're fifty pounds lighter."

"More like a hundred and ten," Jimmy says. "If you're countin.'"

"*Whoa.* How'd you do that?"

"Cut out the carbs. And about half of my stomach."

"Worked, looks like."

"Sometimes extreme measures are in order."

"I'm with you on that." Harkness takes another sip of his whiskey.

Jimmy sidles closer. "Hey, didn't I sell your girlfriend a gun?"

"Ex-girlfriend."

Jimmy nods. "Nasty little Röhm — chrome-plated twenty-five-cal. semi. How'd that work out for her?"

"Almost got us killed." Harkness replays a popular clip from the YouTube channel in his mind, the one that shows his girl Thalia Prochazka, aka Thalia Havoc, squatting down in the narrow streets of Chinatown to blast away at a henchman of the legendary Mr. Mach, nightclub owner and drug lord. The thug lost an earlobe. Harkness got his stolen Glock 17 back. It was messy.

"Well, *almost* don't count except for horseshoes and hand grenades," Jimmy says.

"My algebra teacher used to say that when we got an answer wrong."

"Smart lady," Jimmy says. "Was she a stone-cold fox?"

Harkness summons up Mrs. Ikada from Nagog Middle School with her high-necked gingham dresses and thick glasses that magnified her eyes. "Not unless you like anime."

"'Cuz your girl Thalia was as hot as they get, friend." Jimmy signals the bartender. "Just thinking about her's getting me thirsty. BTW, I seen her around the bar tonight."

Harkness bristles. "What?"

"Yeah, she's here, man. Everyone's here tonight. Everyone shows when a famous shithole like McCloskey's closes down."

"Definitely not just another night," Harkness says. "More like a holiday."

"So now you're gonna buy me a beer, Officer . . .'"

Harkness takes a ten from his stack of change and tosses it closer to the bar. "Harkness."

Jimmy rises off his barstool and jabs his hand in the air. "Damn! That *was* you!"

Harkness stares at Jimmy, wonders what drug just kicked in.

"Damn, damn, damn!" Jimmy is jostling everyone around them and pointing at Harkness. "He shoots, he scores!" Jimmy pantomimes Harkness's toss of Deaf Kid.

There's applause and suddenly the bar in front of Harkness is lined with shots of whiskey and tequila and a dozen beers.

"You're like a fuckin' hero around here, man," Jimmy says. "Saving that deaf kid. Everyone knows Vince."

"He doesn't like that name."

"We just called him that on account of his ears getting messed with."

"What?"

"Van Gogh, man."

"Oh." Harkness sees why Deaf Kid prefers to go nameless. "But I thought he was born deaf."

Jimmy shakes his head. "Nope. His mama popped his eardrums with an icepick when he was six. Said she didn't want him hearing all the bad shit going down in the house. That an' she figured no gang would want a deaf kid."

"That's crazy." Harkness presses his eyes closed for a moment, stunned that Deaf Kid's story could get any worse.

"Yeah, for sure. His mama ended up in MCI-Framingham." Jimmy shakes his head.

Silence descends as Harkness and Jimmy consider the dark side of human nature, neither for the first time. "So what're you doing now?" Harkness asks.

"I'm into sustainable energy."

"Oh yeah?" Harkness turns to give Jimmy the once-over — good suit, gold watch, gleaming Italian shoes.

"Yeah. Most days I hang around my girlfriend's nice place in Jamaica Plain, sustaining my energy."

Harkness laughs, clinks beer glasses with Jimmy. Then he shifts to a new frequency. "I hear you're like the mayor of the Lower South End, what's left of it."

"I do keep my eyes open," Jimmy says.

"Got a question for you," Harkness says. "What do you know about Dark Horse?"

Jimmy freezes up. "Why you askin' me, man? 'Cuz I had nothing to do with that nasty shit. Nothing at all. If this is cop business, count me out."

"No, nothing like that. Just doing a little research," Harkness says. "Heard you know everything that goes on around here."

"That I do," he says. "And I got some stories you won't believe. How much time do you got?"

Harkness points at the shot glasses and bottles around them. "Could be a while."

"Then let's have us a real conversation." Jimmy huddles closer. "Off the record, of course."

Jimmy delivers a novella's worth of information and downs most of the free drinks before stumbling off into the night to Jamaica Plain—leaving Harkness, his new best friend, at the bar, churning through all that he's heard.

When Harkness stands and walks through crowded bar to the men's room, he sees a familiar, crumpled figure lying face-down in a corner booth. Frankie Getler is still wearing his orange emergency vest, surrounded by an array of glasses and bottles. As Harkness passes his table, he puts his hand over Getler's cell phone, deftly palms it, and slips it into his pocket. All without breaking stride.

Harkness feels the familiar rush. Sometimes opportunities are just too good to pass up, even if it means going well beyond BPD protocol. Frankie Getler earned his hundred-dollar squeal fee, but whatever's on his SIM card might be worth a lot more.

In the scrawled, piss-corroded bathroom stall, Harkness cracks open Frankie Getler's cheap phone in seconds, thankful that it's not an iPhone. He pops out the card and slips it in his wallet.

Harkness freezes as a bathroom door opens and someone runs the water, checks out his look in the mirror, and decides it's working, at least for McCloskey's. The door slams.

Harkness leaves the stall and smacks the phone on the edge of the sink to shatter the screen.

Back in the bar, he drops the smashed phone on the floor near Frankie Getler's feet.

Getler stirs and opens his red-rimmed eyes. "Hey, Eddy! What're you doing here in this dump?"

"Same thing you are, Frankie. Hanging out one last night before the bar closes."

"Right." Frankie nods, then paws the sticky table in front of him frantically, sending bottles rolling to the floor as he flails for his missing phone. He bends down and finds his smashed cell. *"Not again, goddamn it!"* He pulls his arm back and throws the phone over the crowd. It ricochets off two walls before skittering under a pinball machine that a couple of guys are trying to steal. Wooden planks from the bar, the booth lights, neon signs bolted to the walls — it's open season on mementos.

Harkness walks on, leaving Frankie to sputter in his booth like a short-circuiting wire, and slips through the crowd.

In the last booth in the corner, face-down on the table, the legendary Thalia Havoc dozes with only bottles and glasses to keep her company.

Harkness slides into the booth across from her and taps the shoulder of her white leather jacket.

"Oh, hey, Eddy," she says, as if she just saw him yesterday. She sits up, runs her fingers through her red hair. "What're you doing here? Taking a little walk down Memory Lane?"

"Sort of," Harkness says. "And you? Last I knew, you were in New York."

"Back in town for a while," she says. "Got some unfinished business." His slippery ex-girlfriend doesn't offer any details and Harkness doesn't ask. "And a sweet holiday gig at the Parker House bar."

"Nice."

She leans forward. "Miss you, Eddy. Miss you tons, man." Her eyes fill with tears and she rubs them away. "We had such —"

Harkness cuts her off. "Not going there, Thalia. You know what my father used to say?"

"'Give me your money, rich sucker'?" Thalia says.

"No," Harkness says. "He used to say that looking back is just a good way to stumble."

"I'm not looking back, Eddy," she says. "I'd be lying if I said I didn't think about you all the way in on the train. Just because things ended so fucked up doesn't mean we're over."

"Actually, that's exactly what it means," Harkness says.

Thalia reaches over and checks out the glasses, finds one with whiskey still in it. "There's someone else, isn't there?"

"Yeah, there is."

"Serious?" She throws back the whiskey.

Harkness nods.

"What, you're going to settle down, find a nice little wifey, buy a house, and have a kid? Stay on the straight and narrow?" Thalia bends forward, eyes turning fierce. "Well, that's just completely fucked up, Eddy. I know you. That's never going to be enough for you. You aren't like everyone else." She waves her hand around at the crowd, more like a mob now. "You're like all the rest of us. Sick and tired of faking it, of pretending like everything's okay when it's not. Late at night after we drank a bottle or two of whiskey, Eddy? The stories that came out of you were little chunks of black ice. That's the Eddy Harkness I know. And the other thing I know? You're not done with your demons, Eddy. And they're definitely not done with you."

Thalia slumps in the booth like an unplugged automaton. Her arm makes one last slash across the table, sending bottles and glasses smashing to the floor, the shattering lost in the roaring crowd. Her eyes go out of focus and she lowers her head down to the beer-drenched table.

Harkness watches Thalia, *Still Life with Hot Mess*. There's much more to say to her, of course. About how life moves on, about how a dark cloud can pass. But he doesn't want to say it and Thalia's not listening. She's just breathing, shoulders rising and falling in gentle waves.

Harkness reaches over and lifts her head gently and puts his scarf underneath, then slips out of the booth, leaving Thalia where he found her.

22

IT RAINED WHILE he was in McCloskey's and the glistening streets smell cold and metallic. Harkness thinks about the other drinking men who stumbled down these same paths in different times, wearing square-buckled shoes, beaver hats, or zoot suits and wide ties — all buffered by beer and whiskey. It's long after midnight but in office buildings people are sorting mail, watching the Tokyo markets, putting proposals together — and their presence, signaled by the bright squares of lights in the darkened towers, reassures him that all is well in the city at night.

Alone except for the occasional rat stirred by his boot steps, Harkness walks through the orange neon of Chinatown, past the silent South Station with the scolding eagle over its clock, across the green-black water of the channel, and into the seaport, where the ambitious and sober are already tapping away on their laptops, where Candace and May are sleeping.

Harkness paws at the wall in the dark, looking for the light switch. The dim apartment makes his head spin. The light snaps on and he sees Candace on the other side of the living room, arms crossed. "Let me give you a hand." She pulls off her plastic hand and throws it at him.

The hand hits Harkness on the chest and rattles across the floor.

"Congrats, Eddy," she says. "I get mad enough to do that about once a year."

"What are you so pissed about?"

"It's like two in the morning, Eddy. You said you'd be home by midnight."

"Sorry, I was in a bar," he says. "Doing some research."

"Doing some shots, smells like."

"That too."

"Thought we decided that was all over, Eddy." Candace stalks toward him and picks up her plastic hand, pops it back on with a quick twist. "Where were you?"

"McCloskey's."

Candace's eyes narrow and her shoulders rise. "That dump you used to go to with Thalia? Don't tell me you're starting that again."

"No way." Harkness tries to drift into the bedroom but Candace blocks his path.

"Those times are over," Candace says. "Really over. No more wild nights. No more rogue-cop shit. If that's the kind of thing you want to keep doing, you need to tell me now. Because I'm starting to actually depend on you."

Harkness sits on the edge of the couch. "That's not it," he says. "It's work — I'm way out in front of an investigation, a big one."

Candace goes into the kitchen and comes back with a glass of water, hands it to him.

"What're you up to, Eddy?"

"I'm trying to fix a big mistake."

"Yours?"

"No."

"Then just let it go. You can't fix everything, Eddy. That's not your job."

"I know."

"You're doing it again." Candace picks up a coffee cup and struggles to stop herself from throwing it against the living-room wall. She sets the cup back down on the table. "Well, don't let me stop you. I mean, you say you like being with me and May, but maybe it's more important to try to get away with more punk-rock-superhero-cop shit, right?" She waves her hands at the last words like they're toxic.

"That's not what I'm doing, not at all."

"All I know is that your day job is dangerous enough without your making it worse," she says. "Just promise me that this Christmas, there's still going to be three of us around here — you, me, and May." Candace wipes her tears on her Replacements T-shirt, which hikes up to reveal a tattoo of a distorted clock on one pale hip with *Time's Running Out* in black script beneath it. "Say it — now!"

"I promise."

"Louder."

"I promise," he shouts.

Escalating screams echo through the apartment.

"Good job, Eddy. You woke May," Candace says as she strides down the hallway.

"You know what?" Harkness yells after her. "You're cute when you're unreasonable."

Harkness wakes in the middle of the night after the emotional squall has passed, Candace nestled against him, May curled up against her, May's ragged stuffed bunny held close to her chest.

He slips out of bed slowly and stands in his BPD T-shirt staring out the window at the thick darkness over Boston, watching the early flights glide toward Logan like slow comets.

He figures it's just a morning-after wakeup, when the alcohol in his system runs out and his body, confused, wants more. In his drinking days, Harkness might have obliged with a maintenance swig from the whiskey bottle. But now, he just sorts through the daily jumble of facts, dreams, worries, looking for whatever woke him.

Jimmy's smooth voice keeps talking in his mind, a podcast for one, demanding to be heard again and again. The confounding detail surfaces like a forgotten name, and Harkness pulls on his uniform and walks quietly toward the door — shoes in one hand, gun belt in the other.

Not quietly enough.

Candace stirs. "Where you going?"

"Early-morning meeting."

"Where?"

"Hamilton School, out in Waltham."

"Is Deaf Kid okay?"

"That's what I'm going to find out."

It's not even light yet when Harkness pulls into the parking lot by the quiet brick main building of the Hamilton School for the Deaf, as elegant as any prep school.

At the front desk sits a tired-looking woman who straightens up as Harkness strides forward and raises his badge.

"Morning, ma'am," he says. "I'm Detective Harkness, Boston Police Department."

She nods, then speaks in the thick, twisted voice of someone struggling with every syllable. "Good morning."

"I'm looking for a student living here, young guy from the Lower South End. We enrolled him a couple of months ago. Nickname's Vince. Last name's Ashmont."

"I think you mean Edward, that's the name he's going by now," she says, slowly.

The news surprises Harkness. "Well, whatever he's calling himself, I need to see him."

"I need to speak with the director of the school first to do that." She struggles so long to get this sentence out that Harkness considers signing. But she's here to talk, to show progress.

Harkness summons up his most compelling cop voice and signs at the same time. "No time for that. It's an emergency. I need you to wake him up and bring him here. Now."

"Yes. Please wait here."

Harkness sits on a bench next to a wall lined with pictures of dozens of smiling kids.

The front-desk woman returns with her hands on the shoulders of a sleepy-looking Edward wearing gray sweatpants and a white V-neck T-shirt.

Harkness signs that he's sorry to wake him up, that this is important.

Edward shrugs, leans forward, and holds Harkness tightly for a long time.

Harkness signs that he has something important to ask about, a secret that shouldn't stay a secret.

Edward looks interested. He also looks like he might fall asleep.

Harkness asks Edward the question that's been circling through his thoughts all night, that he should have asked when he and Patrick found him chained to a radiator in the Hotel Blackstone.

Who killed your uncle?

23

J ENNET ANSWERS THE door to the Jacobsons' garage and smiles at Harkness. "Glad you could make it."

"How could I turn down your invitation?" Jennet texted Harkness with a simple but irresistible message. *I know things you should.*

Jennet walks into the remodeled garage, now meticulously cleaned and organized. There are two twin beds in the back topped by red Hudson's Bay blankets, a cheerful night table next to each. And on the other side of the garage, there's a small kitchen with a hot plate, refrigerator, and microwave.

"I like what you've done to this place," Harkness says. "Very homey."

"Thanks."

"But don't get too used to it."

Jennet's green eyes turn dead as emeralds. "Here to throw me out, Officer Harkness?"

"No, just here to talk, like you said."

"So let's talk." Jennet sits on the big teal couch in front of the flat-screen and pats the cushion next to her.

Harkness brings over a folding chair from the breakfast nook and sits down across from Jennet. "Let me start with something you probably don't want to hear. We know you're working with the Manchester Group, Jennet."

Harkness waits for her to deny it, but she says nothing. "So what do you have to say about that?"

Jennet shrugs. "What makes you think that I'd have anything to do with those creeps? I hate them."

"Well, first of all, Fayerwether asked for information about towns you could wander to, but it was your man Mouse who picked it up from the library," Harkness says. "That's the easy part. Then we found a story about the Community Store scandal."

"Did some digging, did you?"

Harkness remembers Esther's wide smile as she walked into his office carrying a copy of the *Lower South Ender,* culled from a tall stack after two days of reading every page. "It said you were getting paid by the Manchester Group to keep homeless people off the street and make the neighborhood look good."

"It's true," Jennet says with a matter-of-fact shrug. "Can't deny it. You got me. I took money from shitty rich people to help starving poor people. Haul me into jail." She holds out her wrists. "Cuff me."

Harkness stands and lifts up the chair, moves it farther away. "Nothing to say for yourself?"

"Plenty," she says. "Ready to listen for a minute or are you just going to talk all over me?"

Harkness holds up his hand. "I'm all yours."

"Are you familiar with the phrase *by any means necessary*?"

"Malcolm X, right?"

"Yeah," Jennet says. "We took money from the Manchester Group to feed people in the Lower South End for free because the city wouldn't fund us. We called it capital rekarmatization. Taking their dirty money and making it clean again."

"Hard to argue with that," Harkness says. "And now?"

"I needed to get my people out of the Lower South End. By any means necessary. They were stuck in apartments without electricity, without heat. The streets were coated with toxic sludge. So yes, the Manchester Group gave us money to front the wanderer movement. In this case, we shared a common goal—to clear out the Lower South End."

"Why would they give you money?"

"When you pay for the circus, you get to decide when it closes," Jennet says.

"Sounds a little too easy."

"Here's some news. Wall Street paid for the Occupy movement. They channeled the money to make it happen and then shut it off to make it stop."

"That's crazy."

"Oh yeah?" Jennet gives a knowing shake of her long hair. "Whoever pays the bill gets to decide what happens. They get to sidestep lasting change. Happens all the time. The CIA fronted the Vietnam protests. Reagan paid for the pro-Sandinista movement in the eighties. The trick is to take their money and not give up, not let them get their way."

"Sounds like Conspiracy Theory 101 to me," Harkness says.

"Because you have no idea."

"Oh really? I think you're kidding yourself, Jennet. The Manchester Group is clearing out the Lower South End permanently."

Jennet shrugs. "Things change. We took the best option we had at the time. Does that surprise you?"

"A little," Harkness says. "I mean, it's like making a deal with the devil, from what I know about the Manchester Group."

"We made our choice and we'll live with it," Jennet says.

"Seems more like *you* made the choice, Jennet. I'm pretty sure no one in the wanderer movement would like to hear that they're in Nagog thanks to money from the same people who threw them out of their neighborhood. Would they?"

Jennet's green eyes narrow and she takes in a deep slow breath. "Well, I'm pretty sure that none of your friends would like to hear that you raped me." Jennet leans closer, staring at Harkness with some version of anger. She puts one hand on the top of her light flannel shirt and gives it a sudden pull, popping the buttons, ripping the fabric and revealing her delicate black bra.

"*Whoa.* Stop it."

"Mrs. Jacobson has her binoculars trained on the garage door right now, Eddy." Jennet says. "She saw you come in with her own beady, jealous eyes, and she'll see me run out screaming with my shirt ripped. No matter what the truth is, it'll look bad for you," she says. "It's not like you're a stranger to controversy, is it, Harvard Cop?"

"What do you really want?"

"An even trade — my information for yours. And total honesty."

"This from someone about to fake an assault and blame me for it?"

Jennet smiles, pulls her shirt around her. "I didn't do it, did I?"

"Not yet," Harkness says.

Jennet stands up and walks over to the twin beds, shedding the ripped shirt like a husk and reaching behind to unhook her bra. She falls back on the bed, her breasts set in seductive motion. "C'mon, let's have some fun for a while. Gets lonely out here."

Harkness sees speckled shoulders, gentle collarbones, small breasts with generous areolae. He sees a needy young woman on a red blanket. He sees the calculated smile of a political operator who would do anything to get her way.

If Jennet were a man, Harkness would hate her.

"I think I'll take you up on your first offer. Information and honesty."

Jennet springs out of bed, opens a closet, and pulls on a white button-down shirt. "Have it your way, Eddy," she says. "Just know I would have been fine if you'd just fucked my brains out."

Harkness says nothing, desire evolving like a virus, looking for a way to put his body next to hers as quickly as possible. "And what would that have resolved, exactly?"

"Nothing." Jennet pulls the white shirt around her, leaving it un-buttoned. "But it would have been more fun."

"No argument there."

"Now that we've got that figured out, let's get started." Jennet sits back down on the couch, smiling. "You show me yours first."

After Harkness runs through the evidence he has linking Dark Horse to the Manchester Group, Jennet sits quietly, then stands and stalks through the empty room. "That sounds right," she says. "All roads lead to the Manchester Group. Dark Horse is their idea and their fault. They'll do anything to turn the Lower South End into luxury condos. But you're missing one crucial angle."

"What's that?"

"The mayor," she says. "He's Neil Burch's creation — that guy has his hand jammed up inside O'Mara's head like a puppeteer. And he's Fayerwether's chum from way back. They're the two you need to watch. Burch on the street, Fayerwether everywhere else."

133

"Why?"

"The mayor may not have directly been involved with Dark Horse," she says. "In fact, I can guarantee that he wasn't. The guy's not stupid. Deniability is his middle name. But he puts these shitty guys in positions of power and lets them do what they want. So it shouldn't be a surprise that they do terrible things. Dark Horse is just the beginning, Eddy. The more you dig, the more dirt you'll find."

She sits back down on the couch. "Just don't let them off the hook. They rely on people being too scared to go up against them."

Harkness nods. "Your turn to ask the questions."

"I want to know about Nagog," Jennet says. "Who runs the town, who do we need to suck up to, who hates us. Because we hear they're already scheduling another town meeting for January," Jennet says. "We need to be able to stay here until we can go back to the Lower South End."

"From what you're saying, you won't ever be able to go back."

"We can if you can fix it, Eddy. Derail their big plan."

"Nothing would make me happier."

"It's probably impossible," Jennet says. "Just so you know."

"I definitely know."

"Just do what you can. By any means necessary, right?" Jennet leans over, reaches out, and gives Harkness's hand a squeeze. She notices his missing finger and touches its annealed end gently, as if she can rub the damage away.

Harkness slides his hand back. "Let's talk about Nagog," he says.

Jennet reaches for her notebook and flips to a new page. "Okay, Professor Harkness, begin your lecture." She pauses. "Or do you have another lesson planned for this afternoon?"

Harkness stares into her lovely green eyes, the kind that tell beautiful lies. "No," he says. "I think a brief lecture on the power structure of my hometown might help you. But one thing first."

Jennet brightens. "What?"

"Button your shirt, please."

24

THE SUITE OF City Hall offices looks more like a startup lab, with a row of white workbenches and earnest young guys in black T-shirts working at them, some wearing protective glasses like true science nerds. Harkness watches them from the Barcelona chairs in the waiting room — their fast hands, intense focus.

Burch leaves his corner office and rushes toward him, beaming out a manic smile from beneath his shining dome. He's shorter than Harkness remembers and more geeky than scary. "Eddy! Eddy Harkness! Harvard Cop! He shoots, he scores!" He's shouting like a fanboy. "So good to see you again."

Harkness smiles as they shake hands, looks Burch in the jittery eyes. "Good to see you." A lie. Harkness has learned to steer clear of loose cannons like Burch. He's exuding the smell of late-night booze, a sweet stink no amount of toothpaste can cover up. Rumor has it that Burch is a wild man in the bars after-hours.

"Thanks for jumping in during the quote-unquote book riot," Burch says, "catching that idiot book tosser." Though his title is chief technology officer, Neil Burch serves a less visible role as the mayor's enforcer. He waves Harkness into his large, cement-walled City Hall office with windows looking out on the cobblestoned expanse of Government Center.

"Just doing my job."

Burch settles into his brushed-aluminum-and-black-mesh chair and puts his hands on his aqua-glass desk. "Well, you showed how it's done. Beyond the call of duty. Grace under pressure. All that stuff."

Harkness takes a seat on the other side of the desk, notices that it's set a little lower than Burch's chair, a bush-league power play.

"I know my meeting invitation said we needed to talk about the mayor's opioid task force," Burch says. "But first I want to show you something really cool we're working on." Burch rises, twitchy excitement making it impossible for him to stay seated. "I think you'll really like it."

"Sure."

"Okay, so draw your Glock and point it at me."

Harkness shakes his head, wonders if this whole meeting is a setup. "I don't need to tell you the dozen reasons I can't do that, Mr. Burch."

"Neil, please."

"I can't just draw my weapon, Neil. Especially here in City Hall. It violates more regulations than I can count."

"Okay, fair enough," Burch says. "But check this out." He reaches into the drawer and hands Harkness a SIG Sauer.

"Nice." Harkness checks it out — newish, looks like a P226 MK25, except it's tan-colored. He hands the gun back.

"Just like the Navy SEALs use," Burch says. "Except this one's the desert model. You know, for our enemies in the Middle East."

Burch ejects the magazine, turns it to make sure that it's empty, checks the chamber, then pulls back the slide and points the gun at the floor. He pulls the trigger with a loud click. "Now you try." He hands the gun to Harkness.

"I really don't want to."

"I promise, you won't get fired," Burch says. "Nothing bad's going to happen. In fact, nothing at all's going to happen." Burch reaches over and flips a toggle switch next to his phone, then shouts, "FEMP on!"

Harkness stares, wonders what's up. So far, Burch seems more like an overcaffeinated professor than a canny political operator.

"Okay, so try to pull the slide back now."

Harkness holds up the pistol, points it carefully at a leather chair in the corner that might blunt a 9 mm round. But when he tries to pull back the slide, it won't move.

"Can't do it," he says.

Burch throws the switch again. "FEMP off," he shouts. "Try again."

Harkness pulls the slide back. It moves smoothly now, like it's supposed to.

Burch puts up his hand, palm forward. "Hold on," he says to Harkness, then he shouts at the ceiling, "FEMP on!" He nods at Harkness.

Harkness tries to pull the trigger but it won't move.

Another shout at the ceiling from Burch, then Harkness tries again, hears the click of the trigger.

Harkness places the gun carefully on Burch's desk.

"Cool, huh?"

"So what's that all about?"

"Focused electromagnetic pulse, or FEMP," Burch says. "Freezes up moving parts. Metal and otherwise. It's like super glue for guns. Right now, we've got it working in closely confined areas, like about half of my office here." He waves his hand toward the lab. "But soon we'll be able to expand it to larger fields, like a city block. Imagine that — bad guys with guns they can't use."

Harkness nods. "That would be pretty great."

"We can knock out their cell phones too." Burch turns quiet, then looks at Harkness with unalloyed suspicion. "Just so you know, maybe the technology isn't called FEMP at all. Maybe it's something else we can't even tell you about. But it really works."

"Color me impressed," Harkness says, and he is — impressed that one of the buttoned-down mayor's advisers is such a maniac.

"No offense, Harkness. But the old-school police work the BPD's doing is hit-or-miss at best. Cops wander around looking for trouble — on the streets and online. When they stumble across it, they respond. Sometimes it works, sometimes it doesn't."

Harkness nods. Burch hasn't said anything that he disagrees with so far.

"Technology lets us move from man-to-man to zone defense. It boosts efficiency. And it turns cops from blunt objects barging around the city into smart, proactive peace machines."

"Sounds good," Harkness says.

"I thought you'd see it that way," Burch says. "I had you pegged for a forward thinker. Pragmatic and visionary. The kind of guy the mayor really likes on his team. Not like the lard-assed, Dunkin' Donuts–swilling BPD of old, right?"

Harkness lets the slight slide because he's here to charm Burch, not defend himself or the BPD. He's in Burch's world, like an old-school fox in a high-tech hen house.

"Microdrones, digital surveillance, emerging technologies," Burch recites. "It's an exciting time in law enforcement. Every cop has to ask himself, *Do I want to be part of the violent past or the peaceful future?*"

"The future," Harkness says. "Definitely the future."

Burch gives a broad smile and reaches out to shake his hand. "Excellent. Then let me tell you a little secret, Harkness. And it stays in this room. If you tell anyone, I'll have to kill you."

Harkness stares.

"Kidding!" Burch smiles so hard his lips almost disappear. *Ha-ha-ha.* "The mayor's working on a major shakeup of the BPD. In a few months, Lattimore will be out. We'll be replacing him with Lieutenant Landers from A-One, know him?"

"Definitely." Putting on an enthusiastic expression is a challenge, but Harkness does it. "Good man. Saw him just the other day."

"You okay with the change? I mean, I know you and Lattimore are close."

"We're close because I report to him," Harkness says. "If someone else is in the role, I'll be close to him. My job's not about allegiance or friendship. It's about duty and the law, Neil." Harkness recites this careful lie without a trace of outrage.

"Excellent," Burch says. "But this part's harder. We'll be folding Narco-Intel into the Narcotics division. Makes sense to keep like with like."

"So how's that going to work?" Harkness asks, knowing it won't be pretty.

"Everyone in your department will be reassessed and reassigned," Burch says.

Harkness knows what *reassigned* means — fired or put on desk duty.

Burch smiles. "Except you, of course."

"I appreciate that."

"You'll be part of the new Narcotics team. Narco 2.0, we're calling it."

"I like the sound of that," Harkness says.

"In January, we want to announce a narcotics task force that can morph into the new department next year. We'd like your help creating it. Can we count on you?"

A more volatile detective would use this chance to turn the tables on Burch, to ask him why someone in the mayor's office has been prowling around the digital margins of Narco-Intel trying to access records about Dark Horse. He would slam his hand on Burch's fancy glass desk and tell him to fuck himself for breaking up his department and for using such an obvious ploy to keep him quiet.

But Harkness has to play the long game, and play it well.

"Absolutely," he says. "I'd be proud to be part of it."

Harkness reaches into his lowest desk drawer and pulls out the unopened bottle of Jameson that Lattimore gave him. He sets it on the desk in front of him and stares at it, contemplating the consequences of backsliding into a cop cliché.

Patrick barges in. "Hey, Harky . . ."

Harkness turns toward him.

"What's wrong, boss?"

"I just saw the future of law enforcement."

"And?"

"We're not in it."

Silence settles over the office. In the background, they can hear the news channels, the blipping of scanners, detectives shouting.

"You gonna open that, boss?"

"No." Harkness pulls out a desk drawer and puts the bottle away, for now.

"Good call. Did you see this?" Patrick holds out the Business section of the *Globe*, folded to an inside page. "Fayerwether made an announcement today. Picked the lead developer in the Lower South End." He runs his finger down the columns of text. "Called the mayor's landgrab 'a creative public-private partnership for revitalizing the Lower South End.' And guess who that partner is."

.   .   .

Harkness finds the key on his key ring and opens the upper evidence locker. He reaches deep into the locker and runs his fingers along the back wall. There's nothing there, nothing at all.

He steps back and checks to make sure he's looking in the last locker on the left. The other lockers are full of yellow bags, each labeled and bundled for further processing at the main lab. But the top locker is never used—too high, too small.

Just as Harkness begins to run through the possibilities, Esther walks into Evidence. "You know, for a guy who's really great at finding things, you're not very good at hiding them." She unlocks a lower drawer and reaches to the back to pull out a familiar ring box.

"How'd you know that was mine?"

"Patrick told me."

"Why'd you move it?"

"This drawer's safer," she says. "I have the only key. Didn't want your engagement ring hauled downtown by accident. You'd have to explain why you hid it in the same lockers with a bunch of heroin, bloody hoodies, and guns. Not very romantic, IMHO."

Harkness nods, opens the box, and sees that it still holds his family's ring.

"You going to actually use that ring or just carry it around?"

Harkness says nothing, then shakes his head. "I've had it here for three months," he says. At first he told himself he was just waiting for the right time to come along. Then he realized he was stalling. Then he stalled again and again.

"You'll figure it out, boss," Esther says. "If it makes you feel any better, I'd marry you right now if you asked me."

"Really, Esther?"

"Sure!" She bobs with enthusiasm. "Lots of people just get married. More fun than being alone. Tax advantages. You get a bunch of presents from your relatives."

"Sounds great." Even though Esther's in her late twenties, Harkness wonders if the part of her brain that deals with consequences still isn't working yet.

"Meant to tell you, I'm dating Glenn now—your friend at the library."

"Smart guy. And now a lucky guy too."

"Thanks. We hit it off. Maybe we'll get married in a couple of months. Who knows?"

"Anything can happen," Harkness says. "It's a crazy world."

"Here's the way I think about it," Esther says. "All those big decisions people used to get all hung up over? Where to live? Choosing a career? Now people just don't worry about it as much. Maybe you just need to *go with it*. Trust your instincts."

"Thanks, Esther."

"I had an advice column in my high-school newspaper," she says. "It was called Ask Esther. If you need help with anything else, just ask me." Esther drifts out of the evidence room.

Harkness looks at the evidence lockers. Each one holds a story — about a bust, a victim, a deal gone awry. Seeing so many unhappy endings makes it hard to believe in beginnings, Harkness thinks, then decides this line of thinking is total crap, something a jaded detective might mutter on a second-tier cop series.

When he considered the real problem — during stolen moments at work or up late in their apartment — he found himself going back to Thalia's drinks-fueled diatribe. She's right. He's not done with his demons. No one is. Everyone has an empty room inside, one that demons try to break into and colonize. His defenses are strong, but so are the demons. One window shatters and they're back inside.

He puts the ring box in his pocket and takes it with him — not to a new hiding place this time, but home.

25

THINK HE'LL SHOW UP?" Esther pulls her burgundy trench coat around her to ward off the cold and looks out toward Castle Island, its long boardwalk empty.

"He'll be here," Harkness says.

"How do you know?"

"Lattimore's curious," Harkness says. "Always wants to know everything. Particularly when it's about him."

"That why we're out here on the ocean, Harky? On a freaking frozen day." Patrick nods toward the long curve of beige sand and the empty parking lot, infamous from dozens of Mob stakeouts and grainy surveillance photos, now lunar and grim. "Because he'll be curious?"

"That and it's about the most unlikely place to have a meeting ever." They huddle a little closer on the park bench, breathing steam. Harkness points up at a telephone pole. "The neighborhood association bought crappy cameras. None of them work anymore. So we're off the grid."

"We're going to be off to the hospital in about ten more minutes." Patrick shivers. The pigeon-gray sky spits out tiny sparks of snow, carried sideways by the cold wind.

"This is how revolutions start," Esther says. "Three people on a bench, going up against the Man."

"Ain't we supposed to have a bomb or something?" Patrick says.

"We do." Harkness holds up the blue binder.

Esther presses closer to them as they wait on the bench.

"Don't be getting too friendly, girl." Patrick tries to edge away. "Really."

"I'm not," Esther says, voice shaking. "This coat's vintage pleather. Looks good, but it's about as warm as a shower curtain."

"Then why you wearin' it?"

"Seemed like the right coat for a climactic showdown by the ocean."

"That's what we're having today, is it?"

"Yeah," Harkness says. "That's what we're having today."

"There he is." Esther points to the black SUV speeding down Columbia Road. It skids to a halt and Commissioner Lattimore climbs out, wearing a heavy black parka with a fur-lined hood.

They stand and watch as he strides toward them.

"He looks pissed," Patrick says.

Esther stares. "But his coat looks really, really warm."

"I told the car to wait for ten minutes," Lattimore says in lieu of *hello*. "So start talking."

Harkness nods at Esther to begin their pitch. "As you know, everything about Dark Horse is wrong, sir," she says. "It's brown when it ought to be white. It's pure when it looks like black tar. It's packaged in glassine envelopes that stamp collectors use, not in bags. And its logo isn't a crappy rubber stamp. It looks like a graphic designer came up with it." The last two details came from Glenn, who spent a few months "battling the poppy," as he put it, during a rough patch.

"That's what you people got?" Lattimore says. "I came to a frozen beach in Southie to hear stuff I already know?"

"There's more," Patrick says, picking up the narrative. "When the Manchester Group started clearing out the Lower South End last spring, some goons dropped off about three kilos of Dark Horse at the apartment of Levon Ashmont and told him they'd front it to him. He can set the price, sell it, and they'd be back to split the money. Weird deal, but lucrative. He moves some of it through his dealers, and a bunch of people overdose. Right before the Lower South End floods, the goons come back and ask for the rest of the junk. They don't care about the money. They just know it's a good time to get rid of the evidence. He won't give it to them. They kill Ashmont with a heavy shot of Dark Horse."

"You can't be sure of that," Lattimore says. "Dealers OD all the time."

"This one was clean," Harkness says. "I made a mistake when we were in his apartment. Didn't look close enough, just assumed he overdosed — but it was a homicide."

"Who told you that?"

"His nephew," Harkness says.

"Why do we care about Dark Horse still?" Lattimore runs his fingers through his gray hair, turned wild by the cold wind.

"Because the Manchester Group is getting away with murder," Harkness says.

"Then get real evidence and build a case against them," Lattimore says. "That's what we do."

"We've got evidence, and sources." Harkness holds up the binder. "But there are . . . complications."

"Such as."

Patrick counts them off on his gloved fingers. "We got some information from an illegal wiretap down at lockup. Harky stole Frankie Getler's phone to get the goods on the Manchester Group. And I hacked their e-mail server."

"Frankie Getler," Lattimore says, shaking his head slowly. "That guy's batshit crazy."

"But his phone ain't," Patrick says. "And all the other facts we got in this case are solid too, but they came from shaky sources. A musician who dealt Dark Horse, a guy named Jimmy Jazz who's probably a pimp, and Jennet Townsend, who's running the wanderer movement. All of 'em got plenty of priors."

"The Manchester Group's lawyers will gut them," Harkness adds.

"So pull in the DA's office."

"No way," Harkness says. "The DA lives in one of the Manchester Group's luxury apartment towers. From what we can tell, he hasn't paid rent for four years. Then there are the Harbormasters. They're all over this too — Fayerwether, the mayor. We have lists and e-mails that take this all the way to the mayor's office."

Lattimore puts out his hand. "Your gun, Harkness. Now. And your badge."

"Hey, hang on a second," Patrick says.

Esther's eyes open wide.

"Our job is to fight drugs, not the mayor," he says. "I told you not to mess with the Harbormasters and you went against my direct orders. You're relieved of duty effective immediately, Harkness. Gun and badge, now."

In the cold silence that follows, the only sounds are distant seagulls and the jangle of Harkness taking off his gun belt and badge and handing them to Lattimore, who turns and walks toward the idling SUV.

Harkness pauses, like a roadside bomber waiting for the exact second to hit the detonator.

As Lattimore opens the door to the SUV, Harkness takes a step forward and shouts, "O'Mara's appointing Lieutenant Ted Landers commissioner of the BPD in January."

All eyes are on Lattimore, waiting.

Lattimore stops moving, one foot in the SUV, the other on the pavement. He stands frozen for what seems like an eternity, then steps back out and slams the door.

He's stalking toward them again, expensive black parka flying in the wind.

Then Lattimore stands in front of them, Harkness's gear still in his hands. "*What* did you say?"

"Neil Burch told me that O'Mara was going to announce Landers's appointment as commissioner in January. He's disbanding Narco-Intel and firing us all." Harkness skips the part about Burch promising to save his job.

"That's complete bullshit."

Harkness hands him his iPhone and a set of earbuds. "Listen for yourself," he says. "I wore a wire to the meeting."

Lattimore puts the earbuds in and Harkness presses PLAY on the screen. He listens for a few seconds, and then his eyes open wide and his mouth curdles into a lipless grimace.

"I knew O'Mara might replace me," he says. "But not this soon. And not with Lieutenant Landline." He rips the earbuds out and hands the iPhone back to Harkness, followed by his gun belt and badge.

"Excellent job, Harkness. You're back on the force." Lattimore turns to Patrick. "And you, Detective Fitzgerald, leak that report far and wide."

Patrick steps closer. "So what's the plan, sir?"

Lattimore puts one hand on Esther's shoulder and the other on Patrick's. "We're going to go after the head of the snake, Officers — Mayor Michael O'Mara. Strike that. *Former* mayor Michael O'Mara. We're going to destroy him." He pauses. "Or go down trying."

Lattimore's SUV is just a tiny black dot far down Columbia Road. Harkness, Patrick, and Esther shiver in the cold and watch it disappear.

"Well, that was fun," Esther says.

"Nice nail, Harky," Patrick says. "Textbook. Somebody oughta do a case study."

At Narco-Intel, *the nail* is the incendiary, derailing piece of evidence delivered to the jury or leaked to the media at precisely the right time.

The toxic chemicals in the defendant's meth lab killed a litter of kittens.

The assault victim, a photographer, will never be able to see again.

Part of an undigested human ear was found in the psychopathic dealer's stomach.

The nail.

"And how'd you manage to get a wire into that meeting, Harky? Thought Burch was all high-tech and crazy about security?"

"I didn't."

"What?"

"I wrote out what Burch and I said during the meeting and reenacted it with my brother, George. He's really good with voices."

"What if Lattimore figured out it was fake?"

"You know how it goes with evidence," Harkness says. "People believe what they want to believe."

"*Shit,* man," Patrick says. "For a straight shooter, you are one twisted motherfucker."

"Contradictions make the man," Harkness says, dredging up another piece of dark wisdom from his father's bottomless well.

26

S AM REED TOSSES his menu on the table between them. "I'm thinking the breakfast sandwich with egg whites and no meat may be the least deadly thing here." An incongruous collection of autographed photos stare down from the yellow wall — Ronald Reagan, Mike Dukakis, Tip O'Neill, Barney Frank, Mitt Romney, Martha Coakley. Everybody eats at the Fill-A-Buster.

"Smart call," Harkness says. "Not a good time for a cardiac event." The Beacon Hill diner empties out between breakfast and lunch. They're alone except for the fry cooks.

They're sitting at a wobbly table near the window at a place where politicians go to look like they're *of the people* and where neighborhood characters hang out because they *are* the people — underemployed and low on cash. It serves the kind of food middle-aged men like to eat when their wives aren't around — bacon and eggs, hamburgers, souvlaki, gyros, Greek salads piled with feta.

They order and wait.

"I got to say, Eddy, it's really good to see you again. Been a while." Reed smiles, runs his fingers through his sandy hair, cut short and neat.

"You too, Sam." Harkness first met Reed as a rookie patrolling the Lower South End. Reed was a committed community organizer at the time, then the district's much-beloved city councilor, and then a popular but failed candidate for mayor, edged out by O'Mara's coalition.

"Things have been pretty terrible in the old neighborhood." Reed shakes his head. "We've got whole blocks still waiting for basic services."

"What about the big redevelopment project?"

"You know how slowly these things go, Eddy. The Urban Redevelopment Council presents its plan. There's a lot of discussion and debate. I can't see it going anywhere fast."

Harkness says nothing. Even after just a few minutes with Reed, he can tell he's encased in a thick cocoon of denial.

"Just politics as usual—lots of talk and in the end, no action," Reed says. "My job is to make sure that my constituents are protected. And the mayor's people have assured me that they are."

"Really?" Harkness gives Reed a diagnostic stare. His fatal flaw is so obvious, it might as well be a sputtering roadside flare. Professional dispassion, the quality that makes Reed seem so levelheaded during city council meetings, isn't working for him in the middle of a crisis.

The waiter delivers their lunches. Harkness pushes his falafel plate aside. "Sam, the Manchester Group is about to swallow up your entire district," he says. "Do you have any idea what they're up to?"

"Manchester Group? They're real estate developers, right?"

Harkness squelches the urge to shake Reed by the shoulders. "Yeah, and the Nazis were political activists."

"That's a bit incendiary, isn't it?"

"Sam, your district, and your entire base, is about to get dismantled. I think a little incendiary talk might be okay right about now."

"Fair enough," he says, nodding. "I appreciate your candor. I can take it."

"How about this?" Harkness leans forward. "The Manchester Group brought Dark Horse to your neighborhood."

"What?"

"It's deadly heroin disguised as ordinary heroin. Like the Trojan Horse of the opioid wars."

"Why would they do that?"

"To make the area look dangerous and drug-infested," Harkness says. "Albrecht Square is one of the city's jewels. Manchester Group wants it. And they're about to get it."

Reed's face darkens. Now it's his turn to push aside his plate.

"Do you know how many people died from Dark Horse?"

"No," Reed says.

"Twenty-six so far, most in your district."

"But this was before the flood, right?"

"Pretty much," Harkness says. "Then Dark Horse stopped, because the flood was the best windfall O'Mara's colleagues could ever have hoped for. And they most definitely used it. That's what politicians do, right? Take advantage of every opportunity?"

"That's a fair assessment."

"The Manchester Group is about to destroy you, Sam. Unless you do something to stop it."

"Eddy, this is all really disturbing to me," he says.

"I know it's hard to believe," Harkness says. "I'd be glad to show you the evidence, anytime. Then let's talk — and try to fix it."

"Fix what?"

"The leadership."

Reed shakes his head. "You have no idea how politics works. I don't have the votes to take down O'Mara. Couldn't beat him last fall and I still can't. Once the mayor's in office, there isn't a lot you can do about it."

"There are some tactics," Harkness says. "But not the kind you're used to."

"Like?"

"Enforced transparency," he says.

"What's that?"

"We turn into whistleblowers and expose them all — the Manchester Group, the mayor's office, and the Harbormasters," Harkness says.

Reed holds up both hands. "Whoa, do *not* mess with the Harbormasters."

Finally, some emotion, Harkness thinks. "Why not?"

"Do you know who they are? Rumor has it that they were behind the destruction of the West End. And came up with forced busing in the 1970s. Once they get wind of what you're up to, you'll find out just how fast the city can turn really cold and dark."

"It's already cold and dark."

"Look, truth be told, the Harbormasters brought me down," Reed says. "They threw their weight behind O'Mara during the general election and he won. I had no idea what was going on. They're cold-hearted power brokers, Eddy. And if they decide to, they'll crush you."

"Thanks for the warning."

"What are you asking me to do, Eddy? Start a war with the mayor? The Harbormasters? I definitely don't want to be part of that."

"Why not?"

"Because what you're trying to do probably won't work," Reed says. "It's almost impossible to get rid of a sitting mayor. They couldn't even throw Mayor Curley out of office when he was in prison. A recall takes years, if we could make it happen at all."

"So what do you propose?"

"I'd rather keep O'Mara in office for three more years and let the people really see what he's all about. Give him enough rope and he'll hang himself, as they say. Then beat him in the next election by a landslide with an I-told-you-so campaign. That seems like a much more viable option than attacking him head-on."

"Shrewd, very shrewd." Harkness smiles, tosses a couple of twenties on the table for food they didn't touch, and reaches for his black overcoat. "There just may be a politician somewhere under all that *nice.*"

27

W ELCOME HOME," Harkness says as they pull into the unshoveled driveway on Oaktree Court. They look out at the barny McMansion, big as a minor prep school, its many gables dark in the dreary winter afternoon.

"Could be yours," Candace says. "Price is dropping."

The last time he saw the place, Harkness was helping Candace close it up after her father died. An architectural Frankenstein, the house is so charmless that the Nagog Home Team couldn't move it no matter how many apple pies they baked in the kitchen.

"It's so huge, eventually some investment guy will buy it," says Harkness.

"I'll be right back." Candace gets out and opens the back door so carefully that May doesn't even stir in her car seat. "You wait here with Sleepyhead."

Candace lifts up the turkey platter and carries it toward the house. Nora's making Thanksgiving dinner right now in her kitchen. But Candace got up early to roast another turkey to drop off for the anonymous wanderers staying in her house.

Last night's snow left a dusting of white on the driveway, now marked with dozens of footsteps. As Harkness wonders just how many wanderers are in the former Hammond family home, Candace comes running back. She slips and falls, rises to run again. Harkness shuts off the car and steps out, glances back to make sure May's asleep, then locks the doors behind him.

"Eddy, you've got to stop them." Candace is breathing heavily and the beatific smile of someone delivering a carefully prepared holiday meal is gone, replaced by righteous fury. "You're not going to believe it."

Harkness takes her arm and they walk down the icy walkway. As they open the front door and step inside, cindery wood smoke and the feral scent of too many unwashed people in a close space wraps around them like a thrift-shop overcoat. A dark chandelier hangs crookedly in the main room, and the weak afternoon light has already faded. Harkness can make out the forlorn Thanksgiving platter sitting on the cluttered kitchen counter.

They walk farther into the house, feeling a coven-y and cult-y vibe that's setting off Harkness's alarms.

Oil lamps and candles burn on the floor. In the distance wanderers huddle around a wood stove jammed in the center the living room and vented out a window via a long aluminum duct.

"Here's where that duct thingy came from." Candace points to the ceiling, where the drywall's been ripped apart to reveal the house's raw workings, clumps of wires and dark hollows. "They completely fucked up the house, Eddy."

Harkness wonders if Jennet actually encouraged the destruction. "Why's it so dark in here?"

"They turned off the electricity and the heat and now they're burning furniture and branches."

Candace and Harkness walk closer to the huddle of people. They're wearing so many down jackets and overcoats that Harkness can't even tell if they're women or men, young or old. They're just ash-colored figures bumbling around like alt-zombies in the smoke-thick light.

"All right, Boston Police," Harkness shouts, holding up his badge. "Who's in charge here?" His voice echoes through the empty living room. Not much furniture left, just a couple of futons on the floor, stacks of cardboard boxes, and a bunch of beat-up bicycles. Whatever Candace didn't clear out after her father died found its way into the wanderers' wood stove.

"No one's, like, *in charge*," someone mutters. A low wave of laughter rises at the stodgy concept of order.

A shorter wanderer in thick-lensed round glasses walks up to them. "What's up, dudes?" he says in a quiet, California-inflected voice.

"Looks like you guys did a little home renovation," Harkness says.

He shrugs. "The place was like totally energy-inefficient. Forty-eight windows, most of 'em facing north. Figured we'd take it off the grid."

"Off the grid!" Candace's hands are on her hips and she's stalking around kicking at piles of trash. "That's not up to you, fucktard."

Harkness gives her the chill-out look and turns back to the pocket-sized wanderer.

"That's a decision the homeowner gets to make."

"Actually, that's not the case." The wanderer goes over to a stack of books by a shelf marked WANDERER LIBRARY and pulls out a photocopy. "The billeting bylaw allows for, and I quote, 'any reasonable alternations necessary to allow the comfortable habitation of the premises.'"

Candace makes a strangled noise and kicks over a stack of cans.

Harkness points to Candace. "Look, the homeowner here generously handed over the keys to her house, the one you're trashing. And as you can probably tell, she's not happy with what you're doing. So keep the so-called alternations to a minimum and don't burn the place down. That's really the only fair and civilized way to act, right? No matter what the bylaw says."

The wanderer backs off. "Okay, man. We'll do what we can."

Harkness and Candace turn, anxious to get back to May, and walk to the front door, windows on either side covered with burlap.

Candace reaches up to tug on the fabric. "They just nailed it into the wall," she says. "Dad would shit."

"You always hated this house," Harkness says. "Don't forget, you handed over the keys, remember?"

"So I made a mistake," she says. "But that doesn't mean other people get to wreck it. It's going to cost thousands of dollars to fix." She wipes her eyes. "Like we have that kind of money."

Behind them, someone starts playing a plaintive, minor-key folk song on a ukulele.

"Let's get out of here, Eddy," Candace says.

"But they're playing our song."

"Not funny."

As they step outside into the cold, Harkness takes off his jacket and wraps it around Candace.

"Regretting that yes vote, aren't you?"

"Completely," she says.

"Well, you get another shot at it."

"What?"

"There's a special town meeting in January," he says. "The American Landowner people rallied enough NIMBY Nagogians to get a new vote."

"This time, those smelly woven people are out of here," Candace says, her breath steaming in the cold.

"So where are they supposed to go?" Harkness asks.

Candace shakes her head. "Not my problem." She holds her hands up in the cold air and shakes them. "They can wander somewhere else."

They're back in the Chevy, May still fast asleep, when one of the wanderers steps gingerly up the walkway. He's shoeless, bearded, and wearing a flannel shirt and grease-slick overalls that could fit two of him. He looks faux Amish or like he ought to be plucking banjo in an alt-country band.

He holds out the untouched turkey platter.

Candace rolls down her window.

"We're vegan," he says.

28

Y OU KNOW THE origins of Albrecht Square, don't you?"

"No sir, I don't." Harkness does but feigns ignorance to keep Robert Fayerwether IV talking. He's sitting in a leather armchair in the library of the St. Pancras Club — more exclusive than Cedar, Union, or St. Botolph, but nearly empty on a cold mid-December afternoon.

"Well!" Fayerwether holds up his long-fingered hand, palm out, to put Harkness on pause as he focuses on his glass of port. His thin lips busily suck up the sweet wine. Then he bends into his latest lecture, his white hair tumbling forward. "We start during the great wave of German immigration, the 1860s. Sigmar Stark leaves his ancestral home of Nuremberg and quickly becomes a rich man buying and selling land in Boston. The crowning achievement of his life is to create a model neighborhood, the Lower South End, completed in 1876 for the centennial."

Harkness listens as the lecture marches into the twentieth century. Instead of his uniform, he's wearing one of his father's light brown Harris tweed jackets, black wool pants, and a pale blue–striped Brooks Brothers shirt with a dark blue tie. He started with a shiny black one but Candace nixed it, calling it too cop-like. Tweedy and nerdy, thanks to tortoiseshell reading glasses from the drugstore, Harkness looks like he might be the young director of a nonprofit foundation or an unusually buff historian.

"Does Albrecht Square have anything to do with Albrecht Dürer?"

Harkness asks during a lull. He knows that it does — so does anyone who can type and use the Internet.

Fayerwether wags his finger. "Yes, exactly," he says. "I do like it when public servants know their city's history."

Harkness says nothing. They've already bonded over Harvard and now, history.

"Stark had a lifelong obsession with Dürer, who came from his hometown. More specifically, he was fascinated by *Melencolia I*, an engraving from 1514. And he wasn't the only one — it's one of the most well-known prints in the world. Hold on a moment, I'm sure there's a copy of it here somewhere.

"Wheeler!" Fayerwether calls out, and a broom-thin man wearing a black suit and bow tie sweeps into the room. He pauses before Fayerwether and bends down in supplication. "Yes, sir?"

Fayerwether points to the upper reaches of the library shelves, and his manservant beetles around the library, climbing wobbly bookshelf ladders to extract dusty volumes.

Harkness musters up some artspeak he read on Wikipedia. "The engraving is about the overriding order of the universe or something like that, yes?"

"In a way," Fayerwether says, smiling as Wheeler pulls out a thick tome, triumphant. "Yes, that's it."

Fayerwether takes the book from its finder without a word of thanks, thumbs through it, and flops it open. "As you can see, there's a main winged figure of a genius in the foreground, a grounded angel as it were, surrounded by the unused equipment of reason — an empty scale, an hourglass. And it's saying that you have to use what's available to you to bring order to the inherent chaos of your mind as well as the world around you. Order in the midst of chaos — it was a message that appealed to Stark as an . . . urban-planning visionary." He looks across the empty drawing room at the windows facing Commonwealth Avenue when he utters the last words.

Even from his brief time with Fayerwether, Harkness can tell that he'd like to be called an urban-planning visionary, that when he looks in the mirror in the morning he sees a winged genius.

Their conversation lags and Harkness stretches out his arm casually to let the sleeve of his Harris tweed jacket ride up and reveal an elegant 1960s Rolex with a simple steel case and black leather band.

Harkness saw a similar watch on Fayerwether's wrist in a *Globe* photo of last month's Urban Redevelopment Council meeting. Gus "the Chemist" Donovan, drug dealer turned jeweler, is renting Harkness the Rolex for fifty dollars a day.

Fayerwether's owlish eyebrows rise when he spots the watch. It takes only a few shared connections — same college, city, watch — to build trust.

Harkness points to the four-by-four grid of numbers on the print. "Those numbered squares are on the clock tower in Albrecht Square, aren't they?"

"Yes, it's there to remind all passersby of the order of pure reason, no matter what's happening on the streets," Fayerwether says. "See the date at the bottom — 1514? All the rows and quadrants add up to thirty-four. It's a mathematical oddity called the magic square. Like sudoku before there was such an abomination." He reaches out and closes the book firmly. "But enough about history, Officer . . ."

"Harkness," he says.

Fayerwether turns his head and narrows his eyes slightly, as if reading the fine print of Harkness's life. "Any relation to a rascal named Red Harkness?"

Harkness nods slowly, prepares to get thrown out of the St. Pancras Club. "He was my father."

"You don't look much like him," Fayerwether says. "Or act like him."

"That's true." *And for a good reason,* Harkness thinks.

"I remember your father sitting in this very room, decades ago."

"Really?" Harkness remembers his father had a drinking hidey-hole he called "the club," but he had no idea it was the St. Pancras.

Fayerwether's eyes turn cloudy as he drifts into the past. "We were writing the Christmas Revels — the whole club participates. A bawdy send-up of the Nativity play. The wise men are bankers with briefcases stuffed with cash. There's a not-so-Virgin Mary. A martini fountain tinkles away in the corner of the humble stable. I have to say it's . . . quite a laugh."

Harkness smiles, glad that his father charmed Fayerwether instead of ripping him off.

"Red cast himself as the Dollared Dwarf of Dionysus." Fayerwether lets out a dry bark. "Did the whole play on his knees dressed in a priest's cassock, drunk as a . . ." Fayerwether waves his hand to dispel the louche memory and signals the bartender for a refill of port.

"How well did you know my father?"

"Oh, you know, we saw each other on club nights, at lunch at Locke-Ober, or at one of the spring galas," he says. "So, not particularly well but more than a passing acquaintance." He pauses. "I was very sorry to hear about his . . . complications, and his death, of course. Very sorry."

Harkness nods. *Complications* — WASP code for fraud, IRS regulators, Ponzi scheme, disgrace, suicide.

Fayerwether rallies. "But we're not here to talk about the past, are we? Looking back is just a good way to stumble, I always say."

"True," Harkness says.

"You wanted to know about the Lower South End redevelopment plan."

"Right." Harkness adds, summoning up a useful partial truth, "I'm on the mayor's task force. Would be great to hear what's ahead for the neighborhood."

Fayerwether holds up his hand to put Harkness on pause again, then signals Wheeler, who rushes into the library, rushes back out, then returns with a thick cylinder of architectural drawings. He drops them in front of Fayerwether like a black Lab delivering a special stick.

Fayerwether clears newspapers and magazines from a low table and opens the drawings.

Fayerwether smiles when he looks at the designs. "The beauty of Albrecht Square is its architectural integrity. Monumental puddingstone buildings — retail on the street level and mezzanine, spacious flats above. Brilliant!"

Harkness nods but says nothing because silence keeps people talking.

"But the area's not at all beautiful now, by any stretch of the imagination, is it? Particularly after that horrible flood. It's become run down and drug-infested. But it was never redeveloped, so we have the freedom to preserve the original streetscape while adding to it."

He places an overlay drawing on top of the map, adding four towers. "These are early concepts only, of course. Each tower can house about a hundred luxury apartments." He traces his finger from one tower to another. "Here's another wonderful thing about Stark's initial design — it lets us monitor access from four entry points and create a controlled environment."

"Like a gated community?"

Fayerwether waves his hand again to banish the tawdry words, so California. "What we envision is more elegant than that. A high-tech safety zone. We're exploring the possibilities with the mayor's technology fellow."

"Neil Burch?"

Fayerwether brightens at their latest shared connection. "You know Neil?"

"Yes," Harkness says. "A real visionary."

"Absolutely." Fayerwether nods. "We'd like to create a technologically advanced oasis right in the heart of the city."

"What about the people living there now?"

Fayerwether tilts his head slightly. "Familiar with the West End, Officer Harkness?"

"Yes, of course."

"Then you probably know that one of my predecessors at the Urban Redevelopment Council tore it down in 1958 to build the dreadful City Hall Plaza."

"Not a popular move."

"Not at the time. And I'll be the first to admit, City Hall is among the ten worst buildings in modern architecture. But here's the thing." Fayerwether leans forward. "The city tore down forty-seven acres of blighted row houses — including the notorious Scollay Square, the Times Square of Boston. It displaced almost three thousand families but brought Dirty Old Boston into the modern world. And now?"

Harkness waits for Fayerwether to answer his own question.

"Now no one cares." Fayerwether shrugs. "Life continues. People forget. The city moves ahead in waves, and another one's coming, mark my words. The underlying terrain stays the same but the surface changes. We can't will a neighborhood to survive like a sickly pet. The last time I walked through the Lower South End, what I saw was a neighborhood of tawdry bars, minimarkets, SRO hotels, and cheap Chinese restaurants."

"I was there a few weeks ago," Harkness says.

"And what did you see?"

Harkness pauses, works up the right lie. He locks his face in a mask of imperious wisdom. "I saw a neighborhood asking for change."

"Well, it's most definitely going to get it." Fayerwether rolls up his drawings. "In spades."

"Thanks so much for showing me your work."

"Glad to share it." Fayerwether signals the bartender. "Another port for me. And one for my young friend here."

Harkness feels his departmental cell phone vibrate for the second time in a minute. "Excuse me, sir, I have to check this."

"I'm afraid cell phones aren't allowed in the club," Fayerwether says, then looks around the empty library. "But since your father was a member, I suppose we can make an exception."

Harkness reads the text on the screen. "There's news about some Harvard students."

"Oh?" Fayerwether smiles, awaits the good word — they're starting the next Facebook, creating affordable laptops for the developing world, curing Alzheimer's. "What news, then?"

"Two undergraduates dead in a dorm room," Harkness says.

"How awful! What on earth happened?"

Harkness stares into Fayerwether's pale blue eyes. "Looks like they overdosed on heroin."

29

"MEET THE DEAD KIDS." Esther hands Harkness her departmental iPad, decorated with crime scene tape. The first photo shows a young woman with dyed black hair lying on top of a green comforter, eyes wide open, pupils blown, skin mottled and bluish, cheeks sunken. The dead girl wears a white sweatshirt that reads IT'S HOLIDAY TIME, MOTHERFUCKERS spelled out in festive garlands of holly.

"Therese Caldwell, nineteen, Harvard sophomore, from Manhattan, father's a big Wall Street guy," Esther says. "This is her dorm room. No priors. No trouble with the college." She nods toward the hallway, where a cluster of campus cops wait their turn at the crime scene. "And from what I can tell, no previous IV drug use. Looks like a newbie to me. Full blood workups are on their way." Esther may be an oddball but she's solid gold at a crime scene.

Harkness takes a look around the Finster House dorm room with its leaded-glass bay windows facing the snowy banks of the Charles, separate living room, and en suite bathroom. *Plush digs,* he thinks. Except the room is teeming with BPD cops, and the girl who used to live here in collegiate comfort is stone-cold dead.

"Anything else?"

Esther nods toward the bathroom. "We found some prescription drugs in there — high-test Wellbutrin, half-full bottle of Valium, Zoloft. Nothing too weird."

Esther swipes her finger on the iPad screen. "Other dead kid's Jason Kittredge, twenty, Harvard junior from Portland, Maine.

Lived off campus in Central Square in a dumpy hipster house but he's been staying here a lot this fall, the other students on the floor say. Again, no priors, no trouble on campus. This kid's not so fancy — dad runs a nightclub up there. Rock 'n' roll place. Not exactly squeaky clean."

On the screen, Harkness sees a pretty boy with longish brown hair parted down the middle. Jason's dark eyes are wide open, his full lips pale.

"Looks like the lead singer for the Lemonheads," Harkness says. "Forget his name."

"Lemon what?"

"Local rock band from way back. Not a fan."

"Mr. Kittredge was found on the bed next to Ms. Caldwell, in full Hoffman — needle still in his arm," Esther says. "Looks like he shot up his girlfriend, then himself. They'd both been dead for a few hours before anyone found 'em — most of the students have finished exams and cleared out for the holidays."

"This looks like . . ."

"Dark Horse."

"Right."

"But the toxicology report can't prove it," Esther says. "In the bloodstream, dope is dope."

"Gone through the dorm room?"

"Five technicians, two hours," Esther says. "No bags or wrappers, nothing. Looks like they had just enough junk to get high and die."

Patrick walks into the bedroom carrying two cell phones in his hand. "Hey, Harky," he says. "Did a first pass at their phones. Nothing suspicious on hers — just some texts asking Dad for money, the usual back-and-forth with her friends, and sexting with lover boy."

"And his?"

"The dude's phone looks clean too, except for this text thread a few months ago." Patrick holds out the phone and Harkness reads a brief exchange about where to meet up, questions about the price of *the package.*

"When kids are texting to buy drugs, you'd think they'd be a little more clever," Patrick says.

"They think they're invulnerable."

"They are, until they die."

162

Harkness reads further, sees that they ended up meeting at Mc-Closkey's. "Looks like he bought in the Lower South End."

"Back in the day when you could."

"Right."

"What kind of user saves a bag of junk to do months later?"

"Rookies," Patrick says.

"Or hoarders," Esther says.

Harkness and Patrick stare at her.

"Find out who Jason Kittredge was meeting up with in the Lower South End." Harkness hands the phone back to Patrick.

"On it, boss." Patrick walks out of the bedroom, already tapping away on Jason's phone.

"Esther, if there's any extra lab work that can link these deaths to Dark Horse, do it. Get whatever resources you need."

Esther nods, leaves the bedroom clutching a handful of yellow evidence bags.

Harkness closes the bedroom door and locks it. Wet snow falls heavily outside the windows and the afternoon's already fading. The desk drawers are open, floor thick with the debris from hours of searching for the elusive bag.

He walks to the platform bed where the couple died, stares at the twisted beige sheets in the soft gray light. Shoved between the pillows rests a love-worn stuffed bunny, a little bigger than May's but just as threadbare and dirty. He picks it up, finds that the stuffing's compacted and the fur is almost worn off. Therese brought it from home to college — a reminder of her childhood that might have comforted her, but couldn't save her.

Raising it to his face, he smells the sweet-sour funk of years of anxious clutching close to Therese's cheek, leaving it scented with tears, makeup, and cigarette smoke. He sets the bunny carefully back on the pillow. To lose a child is unthinkable. Harkness imagines the Caldwells reeling from a call from the Harvard campus police, their sobs echoing through the Upper East Side. He promises himself that nothing like this will ever happen to May — but knows this promise is impossible to keep.

Harkness pulls out his cell phone and starts to call Candace to make sure May is safe. Then he puts it away, focuses, and sits quietly on the floor. His flickering eyes take in every detail of the room around him. He breathes the air that Therese and Jason breathed. He opens his notebook and runs through the sequence of events.

They both finished their exams yesterday.

Their flights home were scheduled for tomorrow.

The last time anyone in the dorm saw the couple was before dinner yesterday.

There's a half-empty bottle of Prosecco in the minifridge next to the closet.

Harkness imagines their last hours. Therese and Jason set aside a lost day before they had to face up to their families and the holidays. Harkness might have done the same thing back when he was a student. They stayed in her room all night like newlyweds, drinking and talking, reading books, smoking cigarettes. Eventually, Jason took the syringe and junk from his backpack to show Therese that he was a reckless, creative type.

Maybe Therese was scared at first, but not for long. Jason said he knows what he's doing, not to worry. Jason's laptop probably includes a Google search for *how to inject drugs.* They were leading each other down the ancient path of ill-fated lovers. But every moment in this cluttered dorm room was bringing them closer to their last shallow breath.

Harkness half closes his eyes and thinks about the two dead students he saw in Esther's iPad. He imagines them in the room, nestled together on the bed, surrounded by everything they needed — takeout food and Prosecco, cell phones and laptops, music and heroin.

When the storm surge of endorphins washed over them, they forgot their responsibilities and worries — below-expectation grades, shifting personas, cloudy futures. This casting-off is the wonderful part of heroin, like shedding a heavy backpack and running free. The deepening that follows is just as incredible, a gentle dropping-down to a subterranean room where everything is fascinating. Read a book or stare out a window and it's like the best movie ever.

But as their euphoric minds disconnected, their breathing decelerated. When junk tells the body to slow down, then shut down, it does. This decision isn't debatable or revocable. It's the moment when delusion turns darker.

Harkness imagines Therese and Jason hovering in the quiet dorm room like spirits waiting to be set free, then dropping back to earth forever.

Harkness lets the dead kids go, emerges, opens his eyes. Therese kept a journal. The bookshelves over Therese's desk hold dozens of bright orange Rhodia notebooks now scattered on the shelf, secrecy invaded, timeline broken. They've been searched already and revealed nothing but scraps of poems that will never be written.

He reaches for the newest notebook and reads page after page of Therese's looping script, interrupted by taped-in mementos — movie-ticket stubs, receipts, boarding passes, and notes scribbled on bar napkins. She would have kept the heroin bag, particularly Dark Horse with its enticing logo. The bag would be a souvenir of their lost day together, their initiation, rebellion.

Harkness puts the diary back and scans the leaning stalagmites of novels, the slough of books in the corner, the tilted spines along the bookshelf. One book glows like an all-night diner by the side of the highway.

Baudelaire's poems attract an army of young depressives — that's what his mother, a much-beloved English teacher back in her prime, told Harkness. Now that army has lost its latest volunteers, Therese and Jason — young and beautiful, dissatisfied and dead.

Harkness opens *Les Fleurs du Mal*, sees Therese's familiar scrawl on the inside front cover and a date, just a couple of weeks ago. It's a tattered used-book-store copy with the original French on one side, the English translation on the other. He turns the pages, looking for a Dark Horse bag but finding nothing. He closes the book and pulls his thumb along the pages, riffling through them like a card dealer. He holds the book upside down and shakes it.

As he puts the book back on the shelf, Harkness notices that the cloth spine has come unglued at the top but not the bottom. He tries to reach his index finger down into the small pouch in the spine but can't. He takes the book over to Therese's desk, pushes aside her papers and scarves, and shakes it upside down, spine to the desktop. A little glassine envelope flutters out like a flattened four-leaf clover.

Harkness picks it up from the desk and sees the familiar blood-red horse.

. . .

Downstairs, Patrick's sitting in a dark-paneled study room among earnest students. He's got his headphones on and his eyes are locked on the screen of his laptop. Arrayed around him are a couple of empty potato chip bags, some peanuts, and a half-eaten Mars Bar.

Harkness taps on the glass door and Patrick looks up. He nods, closes his laptop, and says goodbye to his new friends. Awkward fist bumps all around.

When he opens the door, a thick wind of coffee, cheese curls, wet socks, and anxiety blows from the room.

"Studying for finals?"

"Figured I'd get more done in study hall than outside in the car. Still snowing out there. Plus, they have an all-you-can-eat snack bar. Did they have that when you were here?"

"Don't think so."

They pull on their heavy jackets and walk out of Finster House. Jammed up on the sidewalk, lights still flashing, their patrol car is covered with about six inches of wet snow. Harkness retrieves the brush and scraper from the trunk and clears off the car while Patrick starts it and cranks the heat.

"Get this," Patrick says when Harkness gets back in the car. "Guess who that text traced to, the one where Jason Kittredge is trying to score?"

"No idea."

"Anthony Incagnoli," Patrick says in a hushed voice. "Ring a bell?"

Harkness pauses, then remembers the connection. "Joey Incagnoli, aka Joey Ink." He pictures the ancient North End felon as he last saw him, reading the *Herald* at a back table at Mr. Mach's Zero Room, a last patch of sleaze on the edge of Chinatown.

"Bingo," Patrick says. "This kid's his nephew. To be accurate, his great-nephew. Twenty-seven years old — long list of priors, including selling bags at nightclubs and a couple of aggravated assaults."

"The apple doesn't fall too far from the tree," Harkness says.

Patrick gives a wise nod. "Especially when it's a bad apple."

"Let's pull this Anthony Incagnoli in for a little chat," Harkness turns onto Storrow Drive, the ice-clogged Charles on their right. Thick snow rushes toward them faster than the windshield wipers can clear it away.

"On it."

"And Patrick?"

"Yeah?"

Harkness says nothing, just holds up the evidence bag holding the Dark Horse wrapper.

30

CANDACE REACHES UP and deftly knots his black bow tie, then gives both ends a gentle pull. "There."

"Where'd you learn how to do that?"

"Dad used to go to a lot of galas and fancy parties when he was already drunk," she says. "Needed help getting ready."

Harkness slips on his black tux jacket and presses down the narrow lapels. "Do I look like a hundred bucks?" That's how much he paid for a thirty-year-old Brooks Brothers tux at Geezer's, the used-formalwear store in Cambridge.

"Maybe a hundred and fifty," Candace says. "You clean up well, for a cop."

"I'll take that as a compliment."

"Wasn't really intended as one."

"You, on the other hand, look fantastic."

Candace spins around in a simple black beaded gown — her mother's, retrieved from her father's house in Nagog. The dress smells a little like wood smoke, but it fits like it was hers all along.

They walk to the full-length mirror on the back of the bedroom door. "Wow, we look like our parents," Candace says.

"Except younger," Harkness says.

"For now."

Harkness reaches into his top dresser drawer to find the long jewelry box. The smaller one that holds the engagement ring remains hidden under his passport, a spare clip for his Glock, and some bullets. His hand's gravitating toward the ring as if it's magnetized. Then he stops himself. The night of the Harbormasters' holiday party isn't the right time to propose. Not at all.

"This might go well with that dress." He hands her the long box.

Candace lifts off the top and takes out an amethyst necklace Harkness bought from Gus Donovan when he returned the rented watch. "Wow, it's beautiful, Eddy."

"Merry Christmas, again."

"I thought we decided that only May would get presents." They spent Christmas morning at Nora's, watching May open box after box, making Christmas dinner, and listening to George's filthy carols, including his greatest hit—"Smear Your Balls with Pumpkin Pie." The days after Christmas have been a blur of tears, toy repairs, and playdates. Exhausted, May's safely asleep at Nathan and Shawna's tonight.

"I think you deserve at least one. Maybe several thousand more," he says. "For now, this will have to do."

Candace leans up and as they kiss, Harkness's hand wanders lower.

"Does your dress have a zipper?"

"It does," she says. "But I'm not going to show you where it is until after the party. Maybe during the party if it's really boring."

In the high courtyard, nasturtiums and trumpet vines cascade down to a lush central garden littered with headless Roman marble statues, low urns, and a carved sarcophagus. An onyx falcon perches in the grass next to a mosaic floor. Isabella Stewart Gardner gathered art trophies all across Europe to cobble together her version of a Venetian palazzo, transforming a swampy marsh on the edge of Boston into a palatial house, now a museum.

"You know, if the city owned this place, the mayor would probably be trying to sell it off," Harkness says as they look out over the garden.

"Why?"

"It's just debris from the past," Harkness says. "That's what we all turn into, eventually."

"I appreciate that festive holiday thought."

The palm trees and topiaries are covered with tasteful white lights. Safe from the latest snowstorm and freed from their families and the holidays, hundreds of guests stand inside the stone cloisters, champagne flutes and cocktails in hand. Their conversations echo through the courtyard, drowning out a Spanish guitarist playing medieval Christmas songs on a low stage.

"Beautiful, isn't it?" Candace says.

"For a crime scene," Harkness says. In 1990, two thieves broke in over St. Patrick's Day weekend and took $500 million in art — a Rembrandt, a Vermeer, a Manet, and more.

"I don't think the museum people want to be reminded about that."

"Largest private-property theft ever," Harkness says. "The robbers were wearing police uniforms."

Candace leans toward him. "Was it you, Eddy?"

"I was in middle school."

Their banter, usually fast and occasionally furious, speeds ahead double-time tonight, and for good reason. Among the hundreds of guests, there's no one they recognize. They talk fast to hide the fact that they're alone in the crowd.

"They're not as scary as I thought they'd be," Candace whispers.

"The Harbormasters?"

"Yeah."

"Most people look okay," Harkness says. "It's what they do that makes 'em scary."

They walk along the cloisters, past bejowled bankers and their bejeweled wives. They pass a woman in a sparkling white dress, her tanned neck encircled by a chain of opals the size of quail eggs.

Candace's gaze narrows. "You know what I'm learning?"

"What?"

"No matter how much you pay for an eye job, you still end up looking like a scared raccoon."

"Good to know," Harkness says.

Candace and Harkness study the crowd like birdwatchers observing an alien flock. Fueled by success and money, the men exude steely confidence. Ambitious bellies are putting cummerbunds and tux-shirt buttons to the test. These men don't need to exert — others do that for them. By contrast, their wives look tough, tanned, and toned, like personal trainers who got to cherry-pick the jewelry counter at Saks.

"Cheery bunch," Harkness says.

"And sexy," Candace adds. "Ha."

"I think they reproduce asexually, like starfish."

"Anything to avoid touching."

Harkness turns to Candace. "I should probably be networking with these guys. May be out of a job pretty soon."

"Somehow, I just don't see you as an investment banker," Candace says. "You'll always be a cop, Eddy."

"We'll see about that."

Harkness keeps escalating Narco-Intel's surreptitious assault on the mayor and the Manchester Group. Patrick's leaking documents like a mini-Snowden. Esther's spreading online rumors. And it's starting to work. A cover story in the *Globe* scrutinized O'Mara's old-boy connections while *Improper Bostonian* chronicled Neil Burch's drunken late-night shenanigans in Lansdowne Street nightclubs. An end-of-year poll shows his approval ratings sinking below 50 percent. But O'Mara's still the mayor, with no end in sight.

"Here's my man Robert Fayerwether." Harkness nods toward the rail-thin éminence grise striding through the courtyard, a long white silk scarf thrown over his confident shoulders. He's agile and deft, conferring briefly with guests who flow toward him like water. Among them are Mayor O'Mara and his puppeteer, Neil Burch, who looks like a hard-boiled egg jammed in a tux.

"Remind me why he invited us?" The invitation arrived via courier, its black envelope marked in silver ink with the crude *X* that the Harbormasters used to scratch on the side of every ship that they deemed worthy of unloading its goods at the port of Boston. Inside, the engraved invitation was definitive. *You and a guest will be attending the annual holiday party of the Harbormasters.*

"I think Fayerwether and I really bonded the other day at the St. Pancras Club," Harkness says. "He knew my father. We both went to Harvard. And we're both working to destroy the city of Boston as it is."

"I'm assuming two of those are true."

"They're all true," Harkness says. "Just in different ways."

A woman in a tan dress steps down into the courtyard, and the

Spanish guitarist stops playing, stands, and raises the microphone for her.

"Good evening," she says with a smile — the first sincere smile Harkness has seen all night. "I'm Katherine Aiello, managing director of the Harbormasters. And I'm here to welcome you to our annual festivities. This is our three hundred and eighty-sixth year of celebrating the great city that we all love so dearly."

Candace pushes her lips toward Harkness's ear. "The Harbormasters have been around for that long?"

"Seems like it."

"That explains why these people look so fucking old," she whispers.

Harkness gives her a silence-inducing stare.

"Not too long ago, you wouldn't have seen a woman up here," Aiello says. "Particularly one with what one of my colleagues once referred to as a vowel obstruction, that pesky *o* at the end of my name that indicates that I am of Italian extraction instead of descended from one of the families that, like all of yours, arrived on the *Mayflower*."

They laugh, politely.

"But times change," Aiello says. "And the Harbormasters have too. Tonight you'll be hearing more about that from our distinguished guests." Aiello's gaze wanders over to Harkness and stops, burning so brightly that he has to look away.

"But first, let me invite you to come upstairs to the beautiful Tapestry Room, where dinner is served."

Upstairs, hundreds of flickering candles illuminate a long rectangular central table and dozens of round tables arrayed alongside. The walls are lined with medieval tapestries showing more deer and bow hunters than the New Hampshire woods in October. Harkness and Candace find their table and introduce themselves to the other people joining them for dinner. There's an investment manager from Fidelity and his bored wife, wearing a diamond that might be visible from space. Next to them sits Jack Desoto, an entrepreneur who runs Hatchet Stump, a software startup whose purpose is incomprehensible to mere mortals. His wife, Genja, has a horse farm on the North Shore that drains a small pile of Jack's money. An MIT genetic scientist, a Commonwealth Insurance executive, a beautiful but chilly Saltonstall heiress, and the striving owner of a lesser advertising agency round out their table.

No one at table 7 is a power broker or Harbormaster. Table 7 is a guest table, which gives Harkness a chance to observe the night's events without worrying about close scrutiny. There's a digital tape recorder hidden beneath Harkness's black cummerbund with a wire that runs down his sleeve and ends at a directional microphone and transmitter disguised as a cufflink. Back at Narco-Intel, Patrick and Esther are listening in. You never know when an unexpected party invitation might turn into a setup.

Harkness looks across the table at Candace, who gives him a careful smile and raised eyebrow that asks, *Can you believe we're actually here?* No, he can't. Like Candace, he's having a hard time reconciling the genial people eating dinner in the Tapestry Room with the reputation of the shadowy, brutal Harbormasters.

They're on their best behavior — but the night is young.

After the main course (dry-aged sirloin, grilled free-range chicken, or toasted Israeli couscous with root vegetables), dessert (maple crème brûlée or chocolate fondant cake), and high-test coffee to perk everyone up, Katherine Aiello steps up on a low dais in front of the largest tapestry and asks for their attention.

"I'd like to welcome our very own Robert Fayerwether IV to the stage," she says. "To take a look back at the year that's just ending and look ahead to the one we're about to begin."

Wild applause. Either Fayerwether is very popular or the nonstop burgundy and sauvignon blanc are kicking in.

"Thank you, thank you." Fayerwether quiets the crowd with his upraised hand, like he's a crossing guard for emotions. "Like the Bible, the biggest news of this year starts with a flood." He gets light applause with that clever phrase. "Followed by an exodus —"

"To the promised land of Nagog!" someone shouts.

Fayerwether shushes the jokers. "Now we're gathered here on the cusp of a new year, celebrating all that's ahead of us," he says in a voice as silky and carefully groomed as his white hair. Fayerwether is more coherent than an elder at the end of a long, wine-infused banquet should be — *A pro*, Harkness thinks with some version of admiration.

"Our city is about to go through a major transformation." Fayerwether wipes his forehead with a white cloth napkin for an extended dramatic pause. "We're taking the Lower South End into a new era. I predict that when we gather here next year, we'll have broken ground to start making our new dream a reality."

They raise their glasses to the urban visionary who is creating new wealth for the already rich.

"I'm an old man, at the end of my career," Fayerwether shouts. "But mark my words. Decades from now, the citizens of Boston will thank all of us for transforming a faltering neighborhood into an oasis of order — despite any ill-considered complaints from the quibbling class."

Fayerwether's vision of the Lower South End as a walled city for the wealthy has triggered a backlash from all quarters — the Boston Architectural College, the Harvard Graduate School of Design, and especially the wanderers and their supporters. After all, it leaves no room for them to come home, ever.

Fayerwether raises his glass high. "To our crowning achievement — the New Lower South End!" He smiles out at the crowd, which breaks into enthusiastic applause, as if he just abolished estate taxes.

When the applause fades, Aiello retakes the stage. "We're fortunate to be here tonight," she says. "It's warm, beautiful, and there's plenty of wine. But outside, it's snowing blue blazes again. So please welcome the man who'll be leaving soon to shovel the entire city, Mayor Michael O'Mara."

Scattered applause echoes through the Tapestry Room. So far, O'Mara has failed to pass the true test of a Boston mayor — getting the snow off the streets before anyone can complain about it.

O'Mara kisses Aiello on both cheeks and steps up on the low stage.

"Thank you, Katherine. Very, very glad to be here." O'Mara lays his hands solidly on the podium, leaning toward the audience like a televangelist.

"You know, the Harbormasters were a disruptive force right from the start," O'Mara says. "They took power because it needed to be taken or this young city would have perished. They kept out the threats. Because of the Harbormasters—of today and those gone by—Boston isn't Cleveland or Providence or Baltimore. It's the shining city on a hill."

Major applause at the JFK reference.

"The rest of my first term is going to be a time of battles and strong words, of arguments and mud-slinging." O'Mara pauses. "And I can't wait!"

Raucous applause. The Harbormasters love a fighter.

"We're re-envisioning the Lower South End because we—the people in this room—know that it needs change. Now, before the drugs and violence can spread throughout the city. If we wait for community activists to get anything done, the city will rot from within and slide into the harbor."

More applause. Harkness imagines what Jennet Townsend would have to say about that.

"Yes, the wanderers have left the city," he says, hitting his stride. "Now that they're gone, heroin is no longer on sale at every bodega in the Lower South End, and I say that's more good news. The vision that Robert Fayerwether and the Urban Redevelopment Council have for the city is brilliant. And I say, if this is change, if this is disruption—then *bring it on!*"

Candace leans over to Harkness and shouts into his ear over the thunderous applause. "It's like he's running for mayor all over again."

"And winning," Harkness says.

O'Mara smiles out at the crowd like a comedian who knows he's killing it. "And for those who say we're moving too fast, I say this: We don't care. We won't wait. Democracy can't catch up to us."

Thunderous applause at the end of the speech, ignoring the casual elitism and the tone-deaf ending, which makes O'Mara sound like a hate-radio talk-show host. He holds his arms in the air to take in all the applause, which goes on and on.

Harkness escapes the Tapestry Room to go downstairs and get Candace a club soda with lime from the bartender. At the end of the narrow side courtyard waits *El Jaleo*, the enormous John Singer Sargent painting of swirling dancers and motionless musicians. A Spanish dancer holds a voluminous white skirt in one hand and points off to the side with the other. Harkness has seen the painting many times over the years — on school field trips, weekend dates, and outings with his mother, who even in the murk of dementia seems to recognize it.

"I've often wondered about that guitar player on the far right," a woman says. He turns and finds Katherine Aiello standing behind him, carrying a glass of red wine in one hand and a small white beaded purse in the other. "Is he sleeping or dead?"

"With musicians, sometimes it's hard to tell," Harkness says.

Aiello smiles. "Just so you know, Detective Harkness, it was me who invited you, not the esteemed Mr. Fayerwether."

"Thanks," Harkness says. "But I have to ask — why?"

"We've been watching you for several years," she says. "It seemed like a good time to connect." Aiello smiles and points to the painting. "But thanks to this overprotected museum, we're being watched by several security cameras. So we're going to spend a couple of minutes appearing to explore the finer points of this magnificent painting while we are, in fact, discussing something far less artistic. If you don't mind, in the interest of brevity, I'll do most of the talking."

"Of course."

"Humans are pack animals, Edward. You know this from your work. They like to congregate in gangs."

He nods.

"It's no different in business or politics," she says. "The real question about a man isn't *who is he?*, because ultimately that's unknowable. What matters is who he chooses to spend time with — who are his friends, his associates?"

Harkness looks at the three musicians leaning against the wall in the painting, thinks of his misfit detectives. "What are you getting at?"

"Sometimes you make a mistake. You misjudge a friend's character or intentions. Or they change over time and you fail to realize it. You'll find this to be true as you get older. You wind up with people who barely remind you of who they were years ago. It's surprising how monstrous friends can get when time twists them in its fist."

"And in this case you're talking about . . . ?"

Aiello pauses. "My good friend Robert Fayerwether is at the end of his distinguished career and looking to leave a shining legacy. There's been considerable discussion among the Harbormasters about the plans he and the mayor have for the Lower South End. Despite the applause tonight, upon close scrutiny, we find them ill-considered and avaricious."

"I voted for him." Harkness takes a sip from his glass. "And I hear you and your friends helped elect him."

"Yes, that's true. But we didn't anticipate the venality of the crew he brought with him."

"And that surprised you?"

"There are levels to everything, Edward. The past year has been shocking to even the most politically jaded among us. We should have backed Reed."

"What can I do about it?" Harkness asks. "Sounds like a job for the Harbormasters."

"We know what you're doing to rally the opposition," she says.

"I can't get Reed to commit," Harkness says. "Says it's impossible to unseat a mayor."

"Things are as difficult or as easy as you make them," she says. And we'll do what we can. But always tactfully and invisibly. That's how we work now. Soft power. And occasionally not so soft."

"Such as?"

"Seated to my right upstairs is a Mr. Bryce Atkins, wonderful scholar, good friend. And of interest to you, he leads the U.S. Attorneys Office. At our urging, he'll be announcing an investigation challenging the legality of the public-private partnership the mayor has entered into in the Lower South End with only perfunctory competitive bidding."

"That'll be a surprise."

"I think the mayor may find the Department of Justice isn't as easily swayed as the locals."

"So what else can we expect to happen, you know, at your urging?"

Aiello points at the dim corners of the painting. "We can only talk about the larger canvas, Edward, not the details. I've found those sort themselves out over time, one way or another."

With that elliptical remark, Katherine Aiello starts to drift away from the painting toward the wide stone staircase back to the Tapestry Room, where her tribe awaits her return.

31

CANDACE STARES OUT at the bleak cornfields from the passenger seat while May sleeps in the car seat behind them. The sides of Route 2 are heaped high with gray salted snow, and the brutal cold sun shines down like a cruel joke played by nature: *Look how sunny it can be and still be freezing.* Harkness's Ray-Bans do little to cut the glare from the ice-glazed fields. They drive in silence, nestled in thick parkas and wool Carhartt caps, stunned by the cold and exhausted by the holidays.

Harkness's phone rings and he hits Speaker.

"Got a late Christmas present for you, Eddy."

"What do you have?"

"According to the rules of order, the mayor's supposed to inform the city council president every time he leaves the city," Glenn says.

"So?"

"O'Mara's gone on a dozen trips that he didn't bother to tell the city council president about," Glenn says. "The mayors' conference in Tampa, a meeting in New York, a special—"

"That's not good enough," Harkness says. "We need something with more teeth in it."

"Look, I've gone through every bylaw that has anything to do with the mayor, Eddy," Glenn says. "There's nothing we can use."

"There's always something. The devil's in the details, right?"

"That's all I've got, Eddy."

"For now."

"What do you want, man?"

"You helped start this whole mess with a regulation no one ever heard of," Harkness says. "Now you need to find another one that helps end it."

"I'm trying, Eddy. I really am."

"Maybe what we need to do is hit the library," Harkness says. "Just you, me, Esther, and all the books in the Boston Public Library. I'll bring the coffee."

Glenn sighs. "You're a fucking pain in the ass, Eddy."

"Clean it up, Glenn. I've got my daughter in the car."

"Oh, then you're just impossible. That better?"

"Much." Harkness clicks off the phone.

Candace takes out her earbuds. "Who was that?"

"A guy who owes me a favor," Harkness says.

"Sounds like you got him looking for a needle in a haystack."

"More like a nail."

Harkness takes the familiar exit toward Nagog and they stare at the landscape, transformed by more snow than they've ever seen. Wind-scoured swirls top the roof of the Nagog Supermarket like buttercream frosting, a range of gray mountains rises in the parking lot of the train station, and every sidewalk has turned into an icy trench.

He pulls the car behind the Nagog Town House, where a dozen tables are lined up in a long row, sprayed with water to create a frozen, sloping path. Despite the cold, the parking lot is crowded with dozens of Nagogians. There's mulled cider courtesy of the Nagog Home Team and a blazing fire in a fifty-gallon drum courtesy of old guys who like to burn things.

Harkness breaks away from Candace for a second and wanders up to Watt.

"Here for the Ice Swap, are we, Eddy?"

"Can't miss the Swap." The Ice Swap is Nagog's end-of-the-holidays event, held the day after New Year's for as long as anyone can remember. It's a way to unload unwanted holiday gifts and an excuse to extend the holiday drinking.

Harkness nods toward the only cop he can see, a young-looking blond guy wearing a Tibetan-looking woven hat with his Nagog Police Department uniform. "You been promoting crossing guards to cops?"

Watt lets out a long, steaming breath. "We're doing the best we can, Eddy," he says. "He's an intern. No one wants to be a small-town cop anymore. These kids think everything's kind of funny. Nothing's a big deal. They're posting photos on Instagram or texting their friends when they're supposed to be on duty."

"You might want to remind them to sharpen up today," Harkness says.

"Worried?"

"Aren't you?" Fights outside the E-Z Mart, early-morning rallies and counter-rallies on the town green, angry opinion pieces in the *Nagog Journal* — it's all leading up to another contentious town meeting.

"The townies are here, the ALA, the wanderers too." Watt nods toward the ice table. "I'd like to think we can all stay civilized."

"Hope so."

A long line of givers wait their turn at the head of the table, where they load whatever they want to swap on a battered wooden Moxie crate and give it a push down the ice-slick course, both sides crowded with potential takers.

First up is a guy in a puffy brown down jacket who shoves a juicer along its way. It flies by a dozen takers until a woman in a red parka pulls it toward her. "I'll trade you a pair of skis, never used!" The juicer owner shakes his head. He has skis. The woman sends the juicer back along its path, where other eager hands reach for it, politely. It's still early.

After the juicer makes several stops along the ice table, a man snags it. "Pair of used snow tires," he blurts out. The owner of the juicer nods. Transaction complete.

The next giver steps up to the front of the line.

"I always wondered why the Swap was so popular," Candace says. "But it is kind of fun."

"Used to be about Yankee frugalness — not wanting anything to go to waste. Repurposing Christmas presents," Harkness says. "Now it's like eBay on Ice."

"What's coming up?" Candace seems to have caught the Ice Swap bug.

"Looks like a waffle iron," Harkness says. "But after that, who knows? That's part of the fun. Could be anything."

"I'm going to check it out," she says. "Hold May?"

"Sure."

Harkness watches as Candace takes her place at the ice table, in the front, right where he needs her. At the end waits a group of wanderers ready to claim all the items the Nagogians don't want. *Good luck with that,* Harkness thinks. Almost everything is useful to a thrifty Yankee. These are people who buy week-old bread, reuse gift wrap, and burn foraged sticks in their fireplaces.

The gaggle of wanderers gets the stink eye from wary Nagogians. Wanderer fatigue is setting in among even their most committed supporters. Over the holidays there was a fire in a carriage house on Main Street, and a fight broke out in a home office in West Nagog. A banner hanging near the mulled-cider hut reminds everyone that a special town meeting is scheduled for January 15, when the fate of the wanderers will be decided.

Harkness gets in line with May perched on his shoulders. A set of free weights, a case of local apple wine, a Kindle, and assorted household odds and ends get shoved down the ice, generating varying degrees of enthusiasm from the takers crowded along the edges.

When he gets to the front of the line, Harkness puts May gently in the wooden crate and hands her the ring box. They've been practicing for this morning every day for weeks. May breaks out in a big grin. "Mama?" she says.

"Yes, *Mama.*"

Harkness pauses, then gives May a gentle push. As she glides slowly down the ramp, even the crustiest of Swamp Yankees have to smile. She's emitting a supersonic squeal of glee as she slides along, one hand waving frantically, the other clutching the ring box.

When May coasts by Candace, she pulls her daughter toward her, confused.

Then May hands her the ring box.

When Candace clicks it open, Harkness shouts from the front of the table, "Will you marry me, Candace Hammond?"

There's chaos, laughter, applause. The Ice Swap has seen many strange items sliding down its ice table—a four-hundred-pound soapstone sink, eighty years of *National Geographics*, and an exerbike with a spandex-clad exer-girl sitting on it. But never a marriage proposal delivered via toddler-gram.

While Candace closes her eyes for a moment, the crowd runs through its collective memory. That both of their fathers killed themselves seems like a strange coincidence. They remember Harkness's mother as a popular schoolteacher and principal who supposedly had an affair with the local chief of police. *She's demented now,* someone whispers. And Eddy Harkness? He was the captain of the Nagog High baseball team. Took the Minutemen to two state championships—the trophies are still in the high school's display case. *That boy went to Harvard! Became a Boston cop and got in some kind of trouble after a Sox game. Didn't he end up emptying the parking meters around here for a while? He shut down that drug lab in the Old Nagog Tavern. That was all over the news.*

They turn their minds to Candace, the town's punky misfit. They remember the horrific plane crash. *Imagine waking up in a field, all cut to pieces, your sister and mother dead.* Her time at the Nagog Bakery isn't forgotten either. *She was terrible. A one-handed waitress, imagine that!*

Beyond these memories, the townspeople see two of Nagog's own in love, ready to start down the sliding slope of life together, letting hope outweigh fear. The crowd begins to clap and cheer, slowly at first, then louder, until May presses her hands over her ears, and Candace waves at them all to be quiet.

"Yes, Eddy Harkness! Yes!" Candace takes the ring and slips it deftly on her finger. May claps.

"But what do you give for it?" A shout from the crowd, then another. "What's your offer?"

Candace turns to look at Harkness and the crowd of Nagogians quiets. "All that I have." She swipes a hand at the tears running down her pale face. "I hope it's enough."

The applause and shouts from the crowd tell her that it is.

32

WE'VE BEEN HERE since seven in the morning, Eddy."
Glenn looks up from the stacks of documents and
books on the green worktable.

Esther raises her head slowly from the table. "How long was I
sleeping?"

Glenn lays his hand gently on the back of her neck. "Just a few
minutes, honey," he says.

"I dreamed about a giant squid," she says. "It had us cornered in a
sea cave."

"That squid's your mean boss." Glenn points at Harkness. "The
one who refuses to let us leave."

"We'll leave when we find what we're looking for," Harkness says.
"And I resent that squid remark."

"Squid are highly intelligent invertebrates." Esther pulls her rust-
colored cardigan around her.

Shadows pass by the frosted workroom window. "See?" Glenn
says. "Everyone else is leaving."

"But you're allowed to stay late, right?"

"Until midnight, Eddy." Glenn holds up the ID tag hanging from
the lanyard around his neck. "Then I turn back into a pumpkin. I
won't be a curator anymore. I'll just be another unemployed guy
with a PhD."

"You'll always be a librarian to me," Esther says.

Glenn smiles. "I guess that's good."

"We have a few more hours." Harkness turns back to his pages from the Boston city charter, more than a hundred pages long. They've split it into thirds to review every line.

"Yeah, but we're done, Eddy. Totally done." They've gone through dozens of city documents looking for any possible justification for ousting the mayor. But every lead they find circles back to the same hard fact—the mayor makes all the decisions and holds all the power.

"Not yet." Harkness walks over to the side table, littered with empty coffee cups, wadded-up paper bags, and sandwich wrappers. He lifts the Dunkin' Donuts Box o' Joe, intended to keep an office caffeinated all day. They've drained it. He shrugs, sits back down at the worktable.

"Aren't you supposed to be tracking drug dealers down and busting them?"

"It's good to be flexible," Harkness says. He holds up his stack of printouts. "I got to say, this doesn't sound particularly *ye olde Boston-y.*"

"This is like the King James Version of the Boston city charter," Glenn says. "A mayoral task force put together a more citizen-friendly version in . . ." He pages through his notes. "In 1947."

Harkness thinks, summons up what he knows about Boston's mayors, glorious and (more often) notorious. "That would be the final term of Mayor James Michael Curley, wouldn't it?"

"I guess so."

Harkness feels the hair on his arms rise. "Is the original still here at the library?"

"It's in the vault in the Rare Books Room."

"Know the combination?"

"No, but I know where it is."

"Go get the old charter, okay?"

"Eddy, the original charter is a badly deteriorating book-length document from the late nineteenth century," Glenn says.

"*Ooo,*" Esther says. "Sounds cool. Go get it, Glenn."

"We're not going to go through all of it," Harkness says. "Just most of it."

Glenn lowers his head to the worktable and moans.

·   ·   ·

"Hold on, right there." Harkness looks up from the worktable.

Esther's reading the original charter aloud as Harkness compares it to the 1947 version. Two hours after they started, they're up to the Declaration of Rights.

"Read that last part again."

Glenn's wearing white conservator's gloves, carefully turning each page of the fragile green book on the table, cleared and cleaned now, as Esther reads out loud:

In order to prevent those who are vested with authority from becoming oppressors, the people have a right to cause their public officials to return to private life by a unanimous vote of the city's elected councilors, who can file a Bill of Address to remove said official. They shall fill up vacant offices by temporary appointments, followed swiftly by regular elections.

Harkness points to a section in the 1947 charter. "That part isn't in my version, Glenn."

"Sure it is. Let me take a look." Glenn carries the book gingerly over to Harkness's side of the worktable. He looks at the original document, then the modern one.

"*Shit,*" he says. "It's not there."

Harkness opens his notebook and makes a careful copy of the full text of the missing section, 17D.

"That Curley guy was a real weasel," Esther says.

"By 1947, Curley had already been thrown in prison for fraud," Glenn says. "Got pardoned by Truman, but he was struggling to hold on to power. Genius politician, but brutal and corrupt. Like Whitey and Billy Bulger rolled into one."

"He definitely wouldn't want the city council to have that kind of power." Harkness closes his notebook and puts it in his jacket pocket. "No mayor would."

"Like an electoral sword of Damocles," Glenn says. "You manage to squeak out a mayoral win, then you can get voted out by the city council, filled with pissed-off pols you've screwed over." Glenn looks at the clause again. "So Mayor Curley's crew just edited out this part and no one bothered to compare. Until now."

"How could anyone?" Harkness stands and circles the table, taking his leather jacket from its hook. "The original was locked in the vault of the Boston Public Library."

"Which is controlled by the mayor and his cronies," Glenn says.

"And still is." Harkness breaks into a broad smile. Now that they've found the nail, their study group is over.

Glenn carefully closes the original city charter and puts it back in its slipcase, stamped in tarnished gold with the city seal. He peels off his white gloves and opens a lower drawer, pulling out a dusty bottle of red wine and a corkscrew. "Been saving this bottle for a night like tonight," he says. "It's an '82 Pavillon Rouge. And guess who gave it to me?"

"No idea," Harkness says.

"It came from the personal wine cellar of Robert Fayerwether IV." He pops the cork and reaches down to get glasses.

"You two nerdy lovebirds go ahead," Harkness says. "Much as I'd like to savor the irony, and the wine, I have to head home. Got some e-mails to write."

"It's like we're sending out a baby announcement," Esther says with a broad and goofy smile. "Congratulations, it's a nail!"

It's cold, but Harkness walks home to the seaport to clear his head after a long day in the library. Late on a January night, the city seems to be hibernating, people huddled in dark bars and warm restaurants, waiting for the thaw. Downtown Crossing looks like an abandoned stage set, gray snow piled high.

His phone vibrates and he takes it out of his pocket. The text is from an old number, one he recognizes instantly.

Some bald fk named Birch an his buds are talkin sht bout u in my bar.
Wnt me to dose hm?

Back at the Zero Room, Thalia used to pour triples, hide an extra shot of Everclear in a whiskey sour, dissolve a Valium in a vodka tonic. Dosing the enemy was her way of getting even, of making bad customers suffer by pushing them over the edge until they passed out, did something embarrassing, or got their asses kicked.

186

As much as he'd like to see Neil Burch dosed into a coma, Harkness just puts his phone in his pocket. Thalia sidling back into his life isn't what he needs now.

When Harkness cuts left down Kingston Street he hears a familiar voice chanting along over drums and bass.

We don't care.
Democracy can't catch us.
We don't care.

It's from Mayor O'Mara's amped-up speech at the Harbormasters' party, sampled and mixed on top of a dubstep track, making his voice sound creepy and disembodied, like it's coming from space. Or an old Thievery Corporation album. Except it's coming from the sound system at Fitzy's, little sonic bites escaping into the cold streets every time the bar door opens.

"Jack," Harkness says. "Unbelievable." Patrick sent the audio file of O'Mara's speech to journalists and bloggers, who used it as proof that the mayor was just another out-of-touch rich businessman, no real surprises there. Harkness e-mailed it to Jack, formerly of the Jackals, and asked him to spread it to all his musician friends and studio rats at Raw Power. It was a long shot. But in a city full of musicians, smart-asses, and college radio stations, he figured something good might come of it.

Now it has.

Harkness's surreptitious audio has been carefully edited to turn an off-the-cuff comment about O'Mara's nimble administration into a damning against-the-people boast:

Democracy can't catch ~~up to~~ us.

It's not exactly his kind of music but it sounds pretty good. Harkness keeps walking down Kingston Street, O'Mara's voice fading with every snowy step.

33

ANTHONY INCAGNOLI RUSHES toward the door when they walk into the interrogation room, but his ankle chains slow him down. Patrick puts an arm out to block Anthony, then shoves him back.

"What is this shit, man?" Specks of spit blow from his wide-open, contorted mouth. If he weren't handcuffed, he'd be swinging at them. "I got a right to call my lawyer. You got any idea who I am?"

"We know exactly who you are," Harkness says.

"You look like an FIA to me." Patrick gives him a hard push toward a metal chair. "That's a Future Inmate of America, case you didn't know."

"We're giving you a few minutes to save yourself," Harkness says. "Or you can be all up in our face and just stay in lockup until you cool down."

"Fuck you, man," he says. "You got nothing on me."

Patrick holds up an iPhone. "We downloaded your life, and it looks pretty shady and druggy."

"You can't do that!"

"Here's a little security tip," Patrick says. "Next time, don't use your birthday as your password."

Anthony starts to rise out of his chair and Patrick shoves him back. "We can cuff you to the chair," he says, "or just keep it civilized-like."

Anthony settles. Harkness nods at Patrick, who gives him one last menacing look before he slams the door.

"That nigger's an asshole," Anthony mutters.

Harkness's right hand flies out, grabs Anthony's long black hair, and slams his forehead down on the metal desk.

Anthony screams.

Harkness lifts his head up and slams it back down again. So much for civilized.

"Stop it, man!"

The duty officer's face appears in the holding room's tiny window. He shakes his head — enough with the shamrock justice.

Harkness waves his free hand. Everything's under control. An emphatic conversation, that's all.

"No N-word, ever again. We're post-racial here. Got it?" He pushes Anthony's shivering, sweaty face into the desk to enhance retention of this life lesson.

"Aw right, aw right, *poft rafel.*" Anthony nods as much as someone with his face pressed down on a desk can.

Harkness lets him go, wipes his hand on his black jeans, and stalks around the room for a minute to settle. He circles back, sits down in a metal chair, and takes a good look across the table at Anthony. Long black hair pulled back, olive skin, tight gray leather motocross jacket, baggy jeans, unlaced boots. He looks like a North End action figure, the kind of handsome guy who might spend his evenings selling Xanax to college girls from his sidewalk table at Café Amalfi. He's a dead ringer for young Joey Ink, now an elder statesman in the city's overcrowded pantheon of notorious felons.

"You got a lot of explaining to do, Anthony." Harkness holds up a clipboard with a couple of photos and printouts on the top and blank paper underneath for credibility. "We pulled your fingerprint from a Dark Horse paper found at the scene of a double overdose at Harvard last week. And we've got your texts with one of the deceased, a guy named Jason Kittredge. Ring a bell?"

"No," he says. "Don't know any Harvard kids."

"Jason looked like this." Harkness flips a printout of Jason's Harvard ID onto the desk.

"Don't remember him."

"Met him at McCloskey's?"

"Got nothing, man."

"Doesn't matter, really," Harkness says. "You're going to get

charged with two counts of homicide this time, not dealing like before. We think your texts show that you knew Dark Horse was pure,
but you sold it low anyway. To people you knew were going to die."

"Whoa," Anthony says, shaking his head. "Way whoa. Wicked
way whoa. You cannot fucking pin that on me. I just sell drugs — I
mean, hyperthetically. It's not like I kill fucking people."

Harkness stares. "The two Harvard kids pushed last year's OD
count over a thousand, in case you're keeping score."

"I mean, what if the mailman delivers some kinda bomb in a
package. Like a dirty bomb with anthrax all over it? It kills the person who gets the package. But is it the fucking mailman's fault? I
think not."

"Gee, Anthony, what a refreshing perspective," Harkness says. "I
guess we should quit bothering the good people like you who sell
drugs. It's really the dead people's fault."

"Damn straight."

In a way, Harkness knows he's right. If Jason, Therese, and thousands of others didn't want to escape their earthy woes for a few
hours, there wouldn't be any Anthony Incagnolis around to make it
happen. Demand triggers supply.

"Look, if I knew that Dark Horse was such over-the-top kick-ass
shit, again hyperthetically, of course, I woulda stomped all over it.
That's just good business."

"Appreciate the insight."

"So what I'm saying is, it makes sense to let me out on low bail,"
Anthony says. "Like soon."

"Good try. But given the drugs and the gun they found in the
trunk of your BMW tonight, plus all your priors, you're not going
to get bail. Not to mention the fact that the sad story of the dead
Harvard kids is everywhere. You're probably looking at ten years in
Walpole."

"That is just completely fucked, man." Anthony's mouth hangs
open at the injustice of the system. He shakes his head at the nightmare he's wandered into. A couple of hours ago he was feeling bul-
letproof, driving into Dudley Square on his way to EDM night at
Interstella, a quart Ziploc of molly tucked under the spare tire of his
black BMW.

Harkness shuts up and lets the pissed-off perp mull his bleak future for a few moments. He pretends to be reading the blank paper on the clipboard while Anthony contemplates the fact that what seemed like another routine trip to the police station now looks like the end of life as he knows it.

"But there *is* another way out."

"What?" Anthony perks up like Pavlov's dog at the sound of a bell.

"Your uncle, Joey Ink."

"What about him?"

"I know him from Mr. Mach's, you know, the Zero Room."

"You're shittin' me." Anthony gives a mistrustful smile. "That place is a fucking dump. He only drank in Chinatown because all the yuppies drove him off of Hanover Street."

"Is your uncle friends with Nicco Malnati?" Harkness knows the answer, waits to see if Anthony lies or not.

"Big guy. Politician? City something. Alderman. Councilor?"

"Right."

"Why the hell do you care?"

"Just answer, Anthony." Harkness looks at his watch. "In a couple of minutes I have to report to the DA."

"Yeah, he knows Malnati. They go way back. Same parish growing up. St. Stephen's."

Harkness stands, pushes his chair in. He slides a card toward Anthony. "Have your uncle give me a call tomorrow. Maybe we can figure something out."

"No," Anthony says.

"Why not? I'm trying to help you. Do you see anyone else in here talking to you?"

"He can't call you. Had throat cancer last winter. Talks through one of those buzzy things. You'd never be able to fucking understand him on the phone."

"Sorry to hear that."

"But he's generally at the bar most nights."

"Which one?"

"Same one as always. The one you said. The Zero Room. In Chinatown."

34

REMIND ME WHY we decided to go outside?" Candace drags the empty stroller behind her down the slushy sidewalk while Harkness carries a wriggling May over his shoulder. Snow falls slowly from the slate-gray sky, and the afternoon light is already fading.

"Been indoors too long," Harkness says. "Good to get some air."

"The air is super-cold," Candace says. "May's nose is going to freeze and fall off."

"Think of it as a family adventure." Harkness spins May around to check the condition of her nose. She giggles.

"Let's buy a coffee, at least." Candace points to the steaming teapot over the Government Center Starbucks. "And a hot chocolate for the squirmer."

They aren't the only ones who want a hot coffee. The line stretches for more than a block.

"We're going to wait in line for Starbucks? That's a first."

"That's how we do it here in the gulag," Harkness says.

The winter has turned from London gray to Oslo grim, with snowstorm after snowstorm and no melting in between. Snow isn't getting plowed because there's no place to put it. Trash is piling up along with the snowdrifts. The schools have canceled more days than they've been in session since the new year began.

As they trudge silently toward the coffee shop, Harkness looks over at City Hall, snow piled around its base. Its gray cement walls and black windows look even more stark than usual—an otherworldly void in the middle of the city. In the plaza below, protesters have cleared away enough snow to huddle around fires burning in fifty-gallon drums.

Harkness sizes up the crowd, puts it at a couple of hundred. Most of the shouters and marchers are neck-bearded young activists, but there are some families too, probably from the former Lower South End. He reads their signs — HEY! HEY! DON'T TAKE OUR NEIGH-BORHOOD AWAY!, JUST SAY NO TO THUGS, and NO MORE DIRTY DEALS!

BPD officers watch the crowd with minimal interest. But there's also a huddle of black-jacketed security guards taking photos and talking into their phones — Burch's crew. Harkness wonders how big the protests have to get before the mayor cracks down and clears them out.

"What's that all about?" Candace nods toward the crowd.

"Protesting O'Mara. There were only a few people there last week."

"Is that why we walked all the way here? Doing a little surveillance on your day off?"

"Kind of." Harkness smiles.

"They must be freezing," Candace says.

"And angry enough to come out on a day like today." All over the city, people are hibernating instead of venturing outside, drinking too much and drifting into depression, turning pasty and getting weird. Domestic violence, overdoses, fires from space heaters — they're all spiking.

As they reach the front of the line, a man walks out of the coffee shop and stops abruptly next to them.

"Edward Harkness?" He's a Central Casting Boston lawyer — thinning silver hair, wire-rimmed glasses, gray fedora, dark overcoat, L.L. Bean boots, battered brown briefcase.

"Yes?"

The lawyer reaches into his briefcase and takes out a cream-colored envelope. "I have a letter for you to deliver to Sam Reed," he says. "Can you do that?"

"Sure." Harkness takes the letter. The man moves on before he can ask any questions.

"Who was that?"

Harkness holds the envelope toward Candace to reveal the familiar silver *X*.

"Them again," she says. "Are they stalking you?"

"I'd like to think they're helping me."

"Open the letter," Candace says.

"It's not for me," he says.

"What kind of detective are you?"

"Good question."

"We need to talk, Sam," Harkness says. "It's important." The last pay phone in Beacon Hill is tilted and ice-crusted, stranded in an alley next to Charles Street Liquors.

"Really?"

"Just meet me at the Fill-A-Buster in half an hour."

"Not sure I can get away."

"You have to," Harkness says. "You've got a city-employee cell phone, right?"

"Sure."

"Leave it in your office so they can't follow you."

"Wow, you're so paranoid, Eddy."

"Not really." The announcement of the U.S. Attorneys Office investigation, the outraged editorials and blog posts, the escalating protests in Government Center — it's all pushing the mayor's office to new extremes.

Harkness hangs up the receiver and listens to the machinery inside the pay phone swallowing his quarters.

The snow falls faster and thicker. Candace and May are in a cab, heading back to their warm apartment. Harkness imagines being with them instead of walking around in the snow, then puts aside the thought. The cream-colored envelope in his jacket pocket calls out for its recipient. He watches a pack of kids slip down Mt. Vernon Street on pieces of cardboard, sliding into the middle of Charles Street, once a major road, now a one-lane, snow-packed bobsled run.

Harkness walks down Charles to Beacon and cuts left, the ice-glazed Boston Common on his right. Beneath the bare branches, Little Dorothy lies on the frozen ground, sweeping her stick arms and legs to make an angel. She stands, her shredded white dress flocked with snow, face a gray annealed void, and points at Harkness as he walks by. He keeps his eyes on the top of the hill — not looking back, not letting the past distract him — leaving Little Dorothy in his wake.

He passes the State House on the left, then turns on Bowdoin Street toward the warm glow of the Fill-A-Buster, which, like almost every restaurant in Boston, is nearly empty as darkness descends at four in the afternoon.

"So how many city councilors do you think you can get to sign the letter of address?" Harkness stirs his coffee. The waitress has brought their orders. They've exchanged pleasantries and complaints about the weather. Now it's time to get to work.

"Are you talking about that old law you sent me?" Reed says. "From the city charter of something?"

Finding the nail is one thing, getting someone to use it is another. Harkness stares at Reed's uncomprehending, winter-pale face, splotched from all the wool he's wearing. "Yeah, that's right."

"Do you know what the city council is, Eddy?" Reed answers himself. "It's like thirteen loose cannons, all pointed at each other. Or, worse, at me. Almost impossible to get a unanimous vote on anything. Someone's always trying to stick his thumb in someone else's eye. It's all I can do to keep them from punching each other or stealing the chairs."

"I'm working on getting you Nicco Malnati from District A-One," Harkness says.

"How?"

"Let's just say I have some leverage. And we may have help getting the other loose cannons lined up."

"Look, maybe we should just let justice run its course, Eddy. The U.S. Attorneys Office is on O'Mara's tail already."

"His lawyers can tie up any case for years, Sam. We need something quick and decisive. You've got people waiting to come home."

"I know," he says. "Believe me, I know."

"I think if you read this, you might be inspired to start lining up your votes." Harkness slips the cream-colored envelope across the table.

"How old-fashioned," Reed says, smiling. "From you?"

"From Katherine Aiello," Harkness says.

"Who?"

"Director of the Harbormasters."

"*Shit*, Eddy." Reed's smile drops. "What've you gotten us into?"

"She can help you."

"Last I knew, they were calling in all their favors to get O'Mara elected."

"They didn't know how much damage O'Mara was going to do."

"Now they want to help me?" Reed looks like someone just told him tomorrow was going to be sunny and in the low eighties. It sounds good, but impossible.

"Yeah. They're as sick of O'Mara as everyone else."

"Did you wonder what they might want in return, Eddy? You're a cop, not a politician. Every favor comes with a bill at the end. And eventually you have to pay up."

A bripping sound comes from underneath their table. Reed takes his cell phone from his pants pocket and checks his texts. "Sorry."

"I told you to leave your cell phone at the office, Sam."

"You're paranoid, Eddy. No one's going to track us down."

Five minutes later, Neil Burch lurches through the front door of the Fill-A-Buster, his bald head covered by a black fur cap, his camo parka unzipped and flying behind him. He sways across the restaurant like a drunken Cossack ready to pillage.

Reed looks at Harkness, shocked. Harkness just shrugs. As the dark winter grinds on, bad habits are turning worse. Even Burch has a void to fill. Everyone does.

But still, it's not even five o'clock.

Burch sits heavily in a chair across the table, his bloodshot eyes going in and out of focus as he begins a rambling, slurry TED talk about how people are either with the mayor or against him — no middle ground. His lab in City Hall has a reputation for frat-boy behavior, long beery lunches, hallway hockey, and serious after-hours drinking. But this afternoon Burch is in champion territory.

The fry cooks watch Burch, wondering if they'll have to throw him out, or worse, clean up after he pukes on their spotless tile floor.

Harkness holds his hand up and asks something he's been wondering about since Burch showed up. "Where were you drinking, Neil?"

"Who cares? I can drink wherever I want. And as much as I want. I'm walking home, not driving. Walked all the way from the Parker House when I found out you traitors were hanging out here."

Harkness nods, senses Thalia's tainting hand behind the bar again.

Reed and Harkness exchange glances — a windfall has just landed at their table and they have to figure out what to do with it. Most politicians would take advantage of the opportunity, the same way that O'Mara's crew capitalized on the hurricane.

"Listen, Neil," Harkness says. "You're really drunk. I think it would be a good idea for you to stand up and walk out of here before you say or do anything you might regret."

"You do, do you?"

"Yeah, I do." Harkness looks Burch in his bloodshot eyes, giving him a way out — but just one.

"Well, I'm not going anywhere," Burch says, eyes almost closing. "I've told you what I'm up to and it's all *good news* for the *city of Boston*. Why don't you two devious bastards start telling me *what the fuck you're up to?*"

They say nothing. Reed sends a quick text under the table.

"I'm a narcotics detective, Neil. I'm just doing my job every day — trying to keep drugs from killing people, and drug dealers from killing each other. That's pretty much it."

Burch shakes his head vigorously and it vibrates like an egg on high boil. "I don't think so. You been nosing around, looking for dirt. Cooking up lies that make us look bad. Don't think we don't know!"

Harkness stays quiet and lets Burch heat up.

"So just cut it out, Harkness," Burch slurs. "Quit fucking with the mayor. We're in power and we're staying in power. Lattimore and all your pals are going to be out. And you know what? I'm taking back my offer. You're going to get fired too, Harkness. How about that?"

"Whatever, Neil." Harkness picks up his fork and starts eating his hash browns. There's nothing that a drunken narcissist hates more than being ignored.

"Quit fucking eating when I'm talking to you," Burch yells.

"My food's getting cold," Harkness says. "And since I'm about to get fired, I guess that means I don't have to listen to you anymore."

Burch reaches over and swipes his arm across the table, sending plates, glasses, and silverware smashing to the floor. The fry cooks roll their eyes. Reed looks like a bomb just went off.

Harkness stares at the mess on the floor, tangible evidence of the exact moment when Burch, platinum-level control freak, officially lost control. "Call me a thrifty Yankee, but I really hate wasting food."

"Shut the fuck up!" Burch's face turns red and sweaty now. "Start telling me what you're really up to."

Harkness tilts his head. "I'm confused, Neil. Do you want me to shut the fuck up or start talking? Because I can't do both at the same time."

Reed leans in, concerned. "Eddy, I think you should —"

"You stay out of this, little man," Burch shouts at Reed. "I'm probably scaring you, aren't I? How about this, does this scare you?"

Burch reaches out and shoves his flat palm into Reed's face, sending blood spraying from his nose onto the table. Reed slumps down with a moan, hands clasped to his face.

Harkness has his arm back, ready to swing at Burch, who reaches into his jacket pocket and pulls out his SIG Sauer with sudden, practiced grace.

The fry cooks retreat into the kitchen, cell phones to their ears.

"Neil, put down the gun," Harkness says calmly, giving Burch another chance to stop his own train wreck.

"Do *not* tell me what to do." Burch points his gun at Harkness. "Just start talking."

"Or what, you'll shoot me?"

Burch fires a shot into the ceiling that sends the stragglers scrambling out the door. He brings the barrel to his lips and blows on it. "How 'bout that, cowboy?"

Harkness just stares at Burch's face, broiling with rage.

Burch's next shot whistles by Harkness's right ear and slams into the wall. Harkness ducks down, head on the table, but inches his hand forward.

The next shot shatters a frame on the wall and sends glass flying. Burch is smiling, gleeful even, glorying in the chaos like a child smashing up his toy box. In the brief lull, Harkness clenches his hand around a plastic bottle of cheap mustard, points it, and squeezes hard — sending a yellow geyser into Burch's eyes.

"Shit!" He raises his hands up, dropping his gun. Harkness grabs one wrist and then the other, twists Burch down to the floor. He keeps a boot squarely in the middle of Burch's back and cuffs him. Burch flails like a fish that's just been landed. Harkness pats down his pockets, then picks up Burch's gun from the broken plates and glass and smeared food.

The blue lights of a BPD cruiser flash in the window, followed by TV news trucks. Harkness keeps his boot pressed on Burch, squirming in the mess he made.

"Ready for your close-up, Neil?"

An hour later, the floor's been swept clean and the cops are gone. The *Globe* photographers and TV crews have taken enough photos to disgrace Burch for several careers. Lattimore personally escorted Burch to District A-1 for processing. He'll be facing serious charges in the morning when he's arraigned, another great photo opportunity. Burch's optics, as the Stooges say, aren't looking very good.

Reed's not looking very good either. The EMTs cleaned up and bandaged his nose (bashed but not broken), but his white shirt is still blood-spattered. He's got his head in his hands and his tidy hair is a mess. He seems to be drifting into a postviolence fugue state.

Two shots of ouzo, provided by the Fill-A-Buster, sit between them, untouched. On the wall behind them, Martha Coakley took a bullet to the shoulder and Reagan narrowly avoided another attempted assassination.

"Never seen anything like that," Reed says quietly.

"Chaos happens."

"Especially around you." Reed pulls on his suit jacket and reaches for his sweater and coat. "Fun as this meeting was, Eddy, I have to head home."

The cream-colored envelope is dotted with Reed's blood. Harkness pushes it across the table. "Read this, Sam. It's important."

"Maybe tomorrow, Eddy." Reed tosses the letter in his briefcase. "I've had enough politics for today."

35

J OEY INCAGNOLI HOLDS down his usual booth in the back of Mr. Mach's Zero Room like a barroom diplomat, smoking a cigarette as he reads the *Herald*, glass of Cynar by his left hand, ashtray by his right.

As Harkness walks across the bar, he notices little changes — the stained orange carpet has been pulled out and replaced with a polished wood floor, the bartenders standing in front of the glowing liquor bottles are young and clean-looking, not the drugged-out, borderline women that Mr. Mach favored back during the dark era when Harkness spent too much time here. He looks for Thalia. His ex used to be one of the bar's most notorious bartenders. But she's gone. And so is Mr. Mach, running from a human-trafficking indictment.

Harkness can't say he misses him.

But Joey Ink's different. He spent long evenings telling Harkness stories about his days with Ray Patriarca and the Angiulo brothers — most along the theme of *how we beat those Irish fucks at their own game.* The game being extortion. Joey seemed to enjoy telling an off-duty cop about all that he got away with, knowing that he was immune from prosecution thanks to a sweet deal with the FBI.

Joey Ink smiles at Harkness and waves at the seat on the other side of the booth.

"How are you, Joey?"

He shrugs, holds up a silver device that looks like an old-school electric shaver. He swallows air, then touches the device to his throat. "Doing okay, Eddy." The robotic words sound nothing like his old voice. "This thing's called . . ." He pauses and swallows again. "An electrolarynx. Sucks."

"Sorry to hear you've had a hard time."

"They cut out my"— he pauses, swallows —"voice box."

"Really sorry."

Joey shrugs. "Everybody's missing"— he pauses, swallows — "something."

There's a lull, then Harkness turns to the business part of their meeting. "Came here to talk to you about your nephew."

Joey swallows, brings the device near again. "Anthony's a good kid."

"Seems like it," Harkness says. "But he's in a lot of trouble."

Joey takes a contemplative sip of his Cynar, raises the device. "I heard."

A waiter comes over — a first in what used to be a stand-five-deep-at-the-bar-and-yell kind of place. Harkness orders a soda water with lime, which earns a raised eyebrow from Joey.

"Cleaned up my act," Harkness says. "Getting married."

"Congrats," Joey buzzes. "Thalia?"

"No."

Joey quiets at the memory of the nasty old days in the Zero Room. "Good."

"Here's the deal, Joey. Your nephew's facing two homicide charges and some serious prison time."

"Jesus."

"I can send him over to the DEA. They want him to roll on his dealers — he knows some big fish they're interested in. If he does, they'll probably let him off with short time. Maybe get him into witness protection."

"Anthony needs to . . ." He pauses. "Get out of town."

"I think you're right."

"So what do you want from me?"

"I need your help with a side project, I guess you'd call it."

Joey rolls his hand in front of him to rush Harkness to the point.

"I need you to talk to your friend Nicco Malnati." A low-profile North End kingpin, Malnati manages to keep getting elected to the city council term after term.

He raises his device. "What about?"

"A vote to throw out Mayor O'Mara."

Joey Ink smiles, raises his device. "I like." He pauses. "That hand-some." Another pause. "Motherfucker."

"Look, I voted for him," Harkness says. "But things have changed. Put in a word with Malnati and I'll try to help Anthony."

"I'll see." He pauses. "What I can do."

All at once, a crowd of people in thick overcoats and scarves blow through the door of the Zero Room and commandeer the tables at the center of the room. They're gawking at the sputtering neon signs, the empty fish tank next to the bathrooms with a flotilla of beer cans on its murky surface.

"Wednesday night." Joey pauses, swallows, raises the device again. "Dive Bar Tour."

That the Zero Room has become a tourist attraction seems impossible to Harkness. Then again, there's a Rat Suite at the Commonwealth Hotel now, turning the city's legendary punk club into an overpriced hotel room.

Joey leans forward. "I'll do what." He pauses, swallows. "I can."

"Does Malnati owe you any favors?" Harkness finishes his soda water.

Joey nods. "Plenty."

"Might be a good time to call them in."

"Don't tell me." Joey pauses, swallows. "What to do."

Harkness holds up his hands. "Got it." He'd forgotten Joey's ice-cold side. Even diminished, he exudes an aura of unalloyed *bad*. Just the kind of character the tour-goers probably love to see — from across the bar.

The news on the flat-screen over the bar catches Harkness's eye. RIOT BREAKS WINTER CALM IN NAGOG. He stands and picks up his coat from the back of his chair. Onscreen, hundreds of protesters carrying torches and signs swarm in front of a blue clapboard house. He recognizes the neighborhood — it's across the street from the town ball field, where he used to spend every spring afternoon. They're interviewing Watt, who squints at the camera, steaming clouds floating from his mouth as he talks to a reporter.

The sound's off, but Harkness can guess what's happening.

36

SHOUTING WANDERERS MARCH in front of Buckholtz's blue, two-story Colonial, the crowd lit by the flashing blue lights of Nagog Police cars and a couple of state police cruisers. Harkness ditches the brown Chevy in a snowbank next to the town ball field and rushes toward the house, flashing his badge to get past the Statie running perimeter.

"Hell no, we won't go! Hell no, we won't go!" Hundreds of wanderers mill around Buckholtz's snowy yard, along with neighbors and TV crews.

Harkness finds Watt at the front of the crowd with a cluster of nervous Nagog rookies keeping the protesters away from the house.

"Welcome to the circus." Watt smiles. "The fun just never stops around here, Eddy."

"Town meeting was tonight, right?"

"Right," Watt says. "They voted to throw the wanderers out a couple of hours ago — by a landslide. WB added some choice comments at the end about what a relief it was to rid the town of freeloaders, freegans, and free-lovers. His words, not mine. And he gave a stern warning to the wanderers to clear out by midnight. So they all regrouped here in his yard. Kind of like a last stand."

"WB inside?"

"Yeah, he's hiding. I don't think he'll be coming out," Watt says, then turns to shout at his men, "Listen up, let's move the crowd another ten yards back."

They stretch their arms out and walk slowly away from the house.

Harkness joins them. The wanderers back up willingly. They may be angry but they're also tired and cold — and smart enough to know there's nothing they can do to change tonight's vote.

The shouting rises suddenly. The front door is moving, pulled inside the dark house, then the storm door, clouded with frost, inches open.

The shouts turn to jeers and booing as Buckholtz totters out, blinking when the TV crews switch on their lights. He's wearing a dark blue bathrobe over his white pajamas and shuffles forward in unlaced L.L. Bean boots.

The wanderers quiet a little when they see that the man they're rallying against is so old, tired, and sad.

Buckholtz wavers on the porch, his hunched shoulders rising and falling with his labored breathing. He's muttering to himself or praying. Spectral, underpowered, he looks like he might slump into the snow at any moment.

He snaps to, as if he's thrown a hidden switch, made an irrevocable decision. He's standing straight and tall now, peering out like a crow seeking shine. Buckholtz reaches beneath his bathrobe, pulls out a shotgun, and levels it at the crowd.

Shouts turns to screams. The wanderers start to run as he fires both barrels in quick succession, the explosions echoing across the yard.

The crowd scatters, slipping and falling, knocking over TV cameras and lights. Bodies drop in the snow. Buckholtz stands at the top of the stairs, smiling at the chaos he's created. Then he tosses his shotgun down. It clatters on the icy sidewalk and he turns back toward his house.

Watt bounds up the steps and tackles Buckholtz. He lifts him like a bag of laundry and drags him down the stairs. Buckholtz shouts as Watt cuffs him, something about the righteous needing no justification.

Harkness shouts at the rookies, *"Call in ambulances, now."* Then he rushes to the jumble of bodies on the ground. Some wanderers are sitting up, stunned. Others cluster around a body. Harkness walks closer and sees Jennet Townsend sprawled in the snow.

Her speckled face is white and marked with grime, long hair

tangled and wet from melting snow, eyes wide open, a front tooth chipped from her deadfall to the frozen ground. Her army surplus parka is half open and blood-slick.

"You've got to help her!" James, her frantic brother, waves him forward with bloody hands.

Harkness kneels down next to Jennet, pale and still. The wanderers step aside and Harkness lifts the coat to reveal two dark cavities in the center of her chest, the pale, shredded flaps of skin giving way to shimmering bone and deep red flesh. A wanderer hands him a T-shirt and Harkness folds it, presses it against the wounds, but it's soaked with pooled blood in seconds.

"It's going to be okay," he says to Jennet but knows it's not. She's already gone, staring up at the bare branches and the distant stars.

Out on the street, the EMTs lift the stretcher into an ambulance. Harkness's hands are dark with Jennet's blood, his mind spinning. Around him, James, Mouse, and the remaining wanderers are crying and shouting. A tear drips down Harkness's face and he wipes it away furiously with his sleeve.

He leaves the group of mourners and walks over to the ambulance.

"I need to see her." He shows his badge.

"Eddy, really. Don't," Watt calls out.

"She was a friend of mine. Just give me a second," he says to one of the EMTs, who nods and pulls back the heavy blanket to reveal Jennet's narrow body, chest covered now with bloody gauze pads that do little to hide the wounds. An abandoned IV line trails from her arm.

"She didn't have a chance," the EMT says. "Two barrels of heavy-grade birdshot to the chest. Died instantly."

Harkness stares at her lifeless body, tracing back the many decisions that led Jennet from the city to this bloodied small-town yard. Some were hers. But a thick vein of guilt runs through these thoughts. Did his advice about Nagog inspire Jennet to picket Buckholtz's house? Should he have warned her how angry and twisted he was? He shakes his head, feels his soul pulled lower. Jennet died the way she lived, doing what she thought was right even when it wasn't. The pale young woman on the stretcher was a survivor who didn't survive, a streetwise innocent brought down by the latest bitter old man unable to control his rage.

He reaches out to close her green eyes, feels her skin cold on his fingertips.

The EMTs say nothing. They never do. They're about stopping pain and death when they can, not explaining why it happened. One replaces the blanket and together they push the stretcher containing the still body that was once Jennet Townsend, good citizen of the Lower South End, into the back of the ambulance.

The crowd is gone, leaving behind the professionals and ghouls. The cameramen have their video of Wade Buckholtz firing into the crowd, screaming wanderers scrambling to get away. The reporters finished their standups in front of the yard and broadcast the latest small-town tragedy.

Disheveled from being tackled and cuffed, WB wears an orange emergency blanket over his bathrobe and leans heavily on his walker next to a Nagog cop. His paper-white face is twisted into a rictus of bafflement, and Harkness wonders if WB even realizes what he's done. His thin gray hair sticks out and his eyes blink. He gives Harkness a sick smile and turns away slowly.

"I want to talk to Buckholtz," Harkness says when Watt walks closer.

Watt's breath steams in the cold. "We've questioned him already."

"Searched his house?"

Watt shakes his head. "Not yet. Why?"

Harkness nods, thinks of the strange look WB just gave him. "Let's give it a once-over, just in case."

They hear the clocks first, dozens of them, all ticking away, out of sync like a crazed cartoon.

"My grandma had one of those." Watt points to a black-cased Waltham mantel clock. "Wonder if it's worth something."

"Probably not," Harkness says. "People always think their family stuff is special." They walk carefully through the house, stopping at the waist-high tower of newspapers, each day of the *Nagog Journal* carefully unfolded and stacked.

"Looks like WB's lost it," Watt says.

"Oh yeah."

A handful of dim bulbs burning in a brass chandelier light the dining-room table, lined with row after row of Mason jars.

"Really late to be canning," Watt says, twisting open a jar. "Seems like—"

"Don't do that," Harkness says, too late to stop Watt from taking a big sniff.

"Sweet Mary, Mother of God." Watt puts the lid back on the jar. Each is carefully inscribed in black marker with the date and time. He moves away from the table and puts his hands on his knees to dry retch. "What kind of man archives his piss?"

"And that's not all." Harkness points to some darker shadows floating in some of the jars.

"I'm calling that TV show, *Hoarder's Heaven,*" Watt says. "No one's going to believe this."

"Sure they will."

"WB's wife must have kept him out of the weeds."

"Kept him from shooting people," Harkness says.

"So that's why people get married?"

"That would be one of the reasons. And a good one."

"I'm sorry." The voice is so soft that Harkness barely hears it as he's about to get in the Chevy. Then he sees the dark figure hunched next to the car.

"What do you want?" Harkness peers into the gloom, feels his right hand tingle, awake and ready to reach for his Glock.

The stranger pulls off his knitted cap to reveal his smoke-bush hair. Mouse, shivering and whimpering. Harkness nods to the passenger door.

"Get in," Harkness says. "Let's have a little talk." He twists the key in the ignition and the Chevy roars to life.

The passenger door opens slowly and Mouse slumps into the seat.

"This car may not look like much, but the heater really works." Harkness twists the fan knob to spread the warm air.

"It's all my fault." Mouse lowers his head into his chapped hands.

"What?"

"I'm the one who told Jennet about that stupid Nagog law," Mouse says. "She started the wanderer movement. And now she's dead."

"Hold on a second," Harkness says. "From what I know, a guy at the library gave you the information about Nagog because Robert Fayerwether asked him to. So you're more of a go-between in this story, Mouse. But definitely go ahead and feel as guilty as you want." Harkness pulls off his gloves and rubs the missing end of his index finger. It always goes numb in the cold.

"Just arrest me, man." Mouse juts both his arms toward Harkness, waiting for the handcuffs. "I'm done."

Harkness peers across the front seat. "Don't think so."

"You said there's still a warrant out for me," Mouse says. "So arrest me. I want everything to be over. No more shooting and shit, man. Jennet was always on me to clean up my act. Said real activists can't be shady."

"I have other plans for you," Harkness says. "Help me out and I'll make sure your warrant goes away. It's important — Jennet would be proud of you. I'm sure of it."

"What're you talking about?" Mouse leans across the seat and Harkness smells damp wool and stale weed.

"Know the story of Exodus?"

"Kinda."

"You're going to be Moses," Harkness says. "You've already got the beard for it."

37

BY THE TIME Harkness gets home, it's after two in the morning and the snow has picked up, tiny flakes sifting down steadily like powdered sugar to cover the old gray snow. He unlocks their apartment door and opens it slowly, trying not to wake Candace and May.

The apartment blazes with light—the television's on with no sound and Candace's laptop is open, the news unspooling onscreen. She and Nora decided to skip town meeting since polls showed the wanderers losing by more than 20 percent. But it looks like she's been monitoring the news from Nagog all night.

Candace lies curled up on the living room rug, a blanket pulled over her.

Harkness puts his hand on her shoulder and shakes her gently. He's reaching down to carry her into the bedroom when she opens her eyes, pulls her arm back, and slaps Harkness in the face with her good hand.

"It's me," Harkness says.

"I know." Candace pulls her hand back and slaps him again and again until he catches her wrist.

"What the hell's wrong with you?"

"I was about to ask you the same thing." She pulls away and stands, backing up slowly, eyes glinting, tear-lined face twisted with rage.

"Been drinking or something?"

"No drinks, weed, pills, nothing." Candace stalks to her laptop and comes back, holding it open toward Harkness. "Look what someone e-mailed me."

On the screen, Harkness sees the sunlit interior of the rehabbed garage. Jennet Townsend lies sprawled on the platform bed, top off, breasts set free, an expansive smile on her face. Harkness stares from the edge of the photo, taken from somewhere up in the ceiling.

"You look like a hungry guy staring at a sizzling steak, Eddy," Candace says. "What the fuck!"

"I went out to Nagog to talk Jennet about the Manchester Group," Harkness says. "She gave me some great information."

"And a really super blowjob?"

Harkness shakes his head. "Nothing happened. Not even a kiss. She ripped her shirt and threatened to make it look like I raped her."

"Oh really? Then what?"

"I didn't go for it and the shirt went back on."

"And the pants never came off? Hers or yours? Tell me the pants never came off."

"No, never."

"Maybe you just wanted one last fling, you know, before you get married. Is that it, Eddy?"

"No," Harkness says. "Nothing happened. What you see there is it — me about ten feet away from Jennet, who pretended to want me. But I did *not* go for it."

Candace's voice shifts into a more desperate key. "You look so *be-fucking-witched,* Eddy, like some guy watching the girl next door undress in front of a window."

"I was just surprised."

"And it's a good surprise when suddenly there are nice tits, isn't it? Every man wants random nice tits popping up in his life, right?"

"Look, I don't know, Candace. I told you what happened. But I have to ask — when did you quit watching the news?"

"They voted to oust the wanderers," Candace says. "That was awesome. Then they showed up at Buckholtz's house, which was a great idea. That's about when I dozed off."

Harkness pauses. "So you don't know what happened next?"

"No."

"Sit down." Harkness points to the couch and Candace sits. He does a quick search and clicks a news clip. "Watch this."

"Police in Nagog have identified the dead woman as Jennet Townsend, thirty-one, of Boston, the activist who founded the wanderer movement." Jennet's face hovers over the newscaster's shoulder. "The alleged shooter is town resident Wade Buckholtz, seventy-seven, who is being held on charges of first-degree murder." A photo of a much-younger Buckholtz appears over the other shoulder.

Harkness clicks the news clip off and shuts the laptop.

"*Whoa,* Eddy. She's dead? What the fuck happened?"

"After the wanderers showed up at Buckholtz's house, he came out on the front steps, really pissed off. He pointed his twelve-gauge and fired both barrels into the crowd. Or, more specifically, into Jennet Townsend. She died instantly."

"*Shit,*" Candace says.

Harkness looks right in his fiancée's scared eyes. "Look, Jennet can't tell you what happened, Candace. So you're just going to have to believe me."

Candace pauses, then starts to cry. "*Jesus,* Eddy. I had no idea. I didn't mean to . . ."

He puts his arms around her. "I'm sorry about the photo, really sorry. But whoever took it and sent it to you just wanted to mess with us. Mostly with me. I'll have Patrick try to figure out where that photo came from."

Candace closes her eyes. "Okay."

Harkness knows they won't be able to trace the sender's bogus e-mail account. But the message is clear: *Don't fuck with us.* Burch may be out of commission, but the Manchester Group has plenty of other cold-hearted fixers onboard.

"The people we're up against will do anything to ruin me, Candace. We can't let them."

"It takes more than a picture, Eddy," she says. "Much more." She reaches over and kisses him, then pulls away slowly and slaps him again.

"What's that for?"

"Just a reminder."

"Of what?"

"Whatever you need to be reminded of."

By the time Harkness finishes writing the letter, it's almost dawn. Candace and May are asleep in the bedroom, and weak winter sunlight is seeping through the apartment. He checks for paper, tries to send the letter to the printer, realizes that it isn't wireless, so he has to find the Ethernet cable and plug it into the laptop. The paper jams. After he clears the wad of paper, the machine produces an okay-looking copy, but on the back there's an article that Candace printed out, then recycled. Harkness finds some clean paper, hits a couple of keys, and pulls the letter from the printer with a sense of triumph.

At first, the chosen communication channel of the Harbormasters seemed foolish but appropriate for a group that started back in the days of quill pens and powdered wigs. But now it makes sense. Cell phones, e-mail, texts — they all leave a trail. Letters send their message, make their request or threat. Then with the touch of a match, they're gone forever.

He looks for a pen in the kitchen, finds only a Sharpie and some crayons. He turns up a stubby pencil from when he and Candace played putt-putt on the Cape last summer, but a golf-pencil signature doesn't seem right.

Finally, he comes up with a not-completely-dried-out pen in a coat pocket and scrawls his signature on the bottom.

It's hard to write a letter in the digital era. Even harder to send it.

Harkness looks for an envelope in the closet where they keep the stack of bills. Nothing. They pay most of them online. The other bills just sit around until someone calls and then they pay them over the phone.

He finds a return envelope from the cable company, but it has an address on it already.

Harkness pulls on his uniform and heavy winter BPD jacket and slips quietly out of the apartment. He takes the elevator to the sixth floor and walks down the hall to Nate and Shawna's apartment. He listens at the door, knocks when he hears voices.

"Hey." It's Nate, ursine and sleepy, pale belly poking out from beneath his gray T-shirt. A redlining body mass index is an occupational hazard of being a craft brewer. "What's up, Eddy?"

"Sorry to bother you," Harkness says. "But do you have an envelope?"

"What?"

Harkness holds up the letter. "Thing that this goes in," he says.

"Oh, that. I'll check." Nate leaves the door open and pads back into the apartment. He asks Shawna where the envelopes are. There's some back-and-forth about whether they actually have any. Jenna's watching educational cartoons at earsplitting volume. Then Nate's back, holding a limp, lumpy envelope in his hand.

"This is all we've got."

Harkness takes the envelope — gray, with smashed seeds dotting it like an everything bagel.

"If you plant it, it grows wildflowers," Nate says. "Supposedly."

"Oh."

"It's left over from last year's solstice-party invitations."

Harkness narrows his eyes. "Would you mind explaining why you didn't invite us?"

"We did! We did!" Nate backs away from the door.

Harkness smiles. "Fucking with you, Nate."

"Shit, Eddy. You've got scary cop down a little too good, man."

"Thanks."

"Not a compliment."

Harkness walks toward the Harbormasters' headquarters, boots crunching in the snow. There are only a few cars parked on the Northern Avenue Bridge next to the building, but two beefy guards stand in front of the doors. As Harkness approaches, they stand up a little straighter and suck in their guts.

"Deliver this, please," he says, handing the letter to the nearer guard.

"Will do, boss," he says.

They don't recognize him as the whiskey-stinking bum they beat up. Now he's just a detective with a message for Katherine Aiello, an old-style letter with news and a request for help — the kind of help that only a Harbormaster can deliver.

His cell phone rings as he walks toward the Chevy. It's Patrick.

"On my way in," Harkness says.

"Got something waiting for you."

"What?"

"Your contract-termination notice, Harky. We all got 'em in our mailboxes this morning. We got a couple of weeks to report to HR and find out if we're getting reassigned or laid off. Narco-Intel is history."

38

THE SNOWY PATH through Freedom City twists through the neat rows of aluminum huts designed by eco-conscious MIT students to replace the tents and lean-to shacks. A volunteer in a heavy black parka pedals a stationary bicycle on a wooden platform. Dozens of volunteers stand in line, waiting their turn to keep the electric heaters and lights on with People Power, as the sign on the platform puts it. Beyond the huts, a huge communal bonfire sends sparks arcing high above Government Center.

In the weeks since Harkness's last visit, Freedom City has grown like a Wild West town. Despite the snow and cold, the people keep coming — nostalgic Occupy activists, students, even some elderly residents of the former West End. They all came to show their support, then stayed because it was more fun than being cooped up in their apartments all winter. The ad hoc protests turned into a nascent town, then the thriving metropolis that Harkness sees stretching out across the plaza. From what he can tell, there must be more than a thousand protesters living in Freedom City, along with reporters from all over the world and a fleet of news trucks here to cover the growing protests against Mayor O'Mara.

The mayor's problems accrued like snow, slowly at first, then in a blizzard. The Burch scandal made his administration seem thuggy and weird. The *Globe*'s spotlight series exploring the links between his administration and the Manchester Group made it look beyond corrupt. And his inept handling of the record January snowfall, the latest natural disaster to hit the city, undercut O'Mara's reputation as a get-things-done mayor.

But despite the growing protests, a hard fact remains, one that everyone in Freedom City knows — O'Mara is still mayor. And he doesn't appear to be going anywhere soon.

Ahead, the shaggy doppel-mayor of Freedom City walks toward Harkness, passing between the rows of huts — smiling at citizens, answering questions, handing out donated coffee. Mouse is wearing a black parka and a blaze-orange motorcycle helmet pulled over his puffy hair. The red third eye painted on the front of helmet makes him hard to miss.

"Hey, Eddy. Pretty fucking incredible, huh?"

"Fantastic," Harkness says.

Mouse points toward downtown Freedom City. "We've got a communications yurt, an infirmary, a library, a central kitchen, and more donations than we know what to do with. Coats, blankets, food, money. People are really generous."

"When they want to be," Harkness says.

"Well, we've hit a nerve."

Mouse waves Harkness back up the steps of City Hall. "Hey, watch this," he says as a clump of guys in parkas and moonboots approach. They're nudging an angry-looking man ahead of them with long sticks. "I'll show you how snow justice works."

Half walking, half sliding, the group comes to the enormous mountain of snow cleared to build the city.

"Stick Men! What's the trouble here?"

"Caught him taking video," one says.

"The city's identifying us all so it can press charges," another adds.

"That's not true!" the prisoner shouts.

"Proof?" Mouse says.

"He was uploading the video to a dark site we know the city's using to gather evidence on us," a Stick Man says. "And he's got a city cell phone."

"I see," Mouse says. "I think a couple of hours in the snow keep should be plenty. Then banish him from the city."

The Stick Men nod and approach the giant snow pile. One steps on the ground in front of the mound and a hidden mechanism kicks in. A door slides open slowly, revealing a dark, icy cavern. The Stick Men shove the offender in and the door closes behind him.

"Impressive," Harkness says. "Who made the giant igloo?"

"MIT students with too much time on their hands," Mouse says.

"What's inside?"

"No heat, no light, nothing," Mouse says. "Some time in the snow keep generally chills anyone out," Mouse says.

"I bet."

"Every city has to keep out the troublemakers, even ours. Especially ours. We want to be a model."

"Just so you know, that wasn't exactly justice. At least, not the kind we learned about at the Academy."

Mouse shrugs. "What happens in Freedom City stays in Freedom City. We just do what we need to do."

"I'm sure the mayor would agree with that approach," Harkness says.

"Hey, don't get picky, man. You're the one who told me to bring the whole wanderer movement downtown and stick it to the mayor. If you don't like it, *you* can run this circus, man. Half of Freedom City can't eat gluten and the other half can't figure out what pronoun describes their gender."

They walk back up the low grade of the plaza, City Hall squatting ahead of them like a cement tomb built by Aztecs.

"There he is, keeping an eye on us. Big Bro." Mouse points to a dark window on the fifth floor. Behind the smoked glass, Harkness can make out a white shirt and dark tie, but he can't see O'Mara's face. As he stares at the window, Harkness imagines O'Mara in a Nixonian huddle with his advisers, trying to figure out how to stanch his hemorrhaging popularity and get rid of Freedom City.

A snowball hits near the mayor's window. For a dollar donation, anyone who wants to can get an Instagram-ready photo taken while throwing a prepacked snowball at City Hall. The line snakes across the plaza.

"I can tell you like what you're seeing." Mouse leans closer and his voice drops. "So you'll tear up my warrant?"

Harkness puts one hand on Mouse's shoulder as they walk through Freedom City. "It's all looking good," he says. "But there's one thing missing."

"What's that?"

"A third act," Harkness says.

39

THE EVOLVING SNOW sculpture known as *Freezing Man* faces City Hall across the plaza. Today he's wearing a tri-corner plywood hat, and one arm is outstretched to give the mayor the finger. Along the edge of the plaza, food trucks dispense free meals to the growing crowd living in Freedom City. Broadcast trucks line Cambridge Street, capturing every moment of Rage Weekend, a galvanizing political protest, urban party, winter music festival — and the third and final act of the wanderers.

Harkness, Esther, and Patrick came up with Rage Weekend during a coffee-fueled brainstorming session pulled together to try to save their department — and get rid of O'Mara by any means necessary. Rage and radical action seemed like the only approach now that their days as detectives are numbered. So they borrowed a concept from the Weathermen. And they held the demonstration on a weekend, making it even more convenient for citizens to join the protests, swelling Freedom City to fill all of Government Center.

"Did you try the bison chili?" Patrick points to one of the food trucks. "Got to say, it's awesome."

"How can you eat at a time like this?" Esther says.

"How can you not? Heard of stress eating?"

"Just because there's a name for something doesn't mean you have to do it." Esther zips up her BPD winter jacket with its fleece collar. Lattimore put Narco-Intel on crowd control, but what they're really doing is waiting — for an impending snowstorm and for news from the city council meeting at the Old North Church. All the detectives on the plaza this afternoon — Fredette, Gray, DeFrancesco, Hendricks, Poole, Tims — are wondering whether they'll have jobs on Monday morning. And looking to Harkness to make something happen. Anything.

They're worried about more than their jobs. They're monitoring drugs no one else in the BPD has even heard of — Retna, Swerve, Brainwash, Front Man, White Alice. They've been listening in on baggage handlers at the airport laundering drug money, tracking down an illusive Mattapan meth dealer, and gathering intel on an online drug mart run out of a Somerville triple-decker. The thought of these investigations and more suddenly going dark on Monday makes Harkness's stomach drop.

Lattimore charges out of the front doors of City Hall, face flushed red, down-jacketed Stooges struggling to keep up with him. "Any word from Reed?"

Harkness looks at his watch. "The meeting just started."

"So does he have the votes or not?"

"Can't be sure," Harkness says. "We've pulled in every favor and yanked every string. We've done things I can't even tell you about, sir. In the end, all fourteen of them have to have the guts to vote for a bill of address to throw the mayor out. But they're the city council."

"Like a deck of wildcards."

"Exactly."

"Get this — the mayor's about to declare a citywide public emergency," Lattimore tells them. "Says there might be more than a foot of snow coming, and he has to keep the citizens safe."

"Like he cares," Esther says.

Patrick shakes his head slowly. "Just another excuse to force people to go home and shelter in place." The mayor's invoked his version of martial law twice already — once during Hurricane X, and once during the winter's unrelenting snowstorms.

"Enough with Bossy McBoss Boss," Esther says. "Everyone's getting tired of being pushed around."

Lattimore looks over at the People's Pulpit, the low wooden platform that faces Freedom City. From MIT professors to singer-songwriters, everyone stands there to address the crowd. "He just ordered me to get up there and tell the crowd to disperse," he says. "I still have to answer to him, at least until Monday morning, when none of us will be around anymore."

Patrick sizes up the crowd. "Probably about ten thousand people here, sir. They're not just going to leave and take the T home, even if you ask them nice-like. What do we do with the folks who stick around?"

"We're supposed to move in and enforce the law. Billy clubs out, Tasers ready to go, busting heads and taking names." Lattimore holds up a sheet of paper. "His lawyers put together a list of violations."

The idea of a street battle against the citizens of Freedom City quiets everyone.

"I want to make one thing clear, people," Lattimore says. "I am *not* going to be the Bull Connor of Freedom City."

Harkness's phone brips. "It's Reed." He reads the slap-typed message, misspelled and in all caps. "Malnati didn't show up for the vote. They can't do anything until he gets there — if he does."

"Shit," Lattimore says. "Thought you had him in your pocket."

"So did I." Harkness points at Patrick and Esther. "Follow me." He turns and starts sprinting to where the Narco-Intel vehicles are parked on Tremont. Patrick and Esther trail after him.

"What am I supposed to do?" Lattimore shouts.

"*Stall*," Harkness shouts. "Don't let anyone leave."

As they run across the enormous snowy plaza, they hear Lattimore's voice booming from the People's Pulpit megaphone. "Attention, please." The megaphone gives out a wail of feedback. "I'm Boston Police Commissioner James Lattimore."

The crowd gathered below turns to listen. The bonfire at the center of the plaza crackles and sends sparks into the dove-gray sky.

"Mayor Michael O'Mara has asked me to tell you that the City Hall Plaza is now closed to visitors due to a major snowstorm approaching the city. He's asked me to shut down this illegally occupied city property, which is in violation of the fire code and other city ordinances."

Major boos from across the plaza — low at first, then louder as the crowd senses a threat.

Lattimore just stares out into the crowd as the noise rises to a roar. Then he puts the megaphone back to his lips and steps forward. "But I'm not going to do that," he shouts.

The crowd goes insane — shouting, whistling, throwing snow in the air.

"You have every right to be here. I will personally ensure that you are safe, warm, and protected. We'll ride this storm out together, right here."

The cheering rises even more.

As they climb in the brown Chevy, Harkness, Esther, and Patrick take one last look at Lattimore, arms stretched up to the sky, taking in the applause, shouts, adoration.

After all, how many chances does a police commissioner have to be loved by so many people?

They drive down Hanover Street toward Nicco Malnati's apartment, the Chevy sliding down the snow-covered road. Ahead, the street's clogged by a crowd parading a dollar-covered statue of a saint.

Harkness slows the Chevy.

"Cool." Esther leans forward in the passenger seat to get a closer look, maybe a photo for her blog.

"A saint day? Right before a nor'easter?" Patrick's in the back seat, laptop balanced on his knees. "Cut down this alley and we can avoid Saint Annoying As Fuck."

Harkness swerves down the alley and guns it, sending trashcans flying.

"Left," Patrick shouts after a few blocks.

Harkness cuts the wheel and skids back onto the street.

"Should be coming up on the right in about a block."

As Harkness drives closer, he sees four black-vested security guards standing at the entrance of Malnati's apartment building.

"Shit, Eddy."

"Get down, both of you." Esther and Patrick duck down. Harkness reaches over and pulls on the green knit cap that makes him look like a guy scalping Celts tickets on Canal Street.

They drive by the building and the guards don't even look at them.

"What're we going to do?" Patrick pulls himself back up.

"Check for someplace else Malnati might be," Harkness says.

"He's back in his apartment, Harky."

Harkness shakes his head. "He's not there."

"How do you know that?"

"I just do," Harkness says. "The guards out front look like a setup. They just wanted us to waste time trying to get in that building when Malnati's somewhere else."

Patrick pounds away. "Magazine profile mentions a girlfriend, Alicia DeVarco. I got her living over on Parmenter Street."

"What's the cross street?"

"Salem."

"Got it."

Patrick looks up from his laptop. "Malnati's got a pile of parking tickets on that block, including one from this morning."

"Hold on." Harkness cuts down another alley and races across the North End's narrow ice-clogged streets, sending Patrick and Esther ducking again. They're one patch of black ice away from the ER.

A gritty collage of takeout menus covers the black-and-white-tiled floor of the apartment building on Parmenter Street. It looks more like a home for students and restaurant line cooks, but DeVarco's name is listed on one of the mailboxes inside the front door. Harkness buzzes the apartment but no one answers.

"You sure this is it?" Esther asks Patrick. "Looks too grubby for a politician's girlfriend."

"Really?" Patrick's eyebrows drift up. "Would you want to date a city councilor?"

"No," Esther says. "Hey, maybe he's not even here. We should try his office."

"No politician around here works the weekends," Patrick says.

"He's here." Harkness points out at the street. There's a black Audi parked illegally. Vanity plate says Dist1POL.

"That's the one that's been getting all the tickets," Patrick says.

Esther looks concerned. "Are we really going to kick down the door or something?"

"We'll just have to huff and puff." Patrick holds up a rectangular metal device the size of a cell phone. "And barge our way in." He presses a glowing green button, then twists a knob slowly until the door buzzes. Harkness pushes it open.

"You guys get all the cool toys," Esther says.

Patrick slips the device back in his pocket and they climb the narrow stairs up to the third floor.

Harkness knocks on the door. "Mr. Malnati," he says politely. "Detective Edward Harkness, Boston Police Department. We need to speak with you." Harkness glances at his watch. The other councilors have been waiting for almost an hour now, if they're even still there.

Nothing happens. They back away and huddle in the hallway.

"I know he's in there," Harkness says softly.

"How do you know?"

"I just do." Harkness gives Patrick a look that dispels any doubts. "You two walk the stairs. Make plenty of noise. Go out through both the doors and wait for me on the sidewalk."

Harkness steps quietly back to Malnati's girlfriend's door. There's no peephole or security camera. He presses against the wall next to the hinge side of the door.

Patrick and Esther clomp down the stairs and slam through the entryway doors. Harkness waits for a minute, then another. After what seems like an hour, he hears a click, and the door opens a sliver, then wider, as someone takes a look around. The door's about to close again when Harkness swivels and forces the door open.

A man in a dark blue suit and white shirt stares at Harkness like he's a Visigoth come to plunder the apartment. He's terrified, his thin lips coming together then moving apart, but he's not saying anything. Inside, the dim living room is all pink marble and watery green walls. It looks like an apartment where a salmon might live.

"Nicco Malnati?" Harkness says.

"How the fuck did you find me?"

Harkness steps inside. "You're supposed to be at a meeting."

"Yeah, Joey Ink explained that to me," he says, walking deeper into the apartment. "But I'm just not feeling that well today, Detective. You know how that goes. You guys call it blue flu when you skip out on work, right?"

"No one calls it that," Harkness says. "That's from some eighties cop show or something. What we call it is being a dirtbag. How much is O'Mara paying you to skip the vote?"

Malnati picks up a pistachio from a bowl on the dining-room

table, cracks it open and eats it, drops the shells in his suit-coat pocket. "Promised me fifty grand."

"I'll double it," Harkness says without a millisecond of thought.

"Oh yeah? Where's a cop going to get that kind of money?"

"I have generous friends."

"I bet you do. But what'll you give me as collateral?"

Harkness reaches over, unclips his badge, and tosses it on the dining-room table with a dead metallic click.

"*Shit*, man," Malnati says. "You must want this vote bad."

"Bad doesn't begin to describe it," Harkness says.

Malnati watches Harkness's glimmering badge spinning on the table. "You really going to come up with a hundred thousand bucks? In cash, mind you?"

Harkness fixes him with his blue eyes. "Yes. And I'll make sure you never get another parking ticket ever again."

"What!" Malnati's mouth opens wide and his eyes bug out. "Are you shitting me?"

"No."

"Deal." He tosses Harkness's badge back to him. Harkness catches it and clips it back on. "You'll rue the day you made this deal, friend. Because I'm like the fucking Koch brothers of parking tickets."

Harkness smiles, wonders if Malnati's next phone call will be to O'Mara's team, trying to cut a better deal.

"You know, Joey told me you were crazy like a fox," Malnati says. "But I already had an inkling."

"Oh yeah?"

"I knew your father," Malnati says.

"Of course you did."

When they get to the Old North Church, Reed's pacing on the snow-lined sidewalk next to Salem Street.

Harkness rolls down the window as Patrick and Esther escort Nicco Malnati to the side door of the church. "Special delivery," he says. "One very influential, expensive politician."

"How'd you get him?"

"How do you think? Money."

"How much?"

224

"More than I have. We'll have a bake sale, Sam. After you get the votes."

Reed shakes his head slowly. "Ever see *Twelve Angry Men*?"

"Sure. All about one righteous man making a stand."

"Well, I've got fourteen angry city councilors stalking around a basement getting jacked up on church coffee and doughnuts. And not a Henry Fonda among them. Wish me luck."

"I'm not going to do that," Harkness says. Snow falls steadily between them. "This vote isn't about luck."

40

THE AFTERNOON DARKENS and the snow turns heavy as Rage Weekend enters its final hours. The citizens gathered in Freedom City huddle in their high-tech lean-tos or stand close to the communal bonfire, which sizzles as clumps of snow fall on the embers. In front of City Hall, Harkness and Lattimore watch as a row of cabs slide up Cambridge Street. The doors open and men and women spill out of the cabs, their faces inscrutable, worried. The city council, all fourteen of them.

A worried glance pings between Patrick, Esther, and Harkness. Lattimore crosses himself, getting most of it right.

A thin man in a long black overcoat walks toward them. As he comes closer, Harkness recognizes Reed, face neutral, eyes on the snowy ground in front of him. He climbs to the People's Pulpit, picks up the red megaphone, and dusts off the snow.

"I'm city council president Sam Reed." His voice booms out over the crowd. People shuffle together for warmth. They stare up at Reed, who stands awkwardly on the platform. He turns, searches the people gathered behind him, and waves Harkness and Lattimore closer.

They climb the steps and stand by him, one on either side. One of the Stooges holds an enormous crimson umbrella over them.

"To the city of Boston, I bring news of an important decision," Reed says into the megaphone. "I just returned from a meeting of the Boston city council in Old North Church, where patriots once sent warnings about threats facing our great city. We face a new, more insidious danger today. Having insinuated himself into politics and bartered his way to the highest office in the city, Mayor Michael O'Mara has pursued a radical and corrupt agenda that has displaced thousands of citizens while benefiting his business interests."

Huge cheers rise from Freedom City, including more than a few shouts of "We Hate MOM!"

Reed exudes a new confidence. His voice sounds stronger and more powerful. Megaphone in hand, he's a leader. Harkness feels a certain pride as he watches the new Reed take action.

"Due to these violations of the public trust and many more, the fourteen members of the city council have voted unanimously to file a bill of address and invoke section seventeen D of the original Boston city charter, which gives us the legal authority to oust a sitting mayor if we feel that individual does not act in the best interests of the city. This is our right as elected officials representing all of Boston's neighborhoods."

The crowd turns silent at the news. On the fifth floor of City Hall, O'Mara and his cronies are probably even more stunned.

"After watching Mayor Michael O'Mara in power for a year, we feel confident that the next three would just bring more damage to this city. We ask the people of Boston to support our decision and show the world that democracy *can* and *will* catch any corrupt politician, no matter how clever or powerful."

The truth dawns on the crowd — O'Mara is out. Wild cheers and shouts rise from the plaza, louder than a Red Sox victory parade, more frenzied than a packed Tremont Street nightclub on molly.

"By the authority vested in me by the Boston city charter, I will take over as interim mayor until a free mayoral election next fall." Reed pauses. "I look forward to serving you — and the city we all love."

As thousands of people in the plaza cheer, Reed turns to Harkness. "I knew you'd get me here," he says. "I just didn't think it would take so long." He gives a tilted grin.

The crowd keeps cheering.

Harkness leans forward. "What?"

"I was sure you'd come through for me, Eddy," Reed says. "I always knew there was a smart guy in there somewhere under all that *chump*." Reed gives a broad smile, then turns to wave at the crowd.

As snow slides in clumps from his leather jacket, Harkness watches the political animal he's helped create and hopes that this one is more evolved and enlightened than ex-mayor Michael O'Mara.

But only time reveals a politician's true intentions.

After the Thaw

HARKNESS AND CANDACE walk toward Albrecht Square, crowded with locals and tourists, all glad to be outside on the first weekend of spring, the smell of ocean salt hovering in the slowly warming air. He's wearing his full BPD dress uniform, a giggling May slung on his shoulder as they walk closer to the grandstand. He considered skipping the event — Harkness likes ceremonies about as much as he does reunion concerts. But Lattimore said it was mandatory.

As they edge through the crowd, Harkness spots Katherine Aiello walking toward him, almost unrecognizable in tan pants and a green fleece vest over a cream-colored shirt. She looks more like a sensible urban gardener than one of the most powerful people in the city.

Harkness passes May to Candace. "Give me a minute."

"Don't get in trouble," Candace says.

Harkness holds up both hands, as if the very idea of trouble is unknown to him.

She laughs, takes May to see what the sidewalk vendors are selling.

"Despite today's event, I don't think you've been sufficiently recognized for your role in this momentous change." Like a true New Englander, Aiello skips any perfunctory greeting.

"Well, that's not the reason I did it," Harkness says. In different ways, O'Mara, Burch, and Fayerwether all posed threats to the city. They had to be stopped, just like any other bad actors.

"But that's the kind of behind-the-scenes work that we appreciate."

"Do *we?*" Harkness raises an eyebrow.

"Yes, we do."

Harkness leans toward Aiello. "I have to ask you, what did you say in that letter to Sam Reed?"

"What letter?"

"The one you had me deliver before the city council vote," he says. "Whatever you said, it really got Reed moving."

Aiello shakes her head. "We didn't say anything."

"Then what was in the envelope?"

"A check for a life-changing sum of money and instructions for keeping it a secret," Aiello says. "Plus a promise of more if he could manage to get with the program."

Harkness stares so long that Aiello finally waves a hand in front of his face. "Honestly, I hope you're not as naive as you seem."

"Maybe I'm just easily surprised."

"Well, prepare yourself." Aiello reaches into her pocket and presses a silver coin into his hand.

Harkness turns it over, sees the date 1630 embossed on one side, the familiar *X* on the other.

"You are hereby nominated to become a member of the ancient and secret order of the Harbormasters," Aiello says in the measured voice of someone serving a summons.

Harkness turns speechless.

"I said you were nominated," Aiello says, "not elected."

"Got it," Harkness says.

"But I have to say, we need new blood. And people under sixty."

"I'm flattered, and by the way, I'm both."

Aiello smiles and reaches up and puts her hand on his cheek. "A sense of humor too. A triple threat."

She disappears into the crowd and Harkness slips the coin into his pocket, then catches up with Candace and May.

Candace gives him an almost suspicious look. "Who was that?"

"My fairy godmother," Harkness says.

"Careful," she says. "They always get you in trouble. Poison mushrooms and so on."

"Don't I know it," Harkness says, leading them toward the Reserved section.

A BPD cop recognizes Harkness and waves them past the rope. They pick up their programs and take their seats.

On a low stage set up at the far end of Albrecht Square, the first speaker is finishing up a brief history of the Lower South End. Behind him hang a row of enlarged photos of the Lower South End during its turn-of-the-century heyday—paperboys in short pants hawking the *Herald-American* in the square, men in gray suits and hats looking up at the square's famous clock.

It's officially Lower South End Day, by proclamation of acting mayor Sam Reed, who's sitting on the dais next to Commissioner Lattimore. Harkness scans the other dignitaries, sees plenty of faces he recognizes—Boston's cast of celebrities and politicians is small, even smaller without the sports heroes. Noticeably absent is the tidy-bearded Robert Fayerwether, quietly removed from the Urban Redevelopment Council and public life.

The crowd applauds as Reed strides to the podium.

"Last fall, Police Commissioner Lattimore stood amid the destruction and desolation and made a promise that this neighborhood would be restored and reborn," he says. "And it has been. Not as luxury condos. But as a much-beloved home to hundreds of families and hard-working citizens."

As the crowd applauds, the commissioner rises from his chair and gives a small wave. Nestled in Harkness's lap, May slaps her hands together and laughs.

Reed continues. "The streets are safe and the scourge of deadly drugs is gone."

Harkness glances over at Patrick and Esther and gives them a knowing look. Streets are never completely safe. Drugs never go away.

"Some good has come from this storm and its political aftermath," he says, deftly referencing O'Mara without saying his name. "The Lower South End is now getting the attention and repairs it needs, and its residents are starting to return in force."

With O'Mara gone, all plans for redeveloping the Lower South End evaporated. As the winter loosened its grip and the snow melted, Reed focused the city's resources on getting the neighborhood up and running again — all while taking full credit for its rehabilitation, of course. The wanderers returned, stores reopened, and the lights started going back on in the dark neighborhood.

Harkness has made his peace with the fact that Reed used him to get into the mayor's office. The first job of any politician is to get elected. The next is to stay elected. That they'll use any tactic to achieve that end shouldn't be any more surprising than that addicts will do anything to stay high.

After all, power, not religion, was the first opiate of the masses.

Over several thankfully uneventful lunches at the Fill-A-Buster, Reed has offered Harkness his sincere thanks. More important, he's kept Lattimore in power and ensured the survival of Narco-Intel.

And he paid Nicco Malnati for his expensive vote.

Reed points to Deaf Kid, squirming in the front row in a black suit, white shirt, and striped tie. "As proof of the remarkable progress made over the past six months, consider Edward Ashmont."

Deaf Kid peers into the crowd, smiles when he finds Harkness.

"During the hurricane, Edward was found chained to a radiator, his uncle lying dead next to him, a drug dealer who fell prey to Dark Horse, an insidious and deadly brand of heroin. He was rescued by a patrol from Narco-Intel, led by Detective Supervisor Edward Harkness, almost drowned by the flood in this very square." Reed points Harkness out. "Detective Harkness is an inspiration to us all and we're lucky to have him here with us today."

Candace gives Harkness her you-are-a-fucking-rock-star look. Harkness can't begin to count the errors in Reed's brief story.

He rises from his white folding chair, smiles, gives a crisp salute, and sits back down, knowing that he's just another dog in this civic dog-and-pony show.

Reed waves Deaf Kid to the podium. "Edward Ashmont graduates this spring from the world-renowned Hamilton School for the Deaf in Waltham, thanks to the generosity of the Boston Police Department."

Applause for the school. And more political capital for Lattimore.

"Since the hurricane, he's had reconstructive surgery and the best speech therapy available," Reed says. "Now I'd like to invite this brave young man to say a few words — the first he's ever spoken in public."

Reed lowers the microphone and points it down toward Deaf Kid, who approaches the podium as if he's walking on a rope ladder across a surging river.

"Hey?" he says into the microphone, then recoils.

Reed gives him an encouraging nod.

"Thank you for saving . . . for saving my neighborhood." His voice is halting but clear. "I am very glad to be here because, because this is my home. This is where I grew up. When I'm done with school, I'll be back. Because the food at the Hamilton School sucks. And I hate it there. Thank you."

Wild applause and a standing ovation reward this moment of unscripted honesty in the midst of a photo op. Harkness lets out a whistle that makes May clamp her hands over her ears. He leans over to kiss Candace as the applause and shouting grows louder.

They pick up May and stand, holding her above the crowd gathered this shimmering spring afternoon — State Street bankers in suits and old men in T-shirts watching from upper-floor windows, wanderers who are done wandering, JJ and his drinking buddies from McCloskey's, an unimpressed Jack of the Jackals, and even Frankie Getler, who looks out over Albrecht Square with his one good eye, adding up the thousands of hours of electrical work necessary to bring it up to code.

No matter how plush and gilded the city becomes or how clean Dirty Old Boston gets, Harkness knows there will always be plenty to complain about — and lots of people eager to do the complaining.

Acknowledgments

Special thanks to:

Dr. Robert Allison, chairman of the History Department, Suffolk University; Peter Drummey, Massachusetts Historical Society; Amy Ryan, former president of the Boston Public Library; the St. Botolph Club; Brian Swett, chief of Environment, Energy, and Open Space, City of Boston; Joyce Linehan, head of policy, Boston Mayor's Office; Nick Mitropoulos, who introduced me to Boston politics; and the many anonymous (but much-appreciated) police officers in Boston, New York City, and Concord, Massachusetts, who contributed their insights.

At Houghton Mifflin Harcourt, thanks to Nicole Angeloro, an angel of an editor, Beth Burleigh Fuller, Katrina Kruse, Michelle Triant, Brian Moore, and Tracy Roe. At Writers House, thanks to Dan Conaway, who took a big chance on me, as well as the great Maja Nikolic and Taylor Templeton. In New York City, thanks to Andrea Schulz, who brought Eddy Harkness to life. And closer to home, a city-size thanks to my brilliant wife, Ann — writer, reader, adviser, and partner forever.